The Trials of
KATE HOPE

The Trials of
KATE HOPE

by Wick Downing

Houghton Mifflin Company
Boston 2008

www.houghtonmifflinbooks.com

The text of this book is set in Baskerville MT.

Library of Congress Cataloging-in-Publication Data
Downing, Warwick, 1931–
Trials of Kate Hope / by Wick Downing.
p. cm.
Summary: At the young age of fourteen, Kate Hope is licensed to practice law
in the state of Colorado in 1973, and with the help of her lawyer grandfather,
and memories of her dead father, also a lawyer, she tries the case of a dog that
is slated to be destroyed for attacking a baby.
ISBN 978-0-618-89133-7
[1. Lawyers—Fiction. 2. Trials—Fiction. 3. Sex role—Fiction. 4.
Grandfathers—Fiction. 5. Colorado—History—1951—Fiction.] I. Title.
PZ7.D7595Tr 2008
[Fic]—dc22
2007047731

Manufactured in the United States of America
MP 10 9 8 7 6 5 4 3 2

This book is dedicated to the memory and courage of
Kate Thornham and Mary Halloran.

Chapter One
Winter 1965

I STARTED CALLING MY DAD ZOZO when I was just a little kid, because of this fascinating scar on his face. He got it in the war at the same time a bomb or something blew off his left arm, but his arm didn't interest me as much as his scar. It started under his left eye near his nose and angled in a straight line to his cheekbone. Then in another straight line it went from his cheekbone to the space between the bottom of his nose and the top of his lip. From there it drooped a little, curving around the top of his mouth to somewhere in the middle of his left cheek.

I'd sit on his lap and trace that old scar with my finger. "Zozo," I said, trying to say "Zorro." He smiled. I called him Zozo after that, because I liked his smile.

But the Saturday after Christmas of 1965, Zozo and Law went skiing. Law was my older brother. I wanted to go with them, but they wouldn't take me along. "You're not ready yet," Zozo said. "Next year, maybe. We'll see."

"You're a girl," Law said, his voice popping all over the place because it was changing. He grinned at me as he opened the garage door. "You'd just get in my way."

"I hate it when you call me a girl!"

"Okay, you're a boy. Try to look like one. Okay?"

He made it sound as though there was something wrong with being a girl. "How can I get ready if I can't even go?" I asked Zozo, watching him put the skis in the rack on top of the old station wagon we had then. His left arm was just a little stub that hung from his shoulder, so he had only his right arm to work with. But he could use it really well and in two seconds, the skis were in the rack, all latched down tight, and they were ready to go.

"You're too young, Katie," Zozo said. "You aren't even seven. Law didn't start until he was ten."

"Girls grow up faster than boys."

He laughed. "We'll see about it next year. Now give me a kiss."

"No."

He shrugged and climbed in the car.

"We'll bake something," Mom said, holding on to me so I wouldn't run into the street after them. "For the boys, for dinner." It was snowing outside, but not hard.

"I don't want to bake anything!" I wailed. "I want to go skiing!"

"You be a good girl," Zozo said, blowing a kiss at me with his right hand. "We'll go see *Snow White* tomorrow." He backed the car onto the driveway and waited for Law to pull the door down. Law stuck his tongue out at me as the door was closing.

I never saw either one of them again. Coming home that night, they swerved to avoid hitting a car that was skidding on the ice. Their car slid off the road and pitched over a cliff.

They were killed.

Chapter Two
Spring 1969

I GLIDED MY BIKE TO A STOP in the driveway of my grandfather's house. There were patches of snow on his lawn, but the streets were dry, and it was warm enough outside for the old man to have his front door open. He lived in the same house he'd lived in forever, and I could see his old face peering over the brick wall that guarded the wraparound porch. I used to hide behind that wall when Law threw snowballs at me, hoping he'd miss and break a window. "Hi, Grandfather," I said.

"Kate darlin'!" he said, recognizing my voice. He's practically blind. "Come give me a hug."

I leaned my bike against the lilac bush by the porch, where buds on the branches were changing into little tiny green leaves. I skipped up the steps and went over to where he sat, kind of like a lump, in an old wooden rocking chair with a low back. Getting behind him, I wrapped my arms around his chest and nuzzled my face in the white hair around his head, then kissed him on his bald spot. "Mom made cookies," I said, peeling off my backpack. "Want some?"

"That would be nice."

He'd changed since the accident, Mom said. He'd given up the law practice he'd been in with my dad, and didn't care about things the way he used to, things that would get him excited and angry, like politics and civil rights and the war in Vietnam. Most of the time he looked like he'd rather be somewhere else and was just waiting for a taxi to take him there—but he always brightened up around me.

"How's your mother?" he asked me.

"She's fine." Why bother him with the truth? It had been three years, but she barely let me out of her sight. The telephone would ring any minute now, and it would be Mom, making sure I was still alive.

"She's fine, is she?" he asked as I pulled the cookies out. There was a table near his chair where he kept his pipe, and I spread them out on a paper towel. "Those cookies smell good," he said, feeling around until he found a cookie. "Mmm," he said, taking a bite. "Drag up a chair, young lady, and have one with me."

I found the weathered old wooden chair that liked to stab me with splinters, pushed it next to him, and sat down.

"I don't want to bake cookies when I get old," I told him, picking one up and biting off a piece. Even though it was delicious, I knew that being a good cook was not what I wanted out of life. "I hate working in the kitchen."

"Well, now. That's not very ladylike."

"I don't even want to be a lady."

He smiled. "You don't, do you? What I'd like to know is this. What are your options?"

"I mean, when people see me, I don't want them to think, 'Isn't she a lovely lady!' I want to work when I grow up and don't ever want to get married or have some man take care of me. I'll just skip the motherhood thing, too, because I don't want babies!" I started getting emotional. "Maybe if Mom had worked all her life and never married Zozo, then . . ."

He leaned over and found my arm. "My pretty one," he said, finding my hand. Pipe smoke surrounded him like a cloud, and I loved the smell. I loved the look of his gnarled old hand, too, like the branch of a tree. "Wish I could hear you better, Kate," he said, "but I see you well enough. Your grandmother didn't like the kitchen either, but I made her stay in it." He shook his head as he thought about it. "She won't let me forget it, either."

"But she's dead, Grandfather. How can she . . . ?"

"Course, things were different in 1922, the year we got married. Married women didn't work in those days. A woman's place was in the home, but that arrangement just didn't suit your grandmother. She'd burn up a perfectly good pot roast and blame it on the oven and insist I take her out to dinner. I think she did it on purpose some of the time so she could get out of the house." He sucked on his pipe, but it had gone out. "She was fearless, your grandmother, and this was when women weren't supposed to be like that. But you didn't want to make her mad." He laughed a little, remembering something as he searched in his pockets for matches. "Have you heard about the Ku Klux Klan yet in that school you go to?"

"The men who wore robes and masks and did awful things to Negroes and Jews and Catholics?"

He nodded as he struck a match and got his pipe going. "One night the Klan planted one of their burning crosses right out there on the lawn of this house," he said, pointing to the place with the stem of his pipe. "I wasn't home, but she was, and when that cross flared up, she tore out of the house with a kitchen knife in her hand and chased five men into their cars and threw the knife at them. They had those silly robes on, and Don Bowman, across the street, was all ready to come to her rescue with a gun, but when he saw how scared they was of a small woman with fire in her eyes, he just laughed."

"Why did they burn a cross on your lawn in the first place?" I asked. "You weren't a Negro or a Jew or a Catholic. I don't get it."

"I was running for the state senate, and gave speeches

about the stranglehold the Klan had on the judges, and how I'd do everything in my power to beat them. We were Unitarians, your grandmother and me, and they said that was worse than bein' a Jew. They were awful people, and your grandmother Maggie hated them with her whole heart. As small as she was—she barely topped five feet—she could make herself heard."

"But you kept her in the kitchen?"

"I did. After your father was born. She didn't like it a bit, but the truth is, in some peculiar way that seemed normal in those days, she thought that was where she belonged." He tapped his pipe. "Of course with all this new women's liberation business, I don't feel good about it now."

The phone rang. "That's Mom," I said. "Want me to get it?"

"If you don't mind."

I ran into the house. The telephone was on a great old mahogany table in the foyer, underneath the steps that led up to the second floor. I yanked it out of its cradle, ready to start a fight. "Hope residence."

"Hi, dear," Mom said. "How's your grandfather?"

That was a disguise. She just wanted to make sure I'd gotten to his house and hadn't been flattened by a trolley bus. "He died," I said. "He fell out of his rocking chair and hit his head."

"Kate, that's not funny. How is he?"

"Mom, I'm okay. I'm all in one piece. We're talking about the Ku Klux Klan and how Grandmother Hope burned up pot roasts in the kitchen."

"O-*kay*," she said, slowly. "Ask him if he'd like to come over for a pot roast tomorrow after church."

"Grandfather!" I yelled.

"Stop that. Go ask him nicely."

I put the phone down and went back out on the porch. "Grampa?" He twisted his head and looked at me out of eyes that could see only blurs. "Mom wants to know if you'd come over tomorrow after church and have pot roast."

"You tell her I can't think of anything in this world I would rather do. Ask her what time."

I went back to the phone. "What time?" I asked Mom.

"Tell him I'll pick him up at three. And Kate?"

"What."

"You don't have to call when you leave. Just come home when you're ready. I love you, dear." She hung up quickly, before I could say anything.

Grandfather was sitting up straighter, and his pipe was going full blast when I sat down next to him. "Let me have your hand, young lady," he said, reaching out with his.

I took the gnarled old thing—it was more than eighty

years old, like the rest of him—and pressed it against my cheek.

"Your mother's still struggling with it, isn't she?" he said quietly.

"With what?"

"The loss of your father and brother." He took a pull on his pipe. "My son and my grandson. It takes time for a grown woman to just let it go, don't you see. It takes time."

"It takes kids a long time too," I said.

"Has to be hard for you, darlin'. How old are you?"

He asked me that every time we were together. It was kind of a habit, I think, like the way some people will say "What?" all the time, even if they've heard you. "Ten," I told him.

"Is your mother still seeing that therapist woman?"

"Just once a month," I said. "She keeps telling my mom to move."

"Now just how is that any of her business?" Grandfather wanted to know.

"She thinks Mom and I need a fresh start in life, and that the house will always remind us of Zozo and Law and keep us planted in the past." I looked at his old house and wondered if he'd thought about moving after Grandmother Hope died.

"How do you feel about it?" he asked me.

"I like my house," I said. "I like being around Zozo and Law. At first it was hard and I cried all the time, but it's different now." He waited quietly for me to go on. "I still cry when I think about them, but I smile too. It's just different. I don't want to leave my friends, either. Mike Doyle?"

"A fine boy. Irish, but then so is your mother."

"His mom drinks a lot, Grandfather. His dad is never around. He kind of needs me."

"Well now. You just be careful about who you start taking care of."

A beat-up green car pulled up next to the curb. An old woman struggled to get out, then emerged and slammed her door shut.

"Who's here?" Grandfather asked.

"A woman, Grandfather. Do you have a girlfriend?"

"Hmph!" But he smiled as she marched toward us. "What does she look like? A pretty young thing, or old and fat?"

"I'll tell you later," I whispered.

"Judge Hope?" the woman demanded, climbing the steps. She was big and tough-looking. "Remember me?"

Grandfather pushed himself out of his chair. "Not yet."

"Your son was my lawyer, but I talked to you as well. You made my husband pay child support. It's Lydia Bartram." She stood directly in front of him and glared into his face. "Surely you remember me now."

"Oh. Well. Of course," he said, but from the way he said it I knew he still didn't.

All of a sudden she started to cry. I jumped up and

kind of led her to my chair. "I need the services of a lawyer, sir," she said, sitting down and pulling a tissue out of
her purse. "Can you help me?"

"I . . ." He sat down too. "Mrs. Bartram, I don't do law
anymore."

"But I'm being evicted, Judge Hope, and it isn't fair!
Isn't the law supposed to be fair? They raised my rent, sir,
and I can't pay it!"

"Well, Mrs. Bartram, Denver's a big town now and
there are lots of lawyers. You'll just have to find someone
else."

"But it would be easy for you. Call them up and
threaten them!"

"Now I remember you," he said, like the memory
itched or something. "It isn't that easy, Mrs. Bartram. A
lawyer can't just pick up the telephone and call up somebody and threaten them."

"I don't see why not. That's what your son did to Fred's
lawyer. That's all he did. I was there when he did it, and
that's all he did!"

"Your husband was in violation of a court order, Mrs.
Bartram. My son said he'd love to send your husband
to jail. This isn't that at all. Now, don't misunderstand
me and go off thinking there's nothing you can do about
the fix you're in, because there *are* some actions a good
lawyer could take. But I can't, don't you see. I don't have

an office or a secretary, and I haven't practiced law in three years, and my license has lapsed, and I just can't do it."

"They'll throw me out, Judge! You're my only hope! I *tried* getting a decent lawyer, but no one would help me!"

Grandfather looked kind of surprised. "Mrs. Bartram, you'll have to excuse me." He pushed himself to his feet and made his way to the screen door. "Kate darlin', I'm getting a bit of a chill out here. Let's go inside where it's warmer."

"You don't have to be rude!" the woman said loudly. "You're like all the lawyers. I thought you and your son were different!"

"Kate, are you coming?"

"I'll be evicted, Judge Hope! You've seen what they do. My things will be scattered all over the sidewalk! Help me. Please!"

He opened the screen door and disappeared into his house, but I felt awful. "Can I help you to your car?" I asked her.

"No!" She bolted out of her chair and stomped her feet going down the steps. But once in her car, she sat for a moment and cried.

"Grandfather?" I knew he could hear me. "Can't . . ."

Suddenly the car lurched away from the curb, and she was gone.

"I didn't handle that well," Grandfather said, coming back outside and sitting in his rocking chair. "Her personality don't exactly endear her to me, and it never did. That woman drove both your father and me to distraction. She certainly did that."

Two weeks later, Mrs. Bartram was the subject of a feature story in the *Denver Post*. HOMELESS WOMAN VICTIMIZED BY SYSTEM, shouted the headline, DIES ON DENVER'S STREETS.

Chapter Three
Summer 1973

IF I'M EVER FAMOUS and someone writes the story of my life, they'll highlight this very day. "On Monday morning, June 11, 1973," the story would say, "with Mount Evans looming on the horizon west of Denver, fourteen-year-old Kate Hope put in her first full day as a lawyer."

Unfortunately for the course of human history, Mom stood in the driveway and had me blocked. "How am I supposed to get to work?" I asked her as I straddled my ten-speed.

"The bus," she said. "Or let me take you, even though you can't stand doing anything the easy way."

"There's nothing very hard about riding a bicycle."

"Honey, won't you just let me drop you off on my way to work? I *hate* it when you're out there dodging cars!"

"I don't dodge them." I stuffed my foot into the toe clip

of the bike pedal and pulled the strap down. "They dodge me." I have Grandmother Hope's genes, everyone says. Like her, I'm only five feet tall, and like her, I have attitude.

"Kate, you scare me to death," she said, inhaling deeply on a cigarette. My own mother smokes! She started smoking again exactly when all her friends quit.

"I'd rather get crushed by a bus than die of lung cancer," I told her, guiding my bike around her and pushing off down the slope of the driveway. I rolled into Hudson Street and banked a hard right, then bent down and tightened the strap over my other toe. "See you tonight!" I was halfway to Sixth Avenue Parkway before she could react.

"Call me when you get to the office?" she yelled after me.

What is it about my mother that makes me grit my teeth? I asked myself as I pumped my bike down Hale Parkway. I loved her, and she loved me, but she still hung on to me way too tightly. She wouldn't let me grow up! She saw me in the world *she'd* grown up in, but that world didn't exist anymore. Mine had body bags, and Vietnam, and *Ms.* magazine. I had no desire to be the nicey-nice girl who grew up next door, like Judy Garland in *Easter Parade*. That may have been Mom's model for life, but it didn't work for me.

A man was riding a bike in front of me, and without thinking I cranked up to pass him. An old guy in his forties, he had a stomach that hung over his belt and he rode with his elbows locked. Would he be willing to take lessons from a fourteen-year-old girl? I could show him how to ride so that it wouldn't rattle his brains, and could introduce him to Mom. She might take *him* on as a project to manage, instead of me. "Hi," I said, pulling up next to him. "Beautiful morning."

He glared at me. "What are you doing on a boy's bike, sweetie?"

Not Mom's type, I decided. Instantly. "Is there a law?" I asked.

"Don't get smart with me," he gasped, his chest heaving with exertion as he tried to keep up.

I didn't want him to have a heart attack, but I couldn't keep my mouth shut, either. "You know something, mister?" I asked him as I pulled away. "I hope you don't have any daughters!"

Grandfather's new law office was not like the one he'd had with my dad. That one was on the ninth floor of the Equitable Building, with a fantastic view of the Front Range. This one was a brick bungalow on Thirteenth Avenue, next to a bail bondsman. It had been built for a so-called bad woman in the 1890s, who—according to Grandfather—hadn't been a bad woman at all. She'd been a prostitute, but that didn't make her bad. She supported a home for unwed mothers, he said, and "most people thought she was nice." But she had to leave town in 1921 when the police started enforcing the law against prostitution, something they hadn't done for at least ten years. "That was a bad day for Denver," he said. "The home for girls closed down in four months."

The house Grandfather used as an office had been built in 1886, which was the year he was born. Both were eighty-seven in 1973, but the old house was in better condition. Even so, it needed some fixing up. Summers in Denver get hot enough to fry the ants on the sidewalk, and our "air conditioner" was a fan in the window.

I pushed my ten-speed up the steps of the porch and locked it to the brass ring planted in the floor. It had been used to tie up horses in the old days. Saddlebags on the back rack of my bike bulged with clothes and lunch. I unhooked them, hung them over my shoulder, and walked inside.

The parlor had been converted into a reception room, with a desk and low counter on the right side, and ancient chairs around a coffee table on the left. The table was covered with magazines. President Nixon glowered at me from the cover of *Time*, his mouth snarling like a bulldog and a finger pointed right at my throat. NIXON FIGHTS BACK, the words on the cover shouted.

Mrs. Roulette, who started working for Grandfather in the 1930s and had been his secretary ever since, needed a hearing aid. She sat at the desk behind the counter with her hands poised over the keyboard of her new electric typewriter like a concert pianist. She hadn't heard me come in. "Hi, Mrs. Roulette!" I said, loud enough to get through.

"Oh!" Her hands jumped off the keys and her bifocals flew off her face. "You startled me."

I dropped my saddlebags on the floor, angry at myself for scaring her, and scurried over to pick up her glasses. They had come to rest by a file cabinet. "I'm sorry," I said, giving them to her. "Are you all right?"

"Yes, dear." She polished them with a hankie that she dragged out of her sleeve. "I may not be as tough as you, Kate. But I'm a pretty tough old bird."

She was, too . . . although when she'd realized Judge Hope wasn't going back to the Equitable Building to resurrect a nice, respectable law practice, it really upset her. How could she work in a house with a history? she'd asked my mom. Next to a bail bondsman? An awful place for a distinguished and reputable lawyer to have his office! But Grandfather told her he had no intention of ever being a reputable lawyer again. "I'm going to be a *real* lawyer, Virginia," he told her. "For people who deserve some justice but can't afford respectability."

"I was not thrilled," she told Mom a few months later. "But so many of our clients are remarkably decent, and they need us—even though some of them haven't bathed in ages. The Judge gives the worst offenders a bar of soap and tells them not to come back until I can stand being in the same room with them." She'd smiled. "They have to pass my sniff test."

She'd even started reading *Ms.* in her spare time, and now, after putting her glasses back on, she found me in them. "Your young man called," she said.

I blushed. "Mike is not my young man!" He may have attached himself to me in grade school, but that didn't make him mine.

"Nevertheless, he'd like you to call him. And your mother . . ."

"Wants to make sure no one ran over me."

"Yes. Your grandfather called too." Her hands returned to her keyboard. "He's not feeling well and won't be in. He wants you to take his place today."

"I'm sorry—*what* does he want?"

"Just until he's feeling better," she said, starting to peck away. "Two or three days, perhaps."

"Mrs. Roulette, I can't take his place," I said. "No one can. He *yells* at people, you know, lawyers and judges and anyone who disagrees with him. *I* can't do that."

"Of course you can't, dear. But—"

"I'm comfortable looking up cases and writing briefs and walking him to the courthouse and filing complaints and things like that. But I can't *handle* anything. The real lawyers would laugh at me."

"You're a real lawyer, aren't you, dear?"

"I don't exactly feel like one. I mean . . ."

"You *are* one, though. You do far more around here than you realize."

"Alvarez," I said, suddenly remembering the motion I'd worked on last week. "It has to be filed *this morning*, and he has to sign it!"

"It's in the machine now. You can run it over to him when it's typed." Her fingers began to find their rhythm, picking up speed. "While I finish it, perhaps you'd talk to Miss Willow?"

The face of an old woman who must have been hiding in one of the big, overstuffed chairs peeked out at me. She had silver-white hair and blue skin, thin enough to see through. "Hi," I said, instantly drawn to her. Whatever her problem was, I had this huge urge to fix it. "Give me a minute or two?" I asked her.

"Yes, dear," she said.

I rushed down the hall to the bathroom and stripped off my bike shorts and shirt. Why do boys think girls don't sweat? I needed a shower but didn't have time for one, so I splashed water all over myself and dried off, then applied a deodorant, sprinkled myself with powder, and slipped into a cotton dress and sandals.

I *hate* being fourteen. My calves are huge, my ankles are thick, my chest is a cavity, and my right elbow is larger than the left one. I frowned at my face in the mirror and fluffed my hair, hoping to bring up a curl, stuck my tongue out at myself, then wiped off the sink and floor and picked up the mess. I trotted to my office.

Grandfather had the large room on one side of the hallway, with a telephone and a wonderful old roll-top desk. My office was one of three small rooms on the other side. In the old days, mine had been called a "crib," and it was barely big enough for a bed. I'd brightened it up with pictures and nice curtains for the window, even though my view was not great. No clouds, blue sky, or mountains out there: just a brick wall, five feet away.

After hanging my bike shorts and saddlebags on hooks in a tiny closet, I zipped across the hall to the Judge's office and picked up the telephone and dialed. "Hi, Mom," I said. "I made it."

"Thanks for calling, dear," she said. I heard the buzz of the newsroom in the background. "I love you."

"I love you too."

Mike would have to wait, I decided, heading down the hall to meet my client.

Miss Willow may have been two inches taller than me, but she was such a frail little thing in her frilly yellow dress! As I guided her into my office, I wanted to take her hands in mine and tell her not to worry. I tried to look capable, even though the furnishings in my office didn't send that kind of message. "Thank you, dear," she said as I offered her the chair in front of my "desk." It was an old wooden table that had looked much nicer on the lawn at the garage sale where I bought it. Now it stood in the corner with a chair behind it, as a bookcase kind of crouched under the window.

My "law library" was in the bookcase: a set of the *Annotated Codes of Colorado,* the *Municipal Ordinances of Denver,* the *State of Colorado Ethics Opinions,* and the *Judge's Bench Book.*

"Dear, do you think you can help me?" she asked as I sat down. She spoke as though she didn't want to hurt my feelings. "Mrs. Roulette said you were a lawyer, but how can that be? You're so young. And you're a girl."

Instant bristle on my part. Girls shouldn't be lawyers, she obviously thought—as did a lot of people, especially other lawyers. But I smiled at her. "It's a long story, Miss Willow," I said, pointing to my license to practice law. It hung behind my desk in an expensive cherrywood frame. "If you'd rather wait for my grandfather, or find someone else, that's up to you. But I *am* a lawyer," I told her, trying to feel like one. "Just ask Mrs. Roulette."

"I can't wait for your grandfather," she said. "I need someone *today.* Do you think you can help me?"

"I don't know. You need to tell me what your problem is."

"It's my dog . . . ," and she started to cry. "They're going to destroy him!" Her delicate frame shook with sobs and she covered her face as though hiding from some unspeakable horror.

"It's okay, Miss Willow," I said, rushing around my desk and taking her shoulders in my hands. "Really." I sat on the edge of the table and smiled into her poor, sad face. "Need a tissue?"

"No thank you, dear." She dragged a hankie out of her dress pocket. "I've never had a lawyer be so nice to me."

"Not even my grandfather?" I asked her.

"Oh my no, dear," she said. "Everyone loves him. But no one thinks he's very nice." Her hand flew to her mouth as if she wished she could keep it closed. "Please don't tell him I said that."

"He *isn't* very nice," I said, "but he's kind of cute." She smiled at that and dabbed off her face. "Who wants to destroy your dog?"

For the next half-hour, words and sobs and tears gushed out of her as I pieced her story together.

She was born in Denver sixty-three years ago, then lived her whole life with her father. "My mother passed away when I was born, you see, which was quite common in those days." She earned a degree in education at Denver University, then taught first grade at Montclair Elementary, but when her dad was diagnosed with cancer, she retired to take care of him. Three years ago he passed away, and—as if by magic—a stray dog attached himself to her. He was a big German shepherd, and she named him Herman. "He's my family now, you see. He's all I have."

He was "big enough for children to ride" and made a wonderful guard dog, which she needed because her neighborhood had "changed so over the years." He was very protective of her and would snarl and bristle at the least hint of danger, but otherwise was quite sweet and gentle.

But two Sundays ago, right around noon, she took him to City Park and spread a picnic blanket near the lake. She tethered him near her picnic basket by jamming a spike in the ground and clipping his leash to it with a thin chain. Then she started to walk to the concession stand to get popcorn for the ducks, but she didn't make it. Two boys, on bicycles with seats that looked like large bananas, ran into her and knocked her down. A nice man made her lie still while someone else hurried to a telephone and called the paramedics.

A huge ambulance with flashing lights arrived, and a man and a woman jumped out and poked her with instruments, then asked her to get up and take a few steps. Everything appeared to be normal, but they wanted her to go to the hospital for x-rays. She refused. Herman had been alone far too long. They made her sign something, and then they drove away.

After hurrying to her picnic spot, she found her basket—still on the blanket—and could see the hole in the ground where she'd pushed in the spike. But Herman was gone! A hungry-looking waif of a thing told her he'd seen a large crowd of people by the lake. A dogcatcher's truck with a big cage in back had driven up, and a big dog had been dragged out of the crowd and put in the cage!

She drove quickly to the animal shelter. It was an awful old house way out on Columbine Street, where the smell of slaughterhouses and meat-packing plants stuck to everything. But it was Sunday and the place was closed. Early the next day, when she went back, a woman behind the counter told her that Herman had been locked up with the dogs who were vicious and would bite. "She told me Herman had bitten a *baby!*"

Then an animal-control officer came up to her and started asking her questions. He wanted to know all about Herman: how long she had had him, and who else he had bitten! "He was an awful man," she told me. "Of course Herman had never done anything like that in all of his life." She asked him why she couldn't take Herman home, and he told her the dog would be quarantined to see if he had rabies, and "if I didn't like it, I should get a lawyer. He seemed to blame *me,* but I had no idea what I'd done wrong."

When he was gone, the woman behind the counter, Maria, let her into the room where the dogs were kept. "I hardly recognized my poor baby," Miss Willow said. "He'd been beaten, and his coat was a bloody mess. And he was cooped up in this tiny cage, in a room full of tiny cages with dogs that barked and snapped. Maria let me stay with him, although I wasn't supposed to touch or pet him, but when no one was looking, of course I did."

For the rest of the week, she took food out to Herman and baked cookies for her new friend Maria, who always found a room where she and Herman could sit together. At least he was out of that awful cage. She stayed with him every day, from eight in the morning until five in the afternoon, as he licked himself clean and allowed those horrible wounds to heal.

"Then Friday morning when I arrived, Maria said there'd be a hearing or something at the courthouse, that afternoon, at two," Miss Willow told me. "I tried to see your grandfather, but he was so busy! Just before two, I hurried to the courthouse but didn't know where to go, and when I found the right room, it was after three and the door was locked. I drove back to the animal shelter, and Maria told me they'd decided Herman was a dangerous dog! Today, the animal-control people will get a court order and have him destroyed!"

The poor woman was crying again and clinging to my hand as though she'd fall off a cliff if she let go.

"You won't let them destroy Herman, will you, dear?"

"No," I said, even though I had no idea how to stop them. "No way!"

Chapter Four

Wᴴᴇɴ ɪ'ᴍ ɪɴ ᴀ ꜰᴜɴᴋʏ ᴍᴏᴏᴅ and way down in the bottom of a pit, sometimes I can lift my way out by staring at this old photograph of my grandfather. It was taken in 1887, on his first birthday. He's sitting up and reaching for something with a look of total focus on his face. His tiny body supports a head that is way too big, with masses of curly hair churning and rippling around it, covering his ears. The cutest little dimple is pasted on his chin.

The dimple is still there, as well as something about him that makes you want to call him "sir." That's the reason most people call him "Judge," even though he's never been one. A lot of lawyers don't see him that way, though. To them, he's just old, and very eccentric. "I don't care what anybody thinks," he says, and he means it. "I have a perspective on the law that comes with experience, and I don't care a whit for appearance. If I'm eccentric, so be it."

He grew up in Glamorganshire, somewhere in Wales, which I'd love to see someday. His family was so poor that he had to work in a coal mine when he was fifteen. When World War I broke out, he fought in the trenches in France. "That was easy for blokes like me," he told me. "We were used to mud and cold, and preferred being outside to working in a tunnel thick with coal dust. The air tasted good—until they filled it up with gas."

He'd glowered when he said that. "Kate darlin', an army of men is far worse than a pack of dogs. Some people think that, in war, gas is good tactics; but the cost in misery and suffering can't be calculated. It would never occur to a dog to fight another dog that way, to poison the very air that all God's creatures take for granted. Dogs don't have the capacity for that kind of madness. Gas destroys a man's lungs and leaves him gasping for air the rest of his life, like a rat in the ocean that can't get a purchase before he drowns."

"Were you gassed, Grampa?"

"I was. It's the reason I came across the water and all the way to Colorado, where the air is good and clean. Although at times I think I was sent here to meet your grandmother." He smiled as a tear trickled down his cheek.

"I see you in her, Katie. There's a magic about you that's just like the magic that was in her. But of course you're the image of your mother."

I had no idea what he meant about magic. That Grandmother Hope was a witch and I was too? And everyone thinks I look like my mom except me. She's taller than I am, has blue eyes instead of my green ones with brown flecks, and is blond. But we both have lots of teeth that show up well in photographs, the way my grandfather's dimple kind of lights up that photograph of him.

He started practicing law in the 1920s, after marrying Katherine Margaret Simpson, my grandmother. She died before I was born. I'm named after her, but everyone called her Maggie instead of Kate. I cannot even imagine what her life was like, as Maggie. What would it do to a grown person to be called something as horrible as that all her life? I stopped making jokes about it, though. Once all I did was suggest to Mom that it shouldn't have surprised anyone that Grandmother Hope died so young. With everyone calling her Maggie, what were her options?

Mom made me sit two inches from her face and threatened me with death if I ever said anything like that again. Grandmother Maggie was a strong woman, full of heart and conviction, Mom told me. She'd also been sweet, gentle, and beautiful, and Grandfather was totally destroyed when she died.

Grandfather didn't stay destroyed for long, though. He went back to his practice with my dad. But when Zozo and Law were killed, he was destroyed forever, he thought, and gave up the law for good.

Then he turned Mrs. Bartram away when she came to him for help, and she died two weeks later on Denver's streets. He beat himself up badly over that, even paying for her funeral—but couldn't forgive himself, or the legal "machine," either, that routinely denied poor people lawyers. "She couldn't afford one," he said to my mom and me, "and died because she had no place to stay. Is *that* what justice is all about?"

That was the only thing he talked about for two months —until Mom said, "Dad. You're making me tired. If you don't like it, *do* something about it."

He looked as if someone had put snow down his back. Then he pounded the table with his fist. "Annie! You're right!"

He didn't return to the practice of law for the money, often giving his clients more money than they paid him for his services. He even sold that great old house he'd lived in for fifty years, and got an apartment in an old hotel, downtown, that was close to his new office.

He didn't dress the way he used to, either. Sometimes when he came to work he'd forget to shave, and the suits he wore were rumpled and stained with tobacco juice. He chewed tobacco at the office, instead of smoking a pipe, and would shout at people who disagreed with him—something he'd never done before—and kick things if he tripped over them. That happened a lot, because he couldn't see.

But Mom loved the old man, and so did I. We liked the fact that he had his life back, even though Mom worried about him because some of the people she knew—lawyers who had known my dad—thought he was crazy.

There were times when he'd make me cringe and die of embarrassment, but I knew he wasn't crazy. In fact, to his clients he was a knight in shining armor, or Prince Caspian in *The Chronicles of Narnia,* infuriated by injustice and oppression. When poor people were "stomped on" by the legal system for the sake of profit, Grandfather became furious. "The law isn't a business!" he'd shout. "It's a profession! The lawyers of today have given her a *terrible* name. They treat her like a product that's for sale to the highest bidder!"

To Mrs. Roulette, he was a constant source of worry. Every time he left the office for the courthouse, she wondered if she'd ever see him again. His confidence in his ability to go from one place to another hadn't changed at all through the years, in spite of the fact that now he couldn't see where he was going.

I was ten when he went back into law. One of the first things he did was ask Mom if I could come down to the office, after school now and then, to help out. He'd take good care of me, he told her. I'd be nice and safe with him. I loved the idea—it got me out of the house—and Mom finally got used to it too. How could she say no?

I loved being the old man's eyes. I'd walk him to court, and later he showed me how to look up cases. When I read them to him at first, I didn't have a clue what any of it meant. But then it started making sense, and I'd ask him questions. Often he'd analyze a case for me, showing how the law could help his clients, and it was fun. Then he showed me how to use legal indexes and statutes and the state and federal reports of cases to find "the law," meaning the answers to legal questions—and one day he asked me to brief a point of law for him. I had to look up the cases on both sides of a legal issue, then summarize each case by writing down its facts, the reasons the court used to decide it one way or the other, and the law of the case.

He thought my brief was "adequate for a twelve-year-old," but he expected improvement. "It's objective enough, and you got the citations right. But it could use a bit of life. You need to keep the judge awake."

With him helping me, I started writing all his briefs, and a few months later he showed me how to write motions for court orders. They weren't hard at all, the way he explained them to me. "They're prayers," he said. "The judge is God. You're asking God to use his power to help you out." We'd sit sometimes in his office and talk about his cases, and when he came over for dinner on Sunday, Mom would listen to us with her patented smile, now and then interjecting some common sense. "She's my clerk," he told Mom one Sunday. "In the old days, that's how the young pups became lawyers. Course *Kate* won't ever be a lawyer, because she's a girl."

The first time he'd told me why I'd never be a lawyer, I was eleven, and it didn't occur to me to disagree with an eccentric old man with perspective. I didn't want to be a lawyer anyway, and neither did any of my friends. We'd stopped playing with dolls, but none of us thought about the future. We were into soccer, and hanging out at Aylard's Drugstore with boys, and the Beatles, and the Rolling Stones.

When he said it again, at another Sunday dinner, I got angry with him. The Friday before, he'd shown me pictures of Mary Lathrop, a famous Denver lawyer in the 1870s. "Where does it say a girl can't be a lawyer?" I asked him.

He laughed. "The fact is, you *can* be one if you want to. You may be only twelve years old, but you think like one already."

At work he started introducing me to women lawyers— even though it would take him out of his way, because there weren't many women lawyers for me to meet. I definitely had the impression that I was being maneuvered, but I didn't resent it. All he wanted was to give me something to think about.

But a few months later, another idea lodged in that massive head of his. He'd just signed a motion I'd written, which asked the district court to stop a landlord from unfairly evicting one of his clients and cited the law on the subject. "This is right on point and don't waste words," he said. "It's good, Kate. You know something?" When he peered at me, I wondered what he saw. "You could be a lawyer *now!*"

"Grandfather. I'm thirteen," I reminded him.

"You look it up and see if I'm not right."

All my friends at Hill Junior High were totally into themselves, and so was I. Would being a lawyer make me a geek, or, like, distinctive? I kind of held my breath as I did the research—and was almost relieved to find out he was wrong. I couldn't be a lawyer. A person has to pass the state bar examination first, I told him. Only graduates of law schools were allowed to "take the bar."

"There's more ways than one to skin a cat," he said. "All you've done is find out how they do it *now.* But that isn't the way it was in the old days, Kate. Find out how it was then, and see if those old laws were repealed. *That's* what a lawyer worth his salt would do."

So I went back to the books, and I found this old law that had been passed and adopted in 1867, when Colorado was still a territory. It said that if a person got a "certificate from one or more reputable counsellors at law," stating that he'd been "engaged in the study of law for two successive years prior to the making of such application," he could be examined by a "standing committee" appointed by the Supreme Court to "examine all applicants, for license . . ."

In other words, take a bar examination.

That old territorial law became a state law. But even if it hadn't, the Colorado constitution had a section that said all the territorial laws would remain in effect until repealed. So although other laws on the subject of bar examinations were passed, that old territorial law had never been repealed. I told the old judge that it was still on the books, and he started whooping with glee.

"What do you think, young lady!" he bellowed. "Have you learned enough law to pass the bar? I could use a partner like you!"

I was not enthusiastic, to be honest. But the expression on his face was the same as the one in his baby picture: total focus. "I can try."

The State Bar Examiners refused my application—which bothered me a little, because I'd looked it up myself and knew the law—but it was a relief, too.

It didn't just *bother* my grandfather, though. It made him mad.

He took them to court, and argued that I was smarter

than most of the "pups out of law school" because my native intelligence hadn't been "ruined by a college education." My mind "hadn't been distorted and configured into something acceptable to the Establishment. It's open, Your Honors, to what most lawyers have forgotten. Justice!"

He won the case—which didn't worry the Bar Examiners at all. They knew I didn't have a chance. That made *me* mad. I took a bar refresher course, taught by a lawyer on weekends for two months. He passed out outlines filled with legal principles on all the subjects we'd be tested on, such as torts, and civil procedure, and criminal law, and wills and estates. But it wouldn't be enough to memorize them, he said. We had to *understand* them, know how to use them. He wanted us to work together in study groups during the week.

No study group for me, though. I worked with my grandfather, who wouldn't give up on a subject until he was satisfied I knew all about it—"and where it fits in the fabric of the common law," he'd say, "which ain't common at all. It's a living thing, in spite of all those who want it to die."

The bar examination was way more difficult than the hardest test I'd ever taken in school. It lasted three whole days! But I passed it. The Supreme Court swore me in on March 22, 1973, which it says right on my Certificate to Practice Law.

FOURTEEN-YEAR-OLD LAWYER, said a headline in the

Post. GIRL, FOURTEEN, A LAWYER, said the one in the *News.* The media were there when I was sworn in by the Supreme Court, and that night I saw myself on TV. I was smiling Mom's great smile and wearing a black dress with a carnation pinned to it. But I kind of looked like a tuna surrounded by sharks. And at school, instant change. My friends thought it was pretty cool, but some of my classmates treated me like a freak, and two of my teachers asked me for legal advice!

The shingle on the front door of Grandfather's office has made it worthwhile, though. It's back to what it was before my dad was killed: HOPE AND HOPE, ATTORNEYS.

Chapter Five

"**W**HO'S THERE?" Grandfather yelled weakly, not sounding well at all. His sad old voice had to struggle to push through the door. "Don't make me guess who it is."

"Me, Grampa." I call him Judge at the office, but this wasn't the office, and I wanted to pet him or something, make him all better.

"Kate darlin'." He opened the door and staggered backward, almost falling down. "Come in."

His face was red enough to erupt into flames, and his skinny white legs dangled, like a puppet's, under a yellow bathrobe. His pale blue feet, in worn-out slippers, looked icy cold. But the silver hair swirling around his head seemed to shoot off sparks, and the eyes that peered out of his face were so bright and alive you would swear they could see through walls. "How are you feeling?" I asked as his bony old hands reached out for things they recognized, and led him to the sitting room.

"Not a hundred percent," he admitted. "It's a good thing I'm as mean as I am, Katie. I'm too mean to die."

He had three rooms on the seventh floor of the Shirley Savoy Hotel. People said that for fifty years it had been one of the finest hotels in Denver. Now it was just one of the oldest. Grandfather liked it because it was only four blocks from the office and he could walk to work, "for the exercise." Mother hated it because when he crossed Broadway he was a moving target. Mrs. Roulette and I hated it too, but so far, in spite of a few near-misses, no one had hit him.

I sat down and opened the briefcase Mom had given me when I passed the bar. "As soon as you've signed this, I'm calling a doctor," I told him.

"No you're not." He dropped wearily into a chair and let his chin fall on his chest. "I'm sick enough now, without some doctor making it worse." He crumpled into the cushions and his eyes drooped shut. "Just let me hear what you have on Alvarez so I can get back in bed."

I pulled the file out of my briefcase—and he fell asleep. He drops off like that at the office, too, only to bump awake five minutes later, all full of himself and feisty. Maybe he doesn't need a doctor after all, I thought, thumbing through the motion and thinking about the case as I waited for him to wake up.

Mr. Alvarez was born in Mexico, but lived in Colorado on a work permit with his wife and five children. His big goal in life was to become a citizen of the United States so that he could make a decent living and take care of his family. But he'd been charged with theft. If he got convicted, he could no longer live in this country. The federal government would deport him and his whole family back to Mexico, and a life of poverty.

He'd been charged with stealing tools from his employer, but it was a lie, and we had a witness who could prove it. The witness wouldn't be at the trial, however. Also a Mexican citizen, he'd been caught working without a permit and had been deported!

The Judge had asked me to write a "motion for an indefinite continuance." It said the case should be continued until our witness came back to Colorado—even though it would be illegal for him to come back. It was a stupid motion, I thought, for lots of reasons. The biggest one was simple: there's no such thing as an indefinite continuance. I made the mistake of telling the Judge what I thought.

"Write it!" he'd shouted at me, which he does when he forgets I'm his granddaughter. Usually he's as old-fashioned as a horse and buggy, even opening doors for what he calls "the gentler sex"—when he can find the knobs. "You might learn a thing or two," he'd said. "That is, if you aren't careful. *I* know there's no such thing as an indefinite continuance. Every jackass knows that. So say in the motion that there *ought* to be." Then he'd frowned in my direction, which was his way of apologizing for yelling at me. "You don't know, young woman," he'd said. "It could make perfect sense, to a judge."

He woke up. "Kate?"

"Hi, Grandfather. Welcome back."

"Don't get snippy now. How long is that motion?"

"Four pages."

"That's about right," he said. "Any longer and the judge won't read it." He clutched his stomach. "Are you satisfied with it?"

"It's not great, Judge. But it's arguable."

"Any authority?"

He was asking if there was a case out there somewhere I'd found that could support the motion. "Not really," I said.

"Well, does it make sense?"

"Not to me," I told him honestly. "It could to a judge."

He snorted at that. "Give me your pen, darlin'," he said. He signed it and tried to push himself out of his chair. "You'd think a man's internal organs would improve with age, the way wine does. Too bad they don't." He started to lose his balance, but I was quick enough to help him. "What does that Willow woman want?" he asked, leaning on my shoulder and letting me slip an arm around his waist. "She was in the office Friday, but she left before I could talk to her."

"Nothing important," I told him as my stomach froze with panic. I wanted to ask him what I could possibly do for her, but didn't. The last thing he needed right now was another problem.

We shuffled toward his bedroom. "Poor lonely old bag of bones," he said. "All she's got in this world is a dog."

We moved near his bed. "Grandfather, let me fix you something to eat?"

"Thanks, darlin'," he said, finding the edge of his bed with his hand and sitting on it. "But I'd throw it up after a while, and it would smell." He chuckled for some strange reason known only to the male members of the human race, who think it's funny for a person to throw up and cause a smell. "Besides, how will I know I'm well if I keep myself stuffed? It's when a man gets hungry that he knows he's well." He shrugged off his bathrobe, revealing purple boxer shorts, and stood up long enough to let the bathrobe fall to the floor. "Leave it there, Kate, so I know where it is and can find it."

I helped him into bed. "Let me at least call Mom?" I asked him. "She'd love to come over and—"

"No you don't." He closed his eyes and pulled the sheet up to his chin. "The last thing I need is a managin' female tellin' me to do this and do that." His eyes closed. "You aren't like that, Katie my dear. Not yet."

It sounded like a warning, which I didn't need. I've always known that the only person I need to manage is me. But I could hardly wait to tell Mom *she* was a managing female. "Will you call me if you need anything?" I asked, hating to leave him when it seemed he might die any second.

"Course. You're my partner." He opened an eye and found me with it, even though I was certain he couldn't see me. "Kate, you're a fine young woman, you are. Your father would be proud of you. So would your brother."

I saw them suddenly, getting in the car and leaving for the mountains on that awful day. "Really?" I whispered as tears squished out of my eyes.

"No question about it."

Chapter Six

I T WAS ALREADY TEN THIRTY when I left Grandfather's hotel. What happened to my morning? The Alvarez motion had to be filed before noon, which I could do. But what about Herman? What if he'd already been put to sleep? I hurried back to the office, torturing my brain for ideas.

When I opened the door, I had to push my way through a crowd of people. Clients? Were they all waiting to see their lawyer? That was me!

Miss Willow's eyes pleaded with mine from a corner of the room, and I nodded at her, trying to keep my cool. "Mrs. Roulette, can I see you a moment?"

"Of course, dear."

She followed me to my room, and I shut the door behind her so no one would hear me scream. "What can I do?" I begged her. "There is no *way* I can see all those people. I don't have *time*. I have to file that motion, and Miss Willow's dog is facing a death sentence!"

She put her hands on my shoulders and smiled at me as though she knew I'd think of something. "Calm down, sweetie," she said. "How would your grandfather handle the situation?"

"He'd decide who has a real problem and tell everyone else to go away." Then came a brainstorm. "*You* know all the clients, don't you?"

"Oh yes."

"And what their problems are?"

She nodded knowingly. "Mrs. Clarvey probably wants to throw her husband out of the house. She's a big woman. The Judge would tell her to pick him up and put him outside. Mr. Thorne often simply wants to change his will. His daughter may have done something to annoy him, and he punishes her by taking her out of it, then telling her what she did to deserve it. Mr. Cleft—"

"Will you screen them for me?"

"What?" She frowned at me with uncertainty. "Dear, what do you mean?"

"Work up a little form? It doesn't have to be very complicated or anything, maybe a place for their name, today's date, their telephone number, and what kind of problem. Then do a quick interview and tell anyone who really needs to see me to come back this afternoon?"

"I'm just a secretary, honey," she said. "Can I do that?"

"You're not 'just a secretary,' Mrs. Roulette." She looked at me as though she wondered what on earth I was talking about. I wondered too, but kept going. "Didn't you read that article in *Ms.* on Pat Nixon?" I asked her. "How she should stop being 'just a wife' and start being a woman?"

"It's a bit late for me to make changes like *that*."

"No, it isn't." She seemed to shrivel before my eyes. "Mrs. Roulette, I really need your help."

She nodded and took a deep breath. "I'll do my best, dear."

"Thank you!" I said. "Use Grandfather's office when you do your interviews, okay? It'll be easier, and you can answer the telephone too." A thought flashed through my mind, someone I could call about Herman. "But let me use it first," I said, hopping across the hall.

"Of course, dear. Would you like to see Miss Willow now?"

"Not yet." I ripped through the telephone book, looking for the number for the animal shelter. It takes forever to find a number when you're in a hurry, but finally I found it. "Maria?" I blurted into the telephone, remembering the name of the "nice woman" Miss Willow had baked cookies for at the animal shelter. "Hi. I'm Kate Hope, Miss Willow's lawyer? Can you tell me what's going on with Herman?"

"Oh! I am so happy you called, Mrs. Hope!"

"Kate," I said. "And it's 'Ms.' Like the magazine?"

"Herman must *not* be destroyed," she said urgently. "He may look like a wolf, but he is a wonderful dog, so strong, so gentle. He would never bite a baby!"

"Where is he now?"

"Here. With me. I take special care of him." Her voice was one step from hysteria. "There's no time to lose. Officer Milliken wants to put an end to the dog today. He will take the paperwork to the city attorney's office himself, and walk it through."

"What does that mean?"

"He will have the city attorney write up an order, ordering Animal Control to 'destroy' Herman! That's what the law calls killing dogs. Then he will take the order to the judge and have it signed, and come back to the shelter, and . . ." Her voice trailed off to a gasp.

"And what?"

"He will see to Herman himself."

I was shocked. "You mean he'll kill him personally?"

"Yes."

"Why?" I asked. "Is he a sadist or something? What's the big hurry? Why does it have to be *today?* What about Miss Willow?"

"He doesn't care about her. It's his wish to be the big hero to the family of this baby, to give them their vengeance. Ms. Hope, is there something you can do?"

My whole body buzzed with static. "Who writes up the orders in the city attorney's office?"

His name was Carl Thomas, and two minutes later, I actually had him on the telephone. Would he talk to me, like, lawyer to lawyer? "I . . . sir, I have a client with a dog," I started.

He laughed. "A lot of people have dogs. Who is this?"

"Kate Hope, sir. I'm with—"

"I know who you are, Kate," he said, then corrected himself. "Miss Hope. I've read about you, and knew your dad. A fine man, I might add. What's this about your client's dog?"

His voice sounded familiar to me, even though I couldn't place it. "There has been this terrible mistake. The dog's name is Herman, and—"

"Is that the German shepherd that bit the Pearsan baby?"

"I . . . well, the *charge* is that he bit a baby, but—"

"It's not a terrible mistake, Kate. The animal-control officer just talked to me, and I'm working on the order now. He'll be here right after lunch to pick it up. Herman will be out of his misery this afternoon."

My body went from buzz to numb. "Please, Mr. Thomas," I begged him. "What can I do?"

"*I* don't know. Ask your grandfather." He sounded angry. "Your client didn't even show up at the hearing, Kate. What do you expect?"

"But—"

"Look, I'm sorry," he said.

I tried to say something, but nothing came out.

"Listen to me, Kate," he said, a bit softer this time. "You're a lawyer now. You win some and you lose some. It's not a bowl of cherries."

"Thanks, I guess," I said.

"I've got another call," he said, and hung up.

Cold sweat covered my forehead. How could I tell Miss Willow that Herman was toast? I grabbed all my notes on Herman and stuffed them in my briefcase, next to the Alvarez motion, then hurried down the hall. "Bye, Mrs. Roulette," I said, waving and smiling confidently at everyone, which is something the Judge said I should always do, no matter what I felt. "Miss Willow?" I asked, finding her terror-filled stare in the corner of the reception room. "Wait here, okay? I won't be long I hope."

Mom's genes may have given me her great smile, but they also gave me her nervous stomach. Why did that have to be part of the package? I probably looked okay to all our clients, but I needed to throw up.

The courts are in the City and County Building, less than two blocks from our office. It's a colossal four-story mass of huge stone bricks that totally occupies two city blocks. It sits there like a Greek temple, with enormous marblelike columns that don't hold up anything except huge marble beams with Roman letters carved on them. Steps spread down from the main entrance on the second floor, like pictures I've seen of those terraced hillsides in China.

As I jogged up the steps, a man coming down them stopped when he saw me, then smiled and got in my way. "Are you Kate Hope, the girl lawyer?" he asked.

"Yes, sir."

He shifted his briefcase to his left hand and stuck out his hand, kind of man to man. "You're hell on wheels, girlie. Thought you were going to run me over on that boy's bike you ride."

"Oh. You're . . ." I held out my hand. He looked almost slender in the lightweight Italian suit he'd changed into.

"Incidentally, I do have daughters, Kate. Two of them." He crushed my hand.

"Aaagh!"

His face beamed with happy malice. "Better strengthen your grip, honey. The law is basically a man's world, know what I mean?" He let go of my mutilated hand.

"I guess it needs some work."

"Another thing, Kate," he said. "I'm Carl Thomas."

"You?" I tried to smile. "Oh."

"I know I was a little abrupt on the telephone. But— well, I'm sorry." He shrugged and trotted on down the steps.

It was cool in the courthouse, like being deep inside a mammoth cave. The high ceilings were twenty feet above the marble floors. I rode the elevator to the fourth floor and hurried down the hall to the office of the clerk for the criminal division. Mrs. Davis, the clerk, was behind the counter. "Hi, cutie," she said to me.

I didn't mind being called "cutie" by Mrs. Davis. It meant I was part of her family. The Judge had introduced me to her right after I'd passed the bar. "She knows more law than most lawyers, Kate," he'd said.

"Judge, you know I can't give legal advice," she had replied. "That's against the law."

"So it is," he'd said to her, then turned to me. "But if you treat her nicely and say please, she might make helpful suggestions."

I hoped she'd give me some helpful suggestions now. "Hi, Mrs. Davis," I said, handing her the Alvarez motion. "This has to be filed before noon."

She leafed through it. "Kate, the DA needs a copy. Have you given him one?"

I took a deep breath. "I forgot. I'll just run back to the office and—"

"You won't make it in time. I'll make you a copy." She took it over to the copy machine. "Five cents a page."

"I don't have any money."

"Pay me the next time you see me." She put the first page of the motion on the glass plate on top and closed the lid. In less than two minutes, the motion was copied. "Do you know what to do now?"

"Give it to the receptionist in the DA's office? And get a certificate of service?"

"Not quite. Have her sign your certificate of service."

"I forgot that, too."

She reached under the counter for a form that said *Certificate of Service* at the top. "Just make sure the receptionist signs and dates this," she said, "and then bring it back to me. Hurry now." She glanced at the clock. "It's eleven thirty."

"You've saved my life." I grabbed the papers, ran across the street to the DA's office, gave the copy to the receptionist, who signed the certificate of service, and then ran back to the clerk's office with minutes to spare.

"You aren't even sweating," Mrs. Davis said as she file-stamped the original at eleven forty-nine. "How are you doing, Kate? Having fun?"

"Not today. Grandfather's sick and . . ."

Two men walked in, so I stopped talking. Neither of them really noticed me as they joked with Mrs. Davis and filed their papers. After they left, Mrs. Davis said, "I'm sorry to hear about the Judge. He's such a dear."

"Mrs. Davis, can I ask you for a suggestion?"

She laughed. "Sure."

After I told her about Herman, she frowned at the clock. It was almost noon. "I'm meeting with some judges for lunch, honey, and can't help you. But I can show you a file. If you're as smart as the Judge says, you'll know what to do." She pulled a file out of the long bank of cabinets in the back and handed it to me, then gave me several clean sheets of legal-size typing paper. "There's a typewriter in the law library. Can you type?"

"Sort of."

"You'll need copies. One for you, one for the court, and one for Carl Thomas." She thought a moment. "Here." She opened a drawer and gave me a key. "This opens that side door. Can you use the copier?"

I didn't know. The office of Hope and Hope didn't have one. "Yes."

"You'll have to be finished at one, Kate. I can't let you stay after that." It was three minutes after twelve. "Think you can do it?"

Mom's great smile appeared on my face. "Piece of cake."

Chapter Seven

THE FILE MRS. DAVIS HAD GIVEN ME was a burglary case! Had she made a mistake? But when I thumbed through it, I understood. The defense lawyer had filed a "Motion for Injunctive Relief, to Prevent the Destruction of Evidence." I could do the same thing, only I'd call mine a "Motion for Injunctive Relief, to Prevent the Execution of a Dog."

I tucked the file under my arm, let myself out the side door, and hurried to the law library.

Mrs. Roulette would not have been proud of the way it looked, with uneven margins and strikeovers and erasure marks. But there wasn't time to worry about that. With two minutes to spare, I left the key on Mrs. Davis's desk and stuffed the motion and all the copies in my briefcase. The city attorney's office was across the street. "Hi," I said, five minutes later, to the receptionist.

"It's Kate Hope!" the receptionist said, smiling at me. She knew who I was, which was nice. All the receptionists, and secretaries, and the women who did all the work that the men got the credit for, knew who I was. I got energy from them too, because they wanted me to succeed. "How are you, honey?"

"Great," I lied. "Mr. Thomas here?"

"He's with someone, but if . . ."

"A dogcatcher? Officer Milliken?"

She nodded.

"Can you sign for this," I asked, giving her a copy of my motion, "and give it to him?"

"Sure, but—"

"I'm in kind of a hurry, or I'd wait."

As she signed the certificate of service, she glanced at the motion. Her eyebrows went up. "You scoot," she said. "I'll see that he gets it."

Next stop was Judge Steinbrunner in Courtroom Six. I hurried into his clerk's office, but no one was there, so I tapped the bell on the counter.

"Who is it!" a man's voice demanded from the judge's chambers.

"It's, ah, Kate Hope, sir," I said.

"You don't say! Well." I heard the man talking to someone, then the sound of a phone being hung up. He came out. A round little man with horn-rimmed glasses and thin gray hair, he looked pleased when he saw me, but not nice. In fact, he looked like a cat who had cornered a mouse. "That was Carl Thomas on the phone, so I was expecting you. Let me see what you have, missy." He took the papers from me and the smile on his face got bigger. "Well, now. Have you ever challenged someone to a duel?"

"Excuse me, sir?"

"Once you start something like this, you can't stop it." He nodded to himself with satisfaction. "Young lady, I want you in my courtroom at two o'clock. Today. Thirty-five minutes from now." He beamed at me. "With your client."

My stomach hurt as I zipped back to the office. "Your young man called," Mrs. Roulette said. "He'd like you to call him."

"Mike Doyle is *not* my young man!" The office had emptied except for Miss Willow, who sat huddled in a corner. "I can't call him now. Miss Willow and I have to be in Judge Steinbrunner's courtroom in twenty minutes."

Miss Willow's eyes popped open and a timid fist covered her mouth. "We do?" she managed. "But I can't go to court looking like this! You'll just have to go without me, dear."

"You look fine, Miss Willow," I said, "and you have to be there. Judge's orders. Let's go."

We drove back in her car, which was a mistake. It would have been faster to walk—and safer, too. She was a complete basket case. When we got to Courtroom Six, I pushed her inside and looked at the clock. We'd made it with one minute to spare.

Mr. Thomas was already there, sitting at one of the tables in front of the bench. He wouldn't look at me, but the big man wearing a brown uniform who sat next to him did. Officer Milliken, no doubt, though he wasn't at all like the picture of him I'd drawn in my mind. I'd drawn a weasel, but this man had a friendly expression on his face and nice brown eyes. "Hello," he said, standing up. "I'm Dan Milliken, Ms. Hope." He stepped over to me and stuck his hand out. Another crusher? "I've got a daughter your age who wants to be a lawyer," he said. "She wants to meet you."

At least he was nice enough not to break any of my fingers when he shook my hand. "If anything's left of me after today, sir, I'd love to meet her."

"I'll tell her," he said, glancing at Miss Willow. His smile disappeared. "Hello, Miss Willow. No hard feelings, okay?"

She wouldn't look at him, which may have been the only mean thing she ever did in her life.

Miss Willow and I sat at the plaintiff's table, where she kind of hid next to me with her head down. Then Judge Steinbrunner's clerk came in through a door that led into the judge's chambers. "All rise!" she said, and everyone stood up as the judge followed her in through the same door. He climbed the steps that took him to his chair behind the bench, and stared around the room through his horn-rimmed glasses, like an owl with a robe on. From his perch he could look down on everyone. As soon as he was in his chair, the clerk said to the rest of us, "Be seated."

"Miss Hope," the judge said to me, holding the motion in his hands, "in all my years on the bench, I've never seen anything like this." I stood up quickly, my knees shaking like a skeleton in a hurricane. "In my experience, dogs get destroyed. They don't get executed. Now, a man can get executed if he commits a certain kind of crime and gets caught and is prosecuted and convicted and all the rest of it, but the law isn't quite as careful about dogs. Why is that?"

"I . . ." I swallowed. What would Grandfather say? "Because dogs can't vote?"

"Well now." He chortled and pushed his glasses back on his nose. "You have a point there. All right, it's your motion. You may proceed."

"Proceed?" I'd been so busy writing and filing the motion that I'd forgotten about what I'd have to do in court. "You mean . . . ?"

"Yes."

The main door into the courtroom opened. The cavalry to my rescue? I turned, hoping it was Mrs. Davis with a suggestion, or Grandfather to take my place . . .

Mike Doyle! He grinned at me and sat down.

"I'm waiting, Miss Hope."

I didn't need Mike there at all! I *hated* having someone I actually knew, *watching me*. "Sir, it's just—my client's dog

59

is going to be executed or destroyed unless something is done about it." My voice was so tiny I could hardly hear it myself.

"You'll have to speak up," the judge barked. "This is a court of record, and what you say is being taped. Now speak up, young lady."

I closed my eyes . . . and saw Neil Armstrong! What was *he* doing in my brain? "The *Eagle* has landed," I heard him say.

If those men had the courage to fly to the moon, I could stand up to an old judge. When I opened my eyes, the judge's scowl didn't seem so awful. I smiled at him. "This is June eleventh, 1973, in the Municipal Court for the City and County of Denver," I said, imitating some of the lawyers I'd watched in court. "My name is Kate Hope and I represent Miss Wilma Willow, who is here. Also present is Mr. Carl Thomas, of the city attorney's office, and Officer Dan Milliken, Municipal Animal Control. You have before you a motion for injunctive relief."

"Well now. That's better."

"The City wants an order from you, sir, to murder my client's dog. I filed this motion to keep that from happening."

"Your Honor, I object to Miss Hope's characterization of the order," Mr. Thomas said, jumping up. "It doesn't say anything about 'murder.' Just last Friday, this Court had a hearing about the dog, and evidence was presented, and the Court found that the dog is a dangerous dog. The order before you is for the dog's destruction."

The judge nodded. "Miss Hope, I'll just supplement the record a bit." He had that tiny smile on his face that I didn't like. "A complaint was filed by the city attorney on June fourth about this dog, and there's a certificate of service showing your client was served with a copy. The complaint alleges that your client's dog is dangerous and should be destroyed. There was a hearing on June eighth, and Mr. Thomas proved to my satisfaction that the dog was dangerous. I told the City they could destroy it once there was a written order. Mr. Thomas said he'd draw it up. I assume he has it with him. Am I right, Mr. Thomas?"

"Yes, sir." He handed a piece of paper to me, but my eyes had blurred over with terror, and I couldn't read it. "Let the record show I've served a copy of the order on the defense." He handed another one to the judge.

"Miss Hope, is there any reason I should not sign this order?"

"It would be cruel and inhuman." How could this happen? I was ready to cry!

"A *legal* reason. This is a court of law."

"I don't *have* a legal reason, sir. But it isn't right! It's not fair! Herman didn't have a lawyer at that hearing. He didn't know what was going on. He had no one there to defend him!"

"Calm down now." The judge's face softened, but not

by much. "I recognize that what's fair is open to interpretation, but in law, it's fair as long as the other side had the *opportunity* to be there and defend. Now, the record shows Miss Willow was personally served with the complaint. She had notice of the hearing. It was her decision, apparently, not to be there. But she could have been, and with a lawyer too, and she could have put on evidence. I have already made a finding of fact in this case and am not inclined to reopen it without a reason. Do you have a reason?"

Miss Willow had been served with papers? She'd never said anything to me about them. "Judge, can I have a minute, please?" I begged.

"You may."

I huddled over Miss Willow like a storm cloud. "Miss Willow, did someone give you some papers about this?" I whispered.

She dug through her purse and pulled out a large, thick envelope. "I think this is what he means."

It was all there. "Why didn't you tell me?" I asked, in a whisper that could be heard in the hall.

The poor thing acted like I'd hit her. "Please don't hate me. I found these on my porch today, when I went home for lunch."

I sat down next to her. "You didn't get these until today?"

"No." She started to sob.

I looked through them for the certificate of service. It

said a deputy sheriff had given her all the papers on June 4, at ten in the morning. "But it says right here that a deputy sheriff *gave* them to you on the fourth!" I hissed at her, trying to keep my voice down.

"But I wasn't even home then," she said. "I was at the animal shelter, with Herman."

"All day?" I asked.

"Yes."

"Did Maria see you?"

"Yes."

I could breathe! "Sir! I have a legal reason!"

"What is it?"

"Miss Willow wasn't served with a copy of the complaint until today! She did not have notice of the hearing!"

"Young lady, the certificate of service says she was served with a copy of the complaint on June fourth, sworn to by a deputy sheriff. Are you calling him a liar?"

"Oh, no. I wouldn't do that. But Miss Willow wasn't home at ten o'clock on the fourth. She found these papers on her porch today."

The judge glared at me long and hard. "So you admit you have them with you now?"

I swallowed. "Yes, sir."

"But you say she just happened to find them on her porch today?"

"Yes, sir," I said again. Miss Willow kept tugging my elbow. "Can I have another minute, please, Your Honor?"

"You have one more minute."

"It's happened before," Miss Willow whispered to me, in her tiny voice. "The mailman has a terrible time."

"What do you mean?"

"People forget the west."

What did she mean? I looked at the envelope. "Your Honor!" I said. "The sheriff's deputy took the papers to the wrong address!"

It didn't take long to explain. There was a 368 Cedar Street, and a 368 West Cedar Street. Miss Willow got their mail, and they got hers. The certificate of service showed that the deputy sheriff had given the papers to someone at 368 Cedar, but Miss Willow lived at 368 West Cedar. Whoever typed the envelope had made a mistake.

"You win, Miss Hope," the judge said. But he wasn't very happy about it. "Mr. Thomas, we'll have to do this again."

"Your Honor, a suggestion?" Mr. Thomas asked as he stood up.

"What is it?"

"We could have the hearing now. Officer Milliken is here, with his reports, ready to testify. The dog's owner is here as well. Miss Hope can cross-examine Officer Milliken to her heart's content and put on any evidence she has. All the due-process protections are in place, and it would save the Court's time."

"Makes good sense," the judge said. "Miss Hope, don't you agree?"

The judge was being awfully nice, and so was Mr. Thomas. "I . . . well . . ." But this time Grandfather's face came into my brain. *He* wouldn't agree. He'd be disagreeable, in fact. *Lawyers aren't hired to get along with judges and other lawyers,* he would say. *Their duty is to protect their clients! To do that, you need time to prepare your case!*

I got the message. I wasn't ready for a hearing now. I hadn't even looked at the reports. "No, sir."

"Very well," the old man said through his teeth. "We'll have another hearing. Mr. Thomas, make certain Miss Hope has copies of all the reports. I don't want to do this a third time because she hasn't had discovery."

"Yes, sir," Mr. Thomas said. "I'll give them to her now." He pulled some papers out of his file. "Let the record show Miss Hope received a copy of the police report and a copy of the animal-control officer's report." He handed them to me.

"So noted," the judge said. "We'll have the hearing in this matter on Friday, June fifteenth, at two o'clock. Anything else?"

"Judge, the hearing will be—I mean—to *you,* sir?" I asked.

"Of course! What did you expect!"

That wouldn't do Miss Willow any good. The judge

had already made up his mind. "We want a jury, sir. A trial to a jury?"

"*What?*" He looked like he was going to jump over the bench and hit me. "A *jury trial* for a *dog?*"

"She doesn't think you can be fair, I guess, Judge," Mr. Thomas said, smiling at me. "But as the Court knows, our ordinances don't allow for jury trials for animals. She's stuck with you, sir."

The old judge started to chuckle. "Well now. A chip off the old block, perhaps." His face glowed the way older people's do when they remember something that happened when they were young. "She has the right, Carl, but it's not in the city ordinances. I remember it because I was in the city attorney's office when a young man fresh out of the district attorney's office brought suit against the city on that very point. Do you know who that young man was, Miss Hope?"

"No, sir."

"Your father." He started writing again. Zozo did that? "He won the lawsuit, but the jury convicted the dog. Ask your grandfather about it."

Tears leaked out of my eyes and I started sniffing and my mouth loosened up. Zozo had come to my rescue, which is what fathers do for their daughters. My heart just seemed to swell up with . . . love?—even though it was horrible, trying not to cry.

"Are you all right, young lady?"

"Yes, sir. I'm fine," I said, wiping my eyes off.

"How much time will you need to prepare?"

Miss Willow handed me a Kleenex. "How much can I get?"

He smiled at that. "What about it, Carl? When shall we try this dog of a case?" He beamed at me over his pun.

Mr. Thomas wasn't very amused, though. "It costs the city fifty dollars a day to keep dogs at the animal shelter," he said. "I'd recommend an early date."

"Do they feed them steak?" the judge asked. "Goodness." He turned a page in his book. "Thursday, June twenty-first, Miss Hope. That's ten days."

"Plenty of time, sir."

"That's the order, then. We're adjourned." He started to get up.

Miss Willow jerked my arm. "Can I take Herman home?" she whispered to me.

"Judge, can the dog go home?" I blurted. "I mean, can Herman be released on bail?"

"The City strenuously objects," Mr. Thomas said. "That animal has bitten a baby. If he bites again, we could be facing a serious lawsuit."

"Miss Hope?" the judge said.

"Sir, we don't know if he bit a baby. That's what the trial will decide. If he goes home, it would save the city fifty dollars a day."

"The evidence was very convincing, Miss Hope. But I'd consider releasing him if I could be absolutely certain your client could control him and he wouldn't bite anyone."

"I'll keep him in the house," Miss Willow whispered.

"My client will keep the dog in her house until the trial, sir," I said.

"The whole time?"

"Well, I guess he'd probably—you know."

"All right. You prepare an order, ordering the City to release the dog to your client until the trial, and ordering her to keep him inside the house except as nature requires him to go outside. Bring it to me this afternoon and I'll sign it. You understand that the dog won't be released until the City has a signed copy of the order?"

"Yes, sir."

"We're in recess, then." He stood up, walked down the steps, and disappeared.

Miss Willow gazed at me like an angel worshiping God. No one had ever looked at me like that. Mike sat there with a big smile on his face too, and I just soaked up all that adoration, tingling inside and feeling wonderful. Then Mr. Thomas got in my way. "You were lucky today," he said, "but don't let that sweet old woman get her hopes up."

"Why not?"

He made a motion with his hand. Slicing his throat.

Chapter Eight

Miss willow wanted to drive us to the office, but that could take forever, so Mike and I decided to walk. She gushed all over Mike when he opened the car door for her and helped her in, which she didn't need. It drives me crazy. He's a boy, so he's a "fine young man" to Miss Willow. But I'm a girl, which makes me a "dearie."

Then Mike tried to take my briefcase out of my hand, as though I needed help too. "Don't," I told him.

His face fell. All the way to the sidewalk. He was brought up to treat women as a different species who constantly need the helping hand of a big, strong man, but wasn't brought up to deal with rejection. I'd wounded his ego.

"Here," I said, handing him my briefcase.

"You were so great," he said, happy now. " 'We want a

jury, sir,' just like Perry Mason. *'What!'* And the way you sprung that trap. 'Miss Willow wasn't served with a copy of the complaint. She didn't have notice of the hearing!' That other lawyer's ears? I could feel the heat."

"Mike, I got lucky."

"It didn't look like luck to me," he said. "You outfoxed him. Want a Coke?"

"Can't. Too much to do." He'd locked his bike to mine and looked really sad when I opened the office door and took my briefcase out of his hand. "Call me tonight?" I asked him.

"Maybe," he said. "If I have time."

Mrs. Roulette was so pleased with me when I told her what had happened that I almost called the Judge to tell him about it too, but I didn't want to wake him if he was asleep. While Mrs. Roulette typed up the order for Judge Steinbrunner to sign, Miss Willow and I read the reports Carl Thomas had given me about the case.

They'd been written by Animal Control Officer Milliken, and Officer Smith of the Denver Police Department, and they were horrible. They said that Ursula Jespersen, age 18 and the babysitter for a family who lived in Cherry Hills, had taken their tiny daughter to City Park. She wheeled the infant in a baby carriage to a location near the duck pond and had stopped to watch the ducks when suddenly a large dog knocked over the carriage, picked up the baby in his jaws, and started to run off with her. But a man charged in and made the dog drop the baby. The brave man held the vicious animal with a dog chain until Officer Smith arrived on the scene and radioed Animal Control.

Miss Willow nearly fainted. "Herman would *never* do something so awful!" she said. "They must have the wrong dog."

Right. But there wasn't time to worry about that now. Mrs. Roulette finished typing the order, and I ran it over to the judge with lots of copies, and he signed them all. The city attorney got one, and Miss Willow took two of them with her to the animal shelter. She was all smiles and tears when she drove off to get her dog, but my brain wouldn't stop whirling around in my head. Zozo had gotten his dog a jury trial, but it hadn't saved the dog.

Clients began to materialize in the reception room, and I spent what was left of the day trying to help them. I used Grandfather's office because it was cooler, there were more chairs, and I love that old roll-top desk he keeps the telephone on.

At six thirty I called Mom. "I'll be another hour at least," I said.

"You're not riding your bike home then," she said. "I'll come get you."

"Mom, please. My legs are twitching and I really need it. I won't be able to sleep!"

"Not without a bicycle light. I'm sorry. You can do deep knee-bends for the twitching."

"Mike has one on his bike. I could ride with him. Ask him if he'll come get me?" He lived on the same block, two houses from mine. "If he won't, then I promise not to argue about it. Okay?"

"Why was it so much easier to be a mother when my mother was a mother? I *always* did what she told me to do. With you, I have to negotiate everything!"

An hour later, when Mike showed up, I still had two clients to go. The first one needed help with a bill collector. I told him I'd write the agency a letter and try to work something out. The second one just needed someone to tell her what she already knew. She had three kids and no money for food because her husband was in jail and couldn't work. And she wouldn't go to the welfare department for food stamps because he had told her he'd beat her up if she did that, when he got out! Just like a man, I thought, not to think things through. His pride had its place, but should his family starve because of it? "Go get food stamps," I told her. "You don't have any other options. Tell him your lawyer said she'll kill him if he beats you." That lightened up the atmosphere. "Tell him too that he can always pay the money back to the welfare department."

According to my grandfather, lots of people actually do that. He doesn't think people are nearly as bad as the public thinks they are.

Mike waited while I changed into bike shorts. He's

useful as an escort to ride home with, even though he could use a poke with a sharp stick. He dawdles around when he rides, like a dog, kind of stopping along the way to sniff things. I had to let him set the pace because he had the light.

But it wasn't awful, even at two miles an hour. It was beautiful out. A huge moon hung over Denver like a big snowball, bright enough to toss shadows. We rode east on Twelfth Avenue from Broadway to Hale Parkway, which is less than four miles when you measure it in distance. But it can also be measured in time, beginning in the last century and stretching all the way into this one. We traveled past the old mansions and huge brick homes near the center of town, then rode through newer neighborhoods with smaller brick houses but bigger lawns. Mom had written an article for the *Post* about the architectural rings around the city, like rings around a tree. If you know how to read them, she'd said in her story, you can walk through history.

We lived near Crestmoor Park. The mountains west of us were on the horizon, and the moon was so bright we could see them clearly, even the patches of snow. The lawns in our neighborhood were landscaped with flowers, shrubs, and leafy trees, and all the gutters were swept clean of debris. No one parked their cars outside at night because the houses had two-car garages with garage-door openers. Usually I feel good about living in such a nice neighborhood, but not tonight. After dealing with some of our clients, I came dangerously close to feeling guilty.

We rolled by Mike's house first, but he had to do his little-old-lady routine by riding with me all the way up my driveway. "G'night, Mike," I said, clicking open the garage door. "You can go now."

I parked my bike, lifted off the saddlebags, and opened the door into the kitchen. "You're late," Mom said, her face one big scold. "It's almost nine."

"Hello, Mother." I dropped the saddlebags on the floor. "How was your day at the office?"

Chapter Nine

My heart sank when I glanced around the reception room at the office the next morning. The place was already packed with clients, and I didn't need another day of dealing with them and all their miserable problems. Some had horrible breath and rotting teeth, and most wore clothes from the Salvation Army, and all of them needed a lawyer. Their fears and anxieties vibrated in my stomach like a jackhammer. I wondered how Grandfather had lasted for eighty-seven years. "Hi, Mrs. Roulette," I said as the telephone rang.

She waved at me, then snatched the phone out of its cradle. "Good morning," she said. "This is Hope and Hope, Attorneys. Can I help you?"

And then I heard the tapping of a blind man's cane. The screen door banged shut and my grandfather teetered there, wearing his brown suit and an old-fashioned string tie. Silver threads were woven into the braids of his tie, which hung down from a polished turquoise rock that he'd cinched to his throat. I was so glad to see him that I could have cried. He glowered around the room like Moses staring down at all the sinners from the mountaintop. "Judge!" "Here's the Judge, praise the Lord!" He'd shaved, but missed patches of whiskers here and there, and a droplet of tobacco juice hung in the stubble on his chin. "My, how nice, we got the Judge back!"

"Kate darlin'. Are you here?"

"Yes, sir."

"Did you get that Alvarez motion filed on time?"

"Of course."

"I knew I could count on you." He glared into the lobby. "Reuben, is that your voice I hear? Did your wife toss you out again?"

"I just don't know what gets into her," a scruffy-looking older man said.

The Judge adjusted his stance and faced him. "It's what gets into *you*. Stop the drinking. Miss Terrell, Mrs. Johnson, you ladies just be comfortable. Mrs. Roulette, hang up the dang phone!"

"It's Judge Tooley, and it's for you, and I am *not* going to hang up on him."

"I certainly hope not. I'll take it in the office. Kate, will you join me?"

"I'd love to." I didn't try to help him, because even though he needs it, he hates it. But when I brushed against him, he put a hand on my shoulder and followed along beside me. Once in his office, he found his desk with one hand and guided himself around it to his chair. I made sure he was standing over the seat and not a patch of air, then sat down across from him. "Is my spittoon where it belongs?" he asked me.

I hate that spittoon with a passion, because when he misses, guess who has to clean up the mess. But if he was well enough to chew that evil stuff without throwing up, he had to be okay. "Can't you just swallow it or something?" I asked him.

"That'd make me sick. Is it where it belongs?"

"Yes," I said, then added, "Please, God, bless him with perfect aim?" I pretended that I was asking for a miracle, which was a game we played. His head twitched in the direction of the spittoon, and a stream of tobacco juice flew through the air, ducking into the brass bowl without touching the sides. "Thank you, God," I said, and he looked satisfied.

Then one of his gnarly old hands found the telephone, and he talked into it. After a good laugh, he hung up. "Judge Tooley heard I was sick and wanted to know if there was anything he could do," he said. "I told him it would help if he'd always rule in my favor. Now, young woman, tell me what I need to know."

I talked for ten minutes without stopping while he sat there like a statue, listening to every word and occasionally chucking a load of tobacco juice into the cuspidor. It's so much nicer on everyone when he smokes his pipe, but he says pipes are for when a man can relax at his home. They don't travel well. A plug of tobacco can fit in a man's hip pocket.

"Did you tell Cartwright to come back with that certificate so his signature can be notarized?" he asked when I stopped talking.

"Won't he know to do that?"

"The man's one of them talking dolls, Kate. He don't know how to think. Better have Mrs. Roulette call him up." He frowned. "Now. What did you tell Mrs. Shumaker to do?"

Mrs. Shumaker had three daughters, but her husband had left her and she couldn't pay the rent. "To leave. She doesn't have a choice."

"You didn't tell her how to get an extra ten days?"

"The statute doesn't say anything about that. It gives *three* days."

"She can go to court!" From his tone of voice I knew I'd made a mistake. "Didn't you explain that to her?"

"No. She doesn't have a defense. I told her to move."

"Kate, she can't pack up her house and find a new place to live in three days! She needs more time than that."

"But Grandfather, it's the law!"

"It may be the law, but that don't make it good legal advice." He scowled at me. "She can go to court and demand a jury trial. That would give her an extra ten days to find a place to live."

"What about legal ethics?" I asked him. "Is it right to advise a client to ask for a trial when you know they don't have a defense?"

"Who cares about that!" he yelled. "Your duty is to your client, the woman with children some rotten landlord is tossing into the street! You do what you can for *her*, and *that's* what's right!"

He yelled at me about some other mistakes I'd made, in a voice loud enough to be heard across the street. I wanted to scream at him, except that it was so wonderful to have him back. So some tears and stuff came out of me instead.

His ears lifted. "Are you snuffling?"

"No!" I said, wiping my nose.

"That's good. The law ain't for whiners." He glared at me with his blind eyes. "Except for them very few mistakes, you did fine and I'm proud of you. Judge Steinbrunner called me up to tell me how you handled yourself in his courtroom. He thinks you'll be a fine lawyer." He snorted. "I ain't so sure, of course, but it's possible."

"Please, God," I said as tears ran down my cheeks, "let me find a Kleenex?"

He frowned and smiled and waited while I put myself

together, and then he issued my marching orders for the day. He and Mrs. Roulette would take care of the river of clients, and I'd work on the two cases that were set for trials. The Alvarez case would be tried next Tuesday, and Herman's would be two days later. "I'm the trial lawyer for the firm, so I'll do the courtroom work. But you'll have to get them ready because I can't see. Any questions?"

I had a ton of them, like how long does it take to really be a lawyer? *I* didn't know how to get a case ready for trial! What if I actually had to *try* one? "No," I said, smiling, because of all the confidence genes Mom had passed on to me. She trots them out, too, when the news editor at the *Denver Post* gives her an assignment she doesn't have a clue about. Grandfather couldn't see my smile, but he could hear the eagerness in my voice.

"Get on with you then, young lady. And send Mrs. Roulette back so we can set this parade in motion."

I'd cranked, riding to work that morning, and could feel dried sweat on my skin. A pit bath wouldn't be enough. I needed a shower.

The shower in the bathroom was state-of-the-art in the 1880s, but there was a problem with it in 1973: it didn't have a hot-water heater. The beautiful porcelain-lined bathtub on ornate brass legs came with an overhead nozzle that sprayed ice water. A wraparound curtain zipped the victim in so the only place to stand was directly under the nozzle. I turned on the water and got stabbed by millions of ice jets, soaped my body, and rinsed it all away, then toweled off. No wonder people in the old days were so tough.

Five minutes later, in my office with the door closed, I shook the wrinkles out of my lavender dress-suit and put it on; then I opened the window, turned on the fan, and got to work. The Alvarez case was set for trial in exactly one week, so I opened that file first. The criminal complaint was on top. I skipped to the juicy part:

> *. . . on or about December 23, 1972, Manuel Alvarez did knowingly commit the crime of theft by unlawfully taking a thing of value, to wit: a power drill, a power saw, and an extension cord, with the combined value of fifty dollars or more but less than five hundred dollars, from Glenn Able.*

The poor man had been arrested on Saturday, December 23, and put in jail. His wife, who could hardly speak English, came to see Grandfather on Tuesday, the day after Christmas, because the office was closed over the weekend and on Christmas Day. Grandfather had understood enough of what she told him to be in court when they brought Mr. Alvarez before a judge. He was marched in with a string of prisoners, all dressed in orange jumpsuits and manacled to one another with leg irons. I'd steered my grandfather to the courthouse that day and watched the whole thing.

"My client pleads not guilty and demands a jury trial," he'd said to the judge, then put up fifty dollars to bail him out of jail. "This man should *never* have spent Christmas

Day behind bars," he'd announced to the world when Mr. Alvarez was released.

The next page in the file was the police report.

On December 23, 1972, at 13:17, I, Reporting Officer Mike Bosse, was on routine patrol with my partner, Dave Cannon. Dispatch sent us to the Able Office Building, 2002 South Bannock, regarding a possible theft of tools by a disgruntled employee.

I'd read enough police reports to understand most of the terms. "Dispatch" meant the radio operator, who talked to all the officers when they were in their cars on "routine patrol."

On arrival, we contacted Gladys Able, WF, dob 7/7/28.

"WF" meant "white female," and "dob" stood for "date of birth." Gladys Able was a year younger than my mom.

She stated that her husband, Glenn Able, had found their maintenance man, Manuel Alvarez, drunk and asleep in the maintenance garage earlier that day. He fired Alvarez on the spot. Alvarez cursed her husband loudly, she said, then left in his truck.

"Cursed her husband loudly"? That didn't sound like the Mr. Alvarez *I* knew, whom I'd met and talked to in the office a few times. He had thick shoulders and no hips, like a boxer, and black hair, soft brown eyes, and a quiet expression. Some men come across as creeps, especially to fourteen-year-old girls. But Mr. Alvarez was the kind of man I knew I could trust.

Yet who knows what happens to men when they drink too much?

Mrs. Able then told the officers that her husband drove to town to attend to some business, and a little after one o'clock Alvarez came back in his truck. The truck was described as a 1959 Chevy pickup with a broken tailgate. As Mrs. Able watched through the office window, Alvarez drove to the maintenance garage and got out.

She observed the glint of a bottle being tipped. Suspect then took an extension cord, and some power tools, out of the garage. He put these items in his truck. As she was terrified of the man, she did nothing to stop him, but as soon as he was gone, she called the Police Department to report the incident.

This was awful, I thought. Mrs. Able was an eyewitness to the crime. She gave the officers Manuel Alvarez's address, which she knew because he worked for them. They drove to his unit in the Santa Fe Housing Projects. His wife told them he was asleep, and refused to let them inside. So they drove through the parking lot and found his truck.

The passenger door was not locked and, due to exigent circumstances, we searched the truck without a warrant.

"Exigent circumstances" was legalese for an emergency situation. It gave the police the right to search without a warrant.

The stolen items were wedged in behind the seat on the passenger side. We photographed them in place: a Black and

*Decker electric power drill, a power saw, and a 50' coil of
extension cord. We secured these items in bags and returned
with them to the Able Office Building, where we contacted
Glenn Able, WM, 47, dob 1/3/25.*

The officers found the stolen items in his truck? Why
did my grandfather think he was innocent? I didn't understand the case at all. What did he expect me to do?

*We showed Mr. Able the items taken from the Alvarez
truck, which he identified as his. He stated that the approximate
value of the items was $350. He also informed the reporting
officers that Mr. Alvarez was a legal alien from Mexico, living
in Colorado with a work permit.*

This was making me sick. But I kept reading. The officers then called Immigration and talked to an agent. They
informed the agent of the allegations against Mr. Alvarez,
then drove back to the projects, arrested Mr. Alvarez, and
took him to jail.

A big pit opened in my stomach like a cave. Mr. and
Mrs. Able would be at the trial to testify for the prosecution, as well as the police officers who had arrested him.
Was Mr. Alvarez really guilty of theft? He'd always seemed
so decent and honest. But how could he be?

The next page in the file was a note in my grandfather's
hand, dated February 9, 1973. He could write notes, even
if he couldn't read them.

*The Ables are liars. Manuel and Juan Lucero worked
that morning for Able, tiling an outdoor patio at the building.*

When they finished, Able said let's celebrate, and poured Christmas drinks for them. Manuel doesn't drink, and it didn't take much to get him drunk. He doesn't know how the tools got in his truck, but he knows he didn't put them there. Manuel also told me that Able owes him over a thousand dollars for work he's done and hasn't been paid for. I told Manuel to bring records to prove it, and we'd sue. Manuel will also find Lucero and bring him in for an interview.

Next was a note of the interview with Juan Lucero.

Lucero remembers the job on December 23rd! Able even paid him for it! Very interesting, because he hasn't paid Manuel a cent. He also remembers the drinks Able poured afterward, like a toast for finishing the job, and a toast to Christmas. But Lucero doesn't want to testify. Afraid he'll get in trouble. Better have him subpoenaed for the trial.

Under that was a note typed by Mrs. Roulette dated March 17. It said Able had been sued, and had filed an answer denying that he owed Mr. Alvarez any money. That case hadn't been set for trial.

Next was a list of witnesses. The prosecution had listed all the people in the police report; our side had named Manuel, his wife, and Juan Lucero. But there was also a subpoena for Lucero in the file, with a note that said, "Two-Fingers can't find him." Then, on May 7: "Can't get Lucero under a subpoena! He didn't have a work permit and has been deported back to Mexico as an illegal alien!"

I felt sorry for Mr. Alvarez, and his family, and my grandfather too. Could this be happening? Wasn't the law supposed to protect the innocent? But without Juan Lucero as a witness, we had no case.

The last page in the file was a checklist of things to do. "Notify client of trial date," and that box had been checked off by Mrs. Roulette. "Contact DA for further discovery," with no check mark in the box. "Contact investigator," also not done. The last thing on the list was "Prepare instructions."

I'd worry about the instructions later, which I could work on anytime. Right away, I'd go to the DA's office for the discovery, then talk to our investigator, Two-Fingers Brock.

He was not like the high-priced investigators who worked for the other lawyers. He didn't have an office, never wore a suit or a tie, and didn't work for anyone except us. Two-Fingers had been a brakeman for the railroad until he lost part of his hand in an accident. Grandfather would lend him money when he needed it, and Two-Fingers would work off what he owed, by finding things out. He was all that Hope and Hope could afford.

And he wouldn't be hard to find. One of the clients I'd talked to the day before had told me where Two-Fingers was.

In jail.

Chapter Ten

I CHANGED INTO HIGH HEELS before walking over to the DA's office, hoping I looked more like a well-dressed professional woman than a fourteen-year-old girl going to a funeral. The heels lifted me two inches closer to outer space, which was nice—now I looked at people's chests instead of their stomachs. And I liked the drumroll sound the heels made on the sidewalk. They announced me as I walked.

The secretary at the front desk smiled when she saw me. "Hi, Kate hon," she said. "Cute outfit. How are you doing?"

I wondered if she really wanted to know. "I don't have a clue," I told her. "It feels like I'm making my life up as I go along."

Her smile grew bigger. "Just remember, kiddo," she said, "we're all on your side." But when I told her I needed to see the lawyer prosecuting Manuel Alvarez, she frowned. "Reginald Applewhite? He's the only lawyer here who won't let us call him by his first name." She dialed him up on the intercom system. "We call him Miss Priss." Two seconds later, she spoke into the microphone attached to her headset. "Mr. Applewhite?" she asked. "A lawyer to see you." She winked at me. "Manuel Alvarez?" Then to me, "Are you filing another motion?"

"No. I'm here for discovery."

She told him, then hung up. "He'll be right out. Good luck," she warned. "He'll test your sense of humor, so keep your cool."

He was a small, thin man with short blond hair who wore a silk shirt, a blue and silver tie, and shoes that gleamed like mirrors. I blushed when he came into the lobby and stood up, but he didn't see me. It was as though I wasn't there. He stared around the room with a frown on his face. "Didn't you tell me an attorney was here on Alvarez?" he asked the nice secretary.

"Yes, sir. Miss Hope."

He looked at me with surprise, and I smiled my hardest at him. His expression pinched into a serious frown. "Well. Follow me."

He didn't walk. He marched. I trailed along behind him, down a carpeted hall and into his air-conditioned office with a carpet, a polished wooden desk, and fluorescent lighting. His desk had one file on it: Alvarez. He waved at the chair in front of his desk and waited for me to sit, then sat down himself behind his desk. "You work for your grandfather and you're that, ah, legal aberration so to speak, aren't you?"

I'd never been called a "legal aberration" before, and didn't know what to say. Not that it mattered.

"That law has been amended, of course," he continued. "Just like our legislature to close the gate after the horse has escaped."

"My grandfather wanted me to say hello," I said, smiling still.

"Really? Nice of him. We've never met." His lips curled into a stupid little sneer because he knew he'd caught me in a lie. Triumphantly he picked up the file. "Why are you taking this case to trial?" he asked, as though accusing me of something terrible. "The man is a thief. We do not need his kind in Denver. If you come to your senses and plead him guilty, I'll recommend no jail and he'll simply be deported."

"Sir, he has a family to support and they'd starve in Mexico. Besides, he didn't do it."

"Of course not," he said sarcastically. "Let me guess how he will prove his innocence. Every member of his family, all twenty of them, will be at the trial, weeping copiously as he denies all knowledge of the tools in his truck." That tight little sneer reappeared on his face. "Incidentally, who is responsible for that ludicrous motion?" He pulled it out of his file and waved it at me in total disbelief. "An indefinite continuance would put a case on hold forever. There is no such animal in the law."

"It's kind of a long shot, isn't it? But it could make perfect sense, to the judge."

"Thank you for that," he said, writing on his copy of the motion. "I intend to quote you. This motion is frivolous, and I'm going to ask the judge to hold you and your grandfather in contempt of court."

I quit trying to be nice and stared at him with the loathing I felt. If looks could kill, he would soon be writhing around on the floor in his death throes.

"Judge Hope will be trying the case, I trust, and not you?"

"Yes."

He leaned back in his chair. "I've heard he often wanders into the wrong courtroom because he's senile and can't see."

"Thank you for that," I said. "I intend to quote you."

At least it canceled the smirk on his face. "Please do. I have nothing against the elderly, but for a man his age, in his condition, to engage in trial work is a mockery of justice. You may quote me still. Your client will have a built-in motion for a new trial, based on incompetence of counsel."

Tears of anger started pushing out of my face—until I remembered that the receptionist had called him Miss

Priss and told me they were all on my side. "Can we talk about what I came here for?" I asked him.

"Of course. Discovery." He pushed the file at me. "You have the right to mine, even though I don't have the right to yours. Take all the time you need."

He didn't make it easy for me. He glared at me as I leafed through the file, then began tapping his fingers impatiently on the desktop. I deliberately took my time, reading through the police report again, even though I had a copy of it in my file. It said photographs had been taken of the tools, but we didn't have copies of them, and there weren't any in his file either. "Weren't pictures taken of the tools?" I asked.

"Yes, but they're missing. No one knows where they are."

"The police report says photographs were taken of those tools in Mr. Alvarez's truck, Mr. Applewhite. I'd like to see the photographs. We need copies of them. They could be exculpatory."

"What a nice big word. Do you know what it means?"

"Yes. Do you need help with it?" I smiled at him. "It means they could prove his innocence."

"I'd like very much to understand how photographs of the stolen items, showing them to be in his truck, could prove his innocence." He made a note. "But I'll ask my officers to look again. Is there anything else I can do for you?" he asked, looking at his wristwatch.

"You might lighten up."

He stared at me with disgust, like the White Witch in *The Lion, the Witch and the Wardrobe* glaring at one of her subjects. "I'm not surprised by that remark," he said, standing up. "Although I must tell you, if you were my daughter, I'd spank you. Good day."

"Thank you for that," I said. "I intend to quote you."

My eyes were smarting and my heart was pounding when I left his office, but I thought—strangely—that Zozo would have been proud of me. "How did it go, hon?" the receptionist asked me, and I knew it wasn't just one of those courtesy questions. She really wanted to know.

I smiled at her, and it wasn't Mom's smile. It was mine. "He certainly tested my sense of humor," I told her. And we laughed.

My next stop was the jail, which could be interesting. I'd heard that inmates whistle at the women they see in the corridors, and wondered if a fourteen-year-old female in high heels with pimples for breasts would draw any glances. The jail, on Curtis Street, was a nice walk from the courthouse: past Currigan Hall and the brand-new Denver Center for the Performing Arts. As long as Two-Fingers Brock was locked up in jail, he couldn't investigate anything for me, but he might be able to tell me what to do.

There were no cells to be seen when I walked into the building and stood in front of the booking desk. A uniformed man with a no-nonsense frown and a crewcut glared down at me. I told him I was a lawyer and needed to see Avery W. Brock, also known as Two-Fingers.

"You're a lawyer?" he asked in obvious disbelief. "I need to see your bar card." I showed it to him. "This doesn't have a picture of you. Let me see your driver's license."

"I don't have one. I'm not old enough."

"If you aren't old enough to drive, how can you be old enough to be a lawyer?" he asked, then tried to ignore me.

But I wouldn't let him. Finally, after a conference with a lieutenant, they stuck me in a small room with gray walls, two chairs, and a table. I had to leave my briefcase at the booking desk. All I could take with me was a legal pad and a ballpoint pen. A few minutes later, the door opened and Two-Fingers, wearing an orange jumpsuit, walked in.

I liked Two-Fingers because he didn't talk down to teenagers and wasn't a creep. He was dark-complexioned, wore thick glasses, wasn't much taller than me, and looked harmless. But he was far from it, according to Grandfather. Twenty years ago he had been the flyweight boxing champion for Colorado. His fists would come at opponents like a buzz saw, Grandfather told me.

"Hey, Kate," Two-Fingers said, smiling at me. "They said my lawyer was here and I expected to see the Judge, so you are a nice surprise." He sat down. "He always brings me something to smoke. You wouldn't have a cigarette on you? I am about to die."

"Sorry. In fact I'm trying to get my mom to stop."

"You be easy on her. I can tell you right now, she's tryin' to stop, and can't. I've quit once a week for the last ten years, but it don't take and it's why I'm back in the coop." I didn't understand him, and he read my expression. "They caught me stealing two lousy packs of cigarettes. I wouldn't have gotten caught if it hadn't been for my hand." He held it up for me to inspect. "I used to be like magic, Kate, the way I could make things disappear. But I fumbled them packs onto the floor." His eyes lit up. "Maybe you and the Judge can reopen my case."

"What case?"

"My workmen's compensation case against the railroad. See, they did this to me." He looked at what was left of his hand. "I get a check every month from the railroad, but a monk in a monastery couldn't live off it. So I supplement my income by relieving grocery stores of excess inventory."

"You take things off the shelves, you mean?"

"But I ain't greedy, Kate. Only what I need. The trouble, lots of times when I take something, it falls out of my hand, and then I get caught. Would that be grounds to reopen?"

"You mean, go back to the Railroad Commission and ask for more money because you can't steal enough to get by?"

He nodded eagerly. "It goes directly to the question of production of income."

"You aren't serious, are you?"

"Not really." He shrugged. "Just tryin' to entertain myself for the next thirty days."

"We need your help, Two-Fingers. I mean, you can't investigate for us just now, but—well, you know, can you consult with me? At your regular rate?"

"On the house," he said expansively. "I owe the Judge. What's your problem?"

We talked about Alvarez first. He propped his feet up on the desk while I took notes on what to do to prove bits and pieces of our case. But when I told him about Herman, he put his feet on the floor and made me go over it again. "Why would a dog do that?" he asked, perplexed. "You say the old lady was knocked down by kids on Sting-Rays? What's a Sting-Ray?"

"A kind of bike, you know, with little wheels and a long saddle."

"Black dudes?"

"I don't know. She didn't say."

"This was City Park, so probably black dudes," he said. I could practically see the wheels turning in his mind. "They knocked her down when?" he asked.

"A little after noon? I don't know exactly. It had to be before the police were called about Herman."

"Get the paramedics' report. It'll tell you when. Lay a

subpoena on them, too. You never know." His mind kept clicking. "How far away from the dog-bite scene?"

"Not far. She'd left Herman tethered at her favorite spot near the duck pond and was on her way to the concession stand for popcorn."

"Don't that seem strange, Kate?" he asked. "Something there doesn't figure. She gets knocked down close to where Herman goes berserk, and I'll bet close to the same time, too. That's got a funny smell to it."

"Like, there's a connection?" I asked, not getting it.

"Why not?" he asked. "If those kids knocked the old lady down and kept right on truckin', did they do something else? Something that got Herman in trouble?"

"Like what?" I asked. "Feed him the baby?"

"Don't go shuttin' off your mind." He thought of something else. "You know Willis Suggs at that school you go to, don't you? One of the black dudes they bus in?"

"Yes."

"Thought so. Willis my nephew. You call him for me, okay? Tell him bring his uncle some smokes." He took my pen and wrote down the telephone number. "Willis keeps his ear on the ground and knows things. Boy's a leader. He was a shoo-in for student body prez at Smiley Junior High, but they bused him to your school instead."

Willis Suggs a leader? He was the biggest troublemaker at Hill. "What if he won't talk to me, Two-Fingers? We're not exactly friends."

"He will. I'll tell him you're cool." He put his hands behind his neck and leaned back in his chair. "That police report said a man charged in and made the dog drop the baby, right? Who was the man? Didn't it name him?"

"That's not in there," I said. "Does it matter?"

"We don't know if it matters, but we need to find out. You got an unidentified man who's a hero, and you got a babysitter. Lots of times things go together. Maybe the babysitter knows who he is."

Coming to see Two-Fingers had definitely not been a waste of time. "A boyfriend or something?"

"Go ask her," he said.

"Am I allowed to do that?"

"Kate. You're the dog's lawyer. You call the shots. You have the right to interview witnesses, so do it." For the next few minutes, with me taking notes as fast as I could, he told me what he would ask and how he'd go about it. "One more thing," he added. "Very important. Whenever you interview a witness, have someone there with you. Take a buddy."

"Why?"

"People change their minds when they get up on the witness stand. They forget what they told you. Or they lie. You need a witness who can prove what they said to you."

Mike. If he'd keep still and let me ask the questions. "This is so great, Two-Fingers." I got up to go. "I wish you'd hurry up and get out of jail. You should be doing the investigating. I'll forget something."

"Probably," he said. "Don't worry about it, girl. You'll do fine."

"Anything I can do for you?" I asked. "Or tell my grandfather?"

"Just be a good lawyer for me and my friends. And tell the old man hello."

Chapter Eleven

I WAS BACK IN MY OFFICE BEFORE ELEVEN. I shut the door, then kicked off the high heels, which were killing me. Could Two-Fingers be right? Did the boys who knocked Miss Willow down do something else? And did the babysitter and the unidentified man connect? I read the reports of the incident again, slowly and carefully this time, for names and details.

Officer Lester Smith got a call about a disturbance at City Park on the south side of the duck pond at 12:14 pm Sunday, June 3, 1973. He arrived on the scene four minutes later, and his initial investigation revealed a dog-bite case. He radioed for Animal Control and ten minutes later, Officer Dan Milliken of that department arrived on the scene. Smith advised Milliken that he (Milliken) was in charge, and gave Milliken his (Smith's) report. Not much.

What he'd seen, and witness interviews. Smith departed the scene at 12:44.

Milliken's report had more details. It said that Ursula Jespersen, age 18, was a live-in babysitter for Monica Pearsan. Monica was the four-month-old daughter of Mr. and Mrs. Farris W. Pearsan, who lived in Cherry Hills. Ursula had taken Monica to City Park, and when they got there, Ursula put the infant in a baby carriage and wheeled her to a spot near the duck pond. As she watched the ducks, suddenly "a large dog knocked over the carriage, rolling the tiny person onto the ground," Milliken's report said. "The animal picked the little girl up with his teeth and started to run off with her."

I visualized a werewolf or something, gripping a small baby by the leg and running away with the infant dripping out of his jaws.

"According to witnesses on the scene, an unidentified man charged the dog and made him drop the baby," the report continued. "The dog was dragging a leash and a chain, and the man held the vicious animal with the dog chain until the police arrived. Had it not been for his brave and spontaneous action, a terrible tragedy would have occurred."

Who was this man? I wondered, thinking about what Two-Fingers had said. Why hadn't he been identified? And why would a dog do what the report said he did? Did Herman need to snack on a baby while waiting for Miss Willow to come back with popcorn for the ducks?

Ursula should definitely be interviewed. Mike didn't know it yet, but he was about to start a whole new life as a private eye.

If Mike didn't have anything to do that morning, he'd probably still be in bed. I padded into the reception area in stocking feet and called him from the telephone on Mrs. Roulette's desk. "Hi," I said. "Did I wake you up?"

"No," he said, then yawned. "Close."

I told him what we'd be doing that afternoon. We'd meet at one o'clock by the clubhouse in Cherry Hills, on our bikes, and ride from there to the Pearsans' house and interview Ursula Jespersen.

I'd ridden my bike out to Cherry Hills lots of times and always drooled with envy over all the lovely homes. Today was no exception. It was an exclusive village of mansions with tennis courts, stables, and swimming pools, about five miles from where Mom and I lived. The clubhouse, with brown stucco walls, sat on an emerald-green lawn away from the street. Mike was waiting for me on the flagstone sidewalk in front. "What took you?" he asked when he saw me. I was fifteen minutes late.

Mike had never been anywhere on time in his life, and I'd thought today would be no different. "I didn't think you'd be here yet," I told him, "and I hate waiting for you."

"Oh."

He didn't look much like Paul Drake, Perry Mason's investigator on television. Paul Drake didn't wear short pants. But Mike's hair had a nice wave, and he didn't have braces on his teeth.

Two-Fingers had given me a short course on how to interview a witness, and I repeated it to Mike before we rode out to the Pearsans' house. Don't call Ursula first and ask if we can come over, Two-Fingers had said. Go knock on the door. Loosen her up a few minutes before asking her anything serious, he'd added. Girl talk. She'd need time to get used to whoever was with me, taking notes.

"Me?" Mike asked.

"You," I said, giving him a legal pad and a ball-point pen.

After the interview, Mike should go over the notes with Ursula, make a few corrections, and have her initial the changes. Then when Ursula testified, if she tried to change her story, her initials would be on Mike's notes proving what she'd really said.

"Easy," Mike said, putting the pad in his backpack. But he looked worried as we rode toward their house, and I hoped I wouldn't have to prop him up when the time came.

We pedaled up a private cul-de-sac to a big stone palace and leaned our bikes against a tree, in a yard as big as a mountain meadow. "Remember, I do the talking," I told him as we walked up the pathway. "You break in only if you don't understand what she says."

"Okay."

A girl a few inches taller than me opened the massive oaken door. She had cover-girl looks, with short, reddish hair and blue eyes, and a complexion and figure to die for. "Miss Jespersen?" I asked.

"Yess?" She stretched the *s* with a nice little accent.

"Hi, I'm Kate Hope and this is Mike Doyle. Can we talk to you a few minutes?"

"I am very sorry, my missus not here. Not here also her husband." She started to shut the door.

"That's okay," I said. "We'd like to talk with you."

"Why with me you wish to talk?" she asked. Then a large shadow loomed behind her.

"Hey," Mike said in a high, squeaky voice. "Ron Benson."

Everyone in Denver knew who Ron Benson was, especially all the girls at Hill. He was a big college football star. "Hi, kids," he said. He was wearing shorts and didn't have a shirt on, showing off his muscles. He needed a shave. "Who're you?" he asked Mike.

"I'm, ah, Mike Doyle, a friend of Kenny's? You know, your younger brother?"

"Yeah, I know Kenny." He smiled at me. "Who's the chick?" he asked Mike.

"She's . . ."

"I can speak for myself, Ron," I said to God's Gift. He'd gone to Hill Middle and East High, and had one more year at Penn State. Then no doubt he would become a professional football player and make a hundred thousand dollars a year. His younger brother Kenny—already more than six feet tall—was in the same class Mike and I were in. "I'm Kate Hope." I stuck out my hand.

He grinned at me as his hand swallowed mine like a shark inhaling a guppy. "The kid who's a lawyer, right?"

His hand warmed up, like it was personal. I have to admit that mine felt good in his . . . until it started feeling trapped. I slid it out. "Right," I said, and dazzled him with Mom's smile. "Ursula? Miss Jespersen? She's a witness in a case I'm working on, and I brought my investigator with me so we could interview her."

"Kenny has a crush on you, Kate. What're you doin', hangin' with this bozo?"

"Not hanging with him," I said. "He's my investigator."

"What'd she do?" He turned to Ursula. "Are you in trouble, baby?"

"I do nothing wrong. What for me you wish?"

"Just to talk, Miss Jespersen," Mike said, forgetting that he wasn't supposed to say anything. "A few questions?"

"Hey, the bozo has a mouth." Ron smiled at Mike, whose ears brightened up a bit. "Come on in, guys," Ron said, opening the screen door. "So you're practicing law.

How come lawyers only practice? Don't they ever get serious?"

"That's just an expression." What a killer house, I thought, looking around. It had marble floors in the foyer and a staircase that spiraled up and up—into the clouds, it seemed. Where did they keep the servants? "Doctors say the same thing."

"Good answer," Ron said. "But you're a lawyer. I'll bet you're full of good answers." He led us to another room, a library, with bookcases on the walls and a polished wooden table with leather chairs. "Sit down. How long will this take?" he asked, looking at his watch.

"Ten minutes," Mike said, kind of staring at Ron. Then he swallowed. "Fifteen, max. But we'd like to talk to Miss Jespersen, you know, without you? It's just quicker."

Those were Two-Fingers' instructions, which I'd told Mike about and then forgotten. Maybe two heads really were better than one, even when one of them belonged to Mike.

"No, you don't," Ron said, sitting down with us. "She's from Denmark and gets mixed up, you know, with the language. I'll stick around and translate."

I smiled at Mike to let him know it was okay. "Ready?" I asked him, nodding at his legal pad. He quickly put it on the table and bent over it with his pen. "You're an au pair, aren't you, Miss Jespersen?"

"How did you know that?" Ron asked.

It wasn't supposed to happen this way, I thought. But we had to go with the flow. "She's called a live-in baby-sitter in the police report," I said to Ron. "But if she's from Denmark—"

"Police report! I thought you said she wasn't in any trouble."

"She isn't," I said quickly, putting my hand on Mike's arm to keep him quiet. He looked ready to butt in. What had gotten into him? "We're here about Herman, the dog who allegedly—"

"'Allegedly'!" Ron jumped up, and in one instant, he grew two feet. "I thought they took that dog out and shot it!"

"Kate," Mike said, staring at Ron. "The unidentified man."

Ron leaned toward Mike and poked him in the chest with a finger. "Unidentified man? What are you talking about?"

"Don't," Mike said, pushing Ron's hand away. "Okay?"

Ron put his hand on Mike's shoulder, near his neck, and squeezed. "Answer my question, bozo. What do you mean, 'unidentified man'?"

Mike did his best not to show any expression, but it had to hurt. "Just that you rescued the baby from the dog."

Ron smiled like a hero and let go. He nodded. "So?"

"So you were there too is all."

"I don't know where this is headed," Ron said, "but I don't like it. You kids know where the door is."

"Look, we'd just like to ask you a few questions about what happened," I said to Ron. "My client is Wilma Willow, and Herman is her dog, and he's all she has in the world. She doesn't have any family except him. And now, you know, the City wants to kill him. Can't—"

"That dog *should* be killed," Ron said. "Ursula, let's show her Monica. She can see for herself."

Ursula nodded. "Come."

She led us up the stairs as Ron kind of blocked Mike out of the way and then put a controlling hand on my shoulder. Gently, Ursula pushed open the door into a large bedroom. "Shh," she whispered. "My little girl sleeps."

A baby crib was in the middle of the room, and an adorable little baby with soft blond hair lay on her stomach with her face to one side. She wriggled, then relaxed into the mattress. Ron pointed at the bruise on her chubby little thigh. "Do you know what you can still see if you look close?" he asked me.

"No."

"Teeth marks."

"What did you think you were doing back there?" I asked Mike angrily as we rode down Clarkson Street. "I told you *I'd* ask the questions. You almost got in a fight with him!"

"Well, how would *you* like it if someone called you 'bozo' and punched you in the chest with his finger and then choked you to death?" he asked me. "I didn't like him calling you 'chick,' either."

Was I angry at Mike? Or at myself, because I let the interview get out of control? At least Mike had stood up to the conceited jerk. "Would you have fought him?"

"I don't know." He wiped off his nose. "At least we found out who the unidentified man is."

"That was all we found out, though."

"So where are we going now?"

"Miss Willow's house." Mike had done that for *me*, I thought in wonderment, then got back on track. "I don't get him."

"*I* get him. He's—"

"I mean Herman. Does he have a split personality or something, like Dr. Jekyll and Mr. Hyde? A nice face for Miss Willow but a monster hiding in him that comes out at night?"

The big clock on top of the City and County Building bonged twice as we jumped the curb in front of Miss Willow's house on West Cedar Street. A little red brick bungalow, it was easily the cutest house on the block, with a grassy yard, flowers in tight little gardens, and bushes nicely shaped and pruned by someone with a flair for it. A light blue picket fence surrounded the yard. We stopped in front of the gate.

Miss Willow, garden shears in her hand, was out-doors. "Why, it's my lawyer and her nice young man!" she exclaimed.

"Hi, Miss Willow," I said as we dismounted and leaned the bikes against the fence. I let the "nice young man" comment slide by. She was wearing a pretty little yellow dress again, and I opened the gate . . . when a big, yellow-eyed animal appeared, stopping me in my tracks. Mike bumped into me and sucked in his breath because the creature looked ready for anything.

"It's all right, Herman," Miss Willow said. The hair on the back of my neck stopped quivering as the dog kind of nodded his head and moved back. We came the rest of the way into the yard, and Mike shut the gate. "He is *so* much better but still can't wear a collar," Miss Willow said.

"Why not?" I asked.

"He's still healing," she said. Herman ambled over to her, and with gentle hands she lifted his face up, exposing his neck. A patch had been shaved and covered with a blood-soaked gauze bandage. "When I first saw him he was an awful mess, the poor darling. Blood had matted in his coat, and one eye had been battered shut and wouldn't open. This raw spot under his neck?" She touched it. "He'd been horribly choked, and it refuses to heal, I think because he can't lick it."

"What happened?" Mike asked.

"The people at the animal shelter told me he'd been beaten before they picked him up," Miss Willow said. "They don't know who did it."

"The unidentified man, I'll bet," Mike said. "Ron Benson."

"Did anyone take pictures of his injuries, Miss Willow?" I asked her. "Or if you have a camera, can we take some now?"

"It hasn't been used in ages," she said, hurrying into her house as Herman reached for Mike with his paw. There was a definite smile on both faces. A minute later there were dog germs everywhere as Herman licked Mike's hand and then his nose. Ugh. By the time Miss Willow got back with the camera, they were good buddies.

But the camera didn't work.

There was something else I needed to find out from Miss Willow before we left . . . "Oh. Do you have a report from the paramedics?" I asked her.

"I'm sure they'll give me one," she said. "Why?"

"We need to know exactly when those boys knocked you down."

"Can I ask her a question too?" Mike asked me.

"Sure," I said. "You're my investigator."

"Did you see a young couple with a stroller anywhere? A big guy and a really pretty girl? A knockout, in fact."

It was a good question, although *I* didn't think Ursula was such a knockout. Miss Willow frowned and shook her head. "I think I saw a baby carriage, if that's what you mean. But I didn't see anyone near it."

I wanted to see the scene of the crime, so we rode out to the duck pond at City Park.

Miss Willow had put her picnic blanket down under a tree in front of the pond, and we thought we found the right place, but weren't positive. An asphalt path circled the pond, which was probably where Ursula had wheeled the carriage. Had Miss Willow seen another one? Was there more than one carriage out there? We rode the path to the concession stand, trying to understand what had happened. "Do you know Willis Suggs?" I asked Mike.

"Yeah."

I told him what Two-Fingers had said, and asked him to find Willis and talk to him. Maybe Willis knew who the kids were who'd run over Miss Willow.

"Okay."

We sat on the grass and watched the ducks. "Were there really tooth marks on that little baby?" Mike asked.

"It looked like it to me."

"I don't get it at all," he said.

"Don't get what?"

"Why did Herman have a baby in his mouth?" We climbed on our bikes. I had to go back to the office, and Mike had to go home. "That dog *likes* little babies, I'll bet. What was he doing?"

I stared at Mike, feeling . . . I don't know . . . trust, or something. It felt good, whatever it was. "Mike?" I said when we got to Twelfth Avenue, where he'd go east and I'd go west.

"What?"

I cuffed him on the arm. "Thanks for sticking up for me today."

Chapter Twelve

THERE WAS NO CHANCE WEDNESDAY to work on Herman's case, and it was dark that night when I rolled into the garage, totally drained. Mom was out for the evening and hadn't even left a light on in the kitchen. I peeled off my pack as the phone rang, and had to turn on the light to find it. "Hope residence."

"How come you never call me back?" Mike asked, all bent out of shape. "I called you twice today."

I could have called Mike, but the truth is, I didn't think of it. Sometimes, he's easy not to think about. "I'm sorry," I said, "but it got really busy at the office. The Judge was there, but he wasn't feeling well, so I had to deal with a zillion problems all day, and I just now got home and was all set to call you, but you called first."

"Yeah, yeah. Sure you were."

"I just this minute came in the door! Cool it." I didn't need any guff from him. "Did you find any witnesses?"

"No, but I talked to Willis Suggs."

"You did?" Amazing, I thought. He actually got off his duff and did something positive. "What'd he say?"

"Said he'd meet me at City Park tomorrow by the pavilion, after he's talked to Uncle Two-Fingers. He said the old guy's cool, even though he gives Willis a hard time about his lifestyle."

"Mike, that's so nice of you."

"Yeah. Then I hung out at City Park for a while, but didn't turn up anything. Even saw Sally Lipscombe, who was feeding the ducks."

Sally was this big flirt at school who had a crush on Mike, of all people. I couldn't stand her, but not because of that. I just didn't like her. "Is she following you?"

"Why would she do that? We just talked. She told me about this big case you have against Ron Benson that all the kids know about now."

"How did they find out?"

"Kenny Benson, Ron's brother? So I played dumb," Mike said, "like I didn't know anything about it, and let her talk."

"What did she say about me?" I asked him.

"She thinks what you're doing is stupid. How could you take the case, is what she doesn't get. The way she made it sound, the Hound of the Baskervilles mangled a baby, and Ron fought the monster off. Why are you defending a dog who'd do something like that to a baby?"

"Did you tell her it's my job?" I asked him angrily. "That I want to save the dog's life?"

"No, I let her talk."

"Well, thanks for standing up for me!" I felt betrayed. It was just like Mike to let a harebrain like Sally say bad things about me! "Of all the people who shouldn't call someone else stupid, it's Sally, who has the brains of a toadstool." I started snuffling. "Damn it," I said. "It makes me mad to have all the kids talking about me, and you doing nothing."

"Hey, I thought I was your investigator," he said. "Did you want me to blow my cover?"

"I don't know. It's just . . ."

"That isn't even what I wanted to talk about," Mike said. "Mom's having a party Saturday, at the lake, and wanted to know if I'd like to have some of my friends up there too. Will you come?"

The Doyles had this great place in the mountains, near Evergreen Lake. I loved it up there. "Who are you asking?"

"Well, you know, the gang. The usual suspects."

"Is Sally going?"

"Yeah. I asked her, anyway."

"Why ask me, then? Look, I'm really tired. I need to get in bed." I started to hang up on him.

"I don't get you," he said, in a tone I didn't recognize.

"I'm not taking Sally. She's going with Kenny Benson. The last time I stood up for you, you wanted me to back off. So around Sally I backed off, hoping she'd tell me stuff that Kenny heard from Ron. Like a good investigator, I thought. Only now you're blaming me for something!" Silence. "Sometimes I don't know how to act around you, Kate."

Real, I thought. Try acting real. But what he said made sense, sort of, and I wondered if it was me. "Okay, I'll go to your party." That didn't sound very generous of me. "I'd like to go, in fact. Thanks for asking." My eyes started to tear up, and I followed that comment with a long snuffle. How romantic, I thought, realizing suddenly what my problem was. I was really tired. "Thanks for helping, too," I said. Just don't expect an apology, I added to myself. "I mean, you've kind of been there for me lately, and it's nice to know I have at least one friend." I wanted to tell him more, except I didn't know what else I wanted to say.

"That's okay," he said, as though he knew I was having a problem. "Go to bed, okay? Maybe you'll feel better in the morning."

I was so tired that I didn't even take a shower before crawling under the covers and wrapping myself around a pillow. Then I had this vivid dream of me waiting at school for my dad to pick me up. I looked just like Judy Garland in *The Wizard of Oz*. "Where are you, Zozo?" I kept asking. Or did I ask for Toto?

I woke up in the middle of the night, still waiting.

*　　*　　*

"Bye, Kate," Mom said the next morning, giving me a kiss.

I nuzzled into her, then realized I was still in bed. "Mom!" I yelped, sitting up. "What time is it?"

"Eight thirty, lazykins." I love it when she smiles at me for no reason, especially when I'm half-asleep and can't fight back. "Your grandfather called me this morning to apologize for keeping you so late last night, and ordered me not to wake you up."

I threw off the covers and bounded out of the sack. "But there's so much to do!" I reached for my bathrobe. "You look nice." She did, too. Her hair was the color of the sun. It floated across her forehead and hung over her ears like a summer cloud. I just wished she'd connect with some guy! . . . although my head couldn't deal with the details. What if he wanted me to call him Daddy?

"Kate darlin'," Grandfather said as I sat down in his office an hour later. "How'd you sleep?"

He looked okay, but not great. "Wonderfully well," I said.

"I just might get some work out of you, then. The Alvarez case. Is it ready for trial?"

"I haven't done the instructions yet, Judge. But I met with Reginald Applewhite, the DA, who's a horrible little man. He thinks you're senile."

Grandfather smiled at that. "That's just fine."

"It is?"

"If we're lucky, he'll underestimate me. Is he holding anything back, or is our file complete?"

"He isn't holding anything back, I guess, but the file isn't complete, either. The officers took photos of the tools and stuff Mr. Alvarez supposedly stole. You know, where they found them in his truck? But they can't find the photos. So he hasn't seen them, but neither have we."

"Umm. What else?"

I told him I'd gone to the county jail to talk to Two-Fingers.

"What's he in jail for?"

"Stealing cigarettes. Judge Tooley gave him thirty days."

"Well, now, jail just might do him good. Did he help you?"

"He's such a nice man, Grandfather. A big help, especially on Miss Willow's case."

"We'll worry about her later," he said. "Kate, what you'll find out about lawyers is that nine-tenths of the time they make it up as they go along. There ain't enough hours in the day to do it right. You'll get used to it. Now, there are a few things we need today." I started taking notes. A few things? Two contracts to draw up, a will, an answer in an eviction case, and a divorce complaint with a temporary restraining order against the husband.

I tried calling Mike, but his mom answered both times and told me he was at City Park with Sally Lipscombe.

Did he have to spend the whole day with her? was what I wanted to know. Investigating what? I started working on the first contract Grandfather wanted me to write, but he interrupted me. I had to look up a statute that he needed now. I found it and started concentrating on the contract again, when he needed a copy of a case we didn't have. So I had to run over to the law library at the courthouse for it. I couldn't get anything done! Mrs. Roulette told me not to worry, but how could I not worry? She said it was just a typical day where the things you start get finished later, when no one is around. The problems of the client who is in your face are always more pressing than work that has to be done for someone else. "Fridays are a bit slower than Thursdays," she said. "You can do those instructions to-morrow." Like I should feel relief or something, knowing that there's always tomorrow.

At seven that evening, Mom came by the office. Mrs. Roulette was still there, but the Judge—not feeling great—had gone home early, for him. I still had a will to write, and needed to call Mike to find out if he'd met with Willis Suggs. But Mom wanted to take me to see a James Bond movie.

"The will can keep," Mrs. Roulette said, "and so will your young man. Go."

Jury instructions are these short little paragraphs the judge reads to the jury, telling them what the law is and what they have to decide. It's the lawyers who write them, and they're a lot of work, because they have to be perfect. The next morning—Friday, when things were usually slower at the office—I called Mrs. Roulette and told her I'd be at the law library with my nose in the books until noon and then with Mike the rest of the day, looking for witnesses. "Your grandfather called a few minutes ago," Mrs. Roulette said. "He's under the weather."

"He won't be coming in?"

"No, dear. Can you?"

Instant mood swing on my part, from fair to foul. "Does it smell in there already?" I asked her, which was mean and cruel of me, but it popped out of my mouth. *They* couldn't help the way they smelled. They couldn't afford soap! "I mean, are there some clients there now?"

"Yes."

The James Bond movie had not been good for me either. I'd dreamt last night that Zozo and Law were in a car chase that ended in a horrible crash. "How did Grandfather sound?" I asked.

"Like death warmed over. I wanted to call a doctor, but he won't hear of it."

"I'll swing by the hotel and—"

"He ordered me to tell you *not* to do that."

"The old bastard."

"Kate!"

Both of my eardrums were drilled simultaneously with sound: Mom from six inches away, and Mrs. Roulette blasting me through the phone. "He *is* an old bastard," I said into the telephone while glaring at Mom. "Will you screen the clients for me, Mrs. Roulette?"

"Of course."

"I'll be in at eleven, okay?" I'd have to call Mike and tell him I couldn't go with him to City Park to look for witnesses.

What had happened to my life? Would Mike still take me to his party? Would I even be able to go?

The temperature was in the nineties at eleven that morning when I locked my bike on the office porch and dreamed of entering an air-conditioned atmosphere instead of a suffocating one that would sweat up my clothes. Mrs. Roulette peered at me over her glasses and smiled, and I checked the lobby for clients. She'd narrowed it to four and each one looked at me as though I was their last hope on earth. "I need a shower," I whispered to Mrs. Roulette. "Be back in a minute."

"Take your time, dear."

But one doesn't take one's time in the shower at Grandfather's office. When I turned the water on, the sudden shock of ice was so intense it was hard not to sing. I controlled myself, toweled off and powdered my body, and put on clean underwear and a light denim dress. It looked strange with saddle shoes, but no one from *Seventeen* would be by that day to take my picture. I moved across the hall to the Judge's office, and Mrs. Roulette sent in the first client.

Then time and space disappeared as I lost myself in other people's problems. They seemed much more fascinating than mine. Was that what happened to Grandfather, too? Had it happened to my dad?

Mrs. Bronson and her five children were being evicted because she couldn't pay the rent, so—just as Grandfather would have done—I told her how to drag it out a few days. Then we called around and found an agency she could go to that would help her find another place to live.

A finance company had foreclosed on Mr. Washington's trailer home, where he lived with his three kids and his mom. She took care of the children because his wife had died of cancer. He hated the finance company with a passion, and wanted to know how much trouble he'd be in if he burned his trailer home down. I told him arson was frowned upon by society and that he could spend the rest of his life in jail, so it was not a good idea even though he'd get a rush out of watching it go up in flames. Then I called the finance company to plead Mr. Washington's case.

The lawyer I talked to turned out to be a decent man, which shouldn't have surprised me, but it did. He gave Mr. Washington three months to catch up on the payments, and he even agreed to cut his own fees in half.

The last two were divorces, which I hated because marriages are supposed to be forever, or at least until death do us part. A fourteen-year-old girl who has lived in one home all her life doesn't have enough experience in the real world to do divorces. Does anyone, when it comes to chopping a marriage vow into bits?

Mr. Hamilton was the defendant in the first divorce case. He worked at night as a janitor, but a sheriff's deputy had yanked him out of bed that morning and served him the papers. The deputy stayed in his room while he dressed, then escorted him out of the house without letting him take anything, even a toothbrush. When Mr. Hamilton came back later to pack a suitcase, his wife wouldn't let him in. The poor man obviously needed more than the clothes on his back.

I called the sheriff's office and finally talked to the deputy who'd booted him out of the house. He felt sorry for my client, and told me he'd call up Hamilton's wife and work something out.

Mrs. Ishmael was next, a beautiful woman with long black hair, a creamy complexion, and dreamy dark brown eyes that looked like they'd seen things that no one should see. A large bruise was wrapped around her left eye and covered her cheek. Her husband had knocked her down, she told me, before throwing her out of their apartment. He'd socked her because she'd tried to stop him from hitting his eleven-year-old son. The boy wasn't hers, she explained, just a stepson to her. So it wasn't really her business, but she couldn't stand it any longer, and thinking about the boy now made her cry. "I've grown to love him," she said. "But I don't have the means to keep him, and he would not come with me even if I did."

I wanted to call the police, but she wouldn't hear of it. All she wanted for herself, out of four years of marriage with the man of her dreams, was the furniture and clothes that belonged to her, and her personal possessions, and her books. She had found a rooming house where she could stay. So I prepared a complaint for divorce, which we took to the courthouse and filed with the clerk, then got a restraining order from the judge and found a sheriff who would serve it on her husband and stay in the apartment long enough for her to move her things. It took most of the day, and she hugged me and kissed me when she said goodbye. "The boy?" she asked. "What of him?"

I'd already talked to my grandfather about him. "Social Services will find him a new home," I said, "as soon as we know you're safe."

So that was what my grandfather did, day in and day out, on his side of the hall. No wonder he kicked things when they got in his way.

Riding home that evening before the sun went down, I felt a huge sense of relief. I'd survived my first week of working full-time in the practice of law. Did that make me a lawyer?

I didn't know. But I knew that tomorrow I'd be in Evergreen with my friends.

Chapter Thirteen

Just before one, Mike trudged over to my house. His mom was already in Evergreen, getting ready for their big party, and his dad was out of town on business. Mom and I would take Mike, which meant I'd sit in back.

Actually, it didn't matter to me where I sat. I was so glad to see him and get out of town and away from all my problems that I didn't mind the arrangement at all. He needed the extra room to stretch his legs, which he still had to tuck under his chin. Mike loomed over everyone at Hill except Kenny Benson, but Mike kind of didn't know how big he was. I liked him for that.

I liked his hair, too, I realized from my vantage point in the back seat. It's jet black and full of waves and curls, like Dustin Hoffman in *Midnight Cowboy* or Cary Grant in some old movie favorites of Mom's. I almost wound one of his curls around a finger, just to see what he'd do, but I resisted the temptation. Instead, I asked him if he'd talked to Willis Suggs again. He hadn't, which didn't surprise me. But Miss Willow would be at City Park the next day around noon, I told him, for her usual Sunday picnic. Two-Fingers wanted us to be there with her because people have habits that tend to repeat. We might turn up a new witness or two. "Can you go?" I asked him.

"Sure."

I leaned back in my seat and opened the window, letting the wind blow through my hair. It felt so wonderful just to relax. In less than an hour we'd gotten to Evergreen and arrived at the Doyles' summer cottage.

We were in a different world. Denver is on the prairie and is mostly as flat as a Ping-Pong table, but Evergreen Lake is surrounded by mountains, grassy meadows, conifer trees, and aspen groves. Snow-covered peaks shimmer in the distance like icebergs, and even when it's hot, it feels cool.

Calling their place a summer cottage was the understatement of the year. It's a big, rambling frame house in a mountain meadow that slopes toward the lake, with a large veranda wrapped around it and a sun deck that steps down from the veranda. Tables, shaded by large patio umbrellas, were spaced around the deck, and their huge lawn stretched all the way to the shoreline. A big asphalt parking lot was behind the house, and the lot was nearly full. "Who are all the people?" I asked him.

"Friends of Mom's, I guess," he said. "I don't know who she asked."

The Doyles made the society page on a regular basis. They entertained a lot, and were part of what my mom called "the country-club scene." But they weren't snobs. They were nice to their servants.

Mrs. Doyle came out to greet us with a drink in one hand, a cigarette in the other, and a hostess smile on her face. Taller than a lot of men, she loomed over Mom and me but not Mike. "Hi, Annie," she said to my mom, whom everyone warms up to because of her smile. "So nice of you to bring my son!" When they hugged, I was afraid her cigarette would set Mom's hair on fire. "You too, dear," she said, bending down and giving me a kiss. "You're certainly keeping Mike busy these days. I hardly see him."

She herded Mom and me toward the house, chatting us up about how nice we looked and telling me how proud she was to know the sweet little girl from Hudson Street who really could be president someday, while Mike trailed along behind like an ugly duckling. I thought she could have been nicer to her only child. But I guess there are times when Mom treats me like part of her background.

Some adults had spilled out onto the sun deck from the veranda with drinks in their hands, and others stood around the horseshoe pits. Most of them were well-dressed and distinguished-looking, like a collection of important people. Was this just a party, I wondered? Or was something being celebrated?

At least the kids I saw looked normal. Three or four of them were trying to string a volleyball net between posts. "Go help," Mrs. Doyle ordered Mike, pointing her head toward them. I started to go with him. "Not you, Kate," she said. "There are some people here who are dying to meet the youngest lawyer in town. And Annie, I've asked about a hundred single men who are dying to meet you."

"How nice," Mom said. "But what's the occasion? I'm in shorts."

"You look fine," Mrs. Doyle said, not answering Mom's question.

She sat us down on the veranda, where it was cool and out of the sun, with Mom next to some man and me next to Justice Spriggs of the Colorado Supreme Court. I tried not to watch the kids who were playing volleyball, even though Sally Lipscombe and Mike were huddled on one side of the net over strategy or something. Their heads were stuck together for the longest time. Kenny Benson was laughing and talking on the other side with Linda Frailey. Then the two Jimmys showed up. Big Jimmy got over on Mike's side, while little Jimmy went with Kenny's team. As they played and had fun, I tried to make conversation with Justice Spriggs.

We didn't have much in common. He'd never tried a dog-bite case, and I knew absolutely nothing about antitrust litigation. Then some doctors, psychiatrists, and business people joined us. They were all telling stories, and it was like I was expected to join in.

"You must be proud of Kate, Annie," Mr. Oleander said. If the hundred men Mrs. Doyle wanted to surround Mom with were all like him, she'd be safe. He's a little taller than she is, twice as heavy, and sweats buckets. But he's a pretty nice man who's even proposed to Mom, and wants me to call him by his first name, which I'd do except I never remember what it is. "Imagine. When she's thirty, she'll have been a practicing lawyer for fifteen years!"

All at once, Janet Young—another friend from Hill— muscled her way into the conversation. Janet's hair hangs over one eye, like a Veronica Lake peekaboo bang. "Kate, we need you," she said, grabbing me by the hand. "It's four against three."

Justice Spriggs looked relieved. "Off with you, young lady," he said, "or I'll hold you in contempt of court."

"Thank you, Your Honor," I said. "I won't object!"

My legs were twitching, in fact. I can't spike a volleyball because I'm way too short, but I can keep the ball in play. My specialty is making my teammates look good.

We started a new game, with Sally and me as captains. I lost the toss, so she chose first and picked Mike. Sally is as subtle as a sledgehammer sometimes. Her flirts are as big and solid as bricks, and I hoped she'd trip over one and break her leg. I chose Kenny, who's a much better player than Mike—at least when his mind is on the game rather than on girls. Sally picked Big Jimmy, so I took the little one; then she picked Janet, and I wound up with Linda— who either laughs at herself when she misses a shot, or cries, which makes her a serious distraction.

"What's with your case against my brother?" Kenny asked me before we started. He made it sound like a big joke. "Ron says you're actually defending some rotten dog who took a chunk out of a baby girl's leg. Don't you like babies?"

"Your brother's a dog beater," Mike said, before I could open my mouth. "An All-American dog beater."

"Be careful what you call my brother, Mike," Kenny threatened.

"Really. Can't he take care of himself?"

"Mike!" I said angrily. "That isn't even nice." What had gotten into him? "Let's just play volleyball and have fun, you guys, okay?"

But the game deteriorated into a duel between Kenny and Mike. Even though Kenny was on my team, I secretly rooted for Mike. So did Sally, who made no secret of it. She'd grab Mike and hug him when he made a good shot. Kenny expected me to get physical with him too, but he's definitely not my type. I kept my praises verbal, even when he tried wrapping me up in his big, strong arms, as though he were his brother, the football star. I'd twist out of his grip.

But Mike was no match for Kenny, even though he's just as big. It's like he doesn't trust himself, and makes too many mistakes. Still, he wouldn't give up. Kenny drilled him with the ball on a high leaping spike, and it was like Mike had to watch the ball hit him. He didn't even turn his head and take the shot on his cheek. His nose bled all over the place and I thought he should quit. "No way," he said, mopping the blood off his face with a towel. "Have you guys had enough?" he asked, staring right at Kenny.

My side beat Sally's team, 15–7.

After the game, Kenny tried cornering me, and Sally made a beeline for Mike. But I didn't want her getting her claws into my investigator, so I got between them. "Let's go for a hike," I said to the three of them. "Three Sisters?"

The others stayed behind to play horseshoes, but Sally and I wrapped up some snacks from the hors d'oeuvre tray and loaded them into backpacks with pop and water. "So what's going on with the case?" Kenny asked me as we hiked an old jeep trail Mike knew about that would lead us to our destination. Kenny had all the innocence of a spy. "Think you'll win it?"

"I hope so," I said, trying a ploy of my own. "The dog belongs to this poor woman who will die if we lose."

The view from on top of the tallest of the Sisters is what people come to Colorado to see, with purple and white mountains silhouetted against a turquoise sky. Above the horizon, the sky fades into deep, luminous blue that white clouds drift through. I can stare at the clouds for hours, watching the faces from my past and being a witness to my future. Along the way, it seemed like Mike and Kenny were becoming friends, which was nice, I thought— until I realized it wasn't necessarily true that they liked each other. They'd snuck beer into their packs, and offered a bottle apiece to Sally and me. I quietly fed mine to the ants, then led the way back.

Toward evening, as the sun dropped behind the mountains, Mrs. Doyle served a buffet dinner of barbecued steaks, chicken, hamburgers, and slices of lean roast beef. I wished I could give the leftovers to clients and the steak bones to Herman, even though most of our clients— because of their pride—would have been offended if I'd offered to feed them. Not Herman who wouldn't have been offended. Pride isn't an obstacle to a dog.

Mrs. Doyle became tipsy and talkative, which was to be expected. I put a few things on my plate and wanted to go sit with the Hill crowd, but she guided me to a circle of over-thirties, just knowing I'd rather eat with grownups. She served me a glass of punch and sat me next to Mr. Roberts, who was a lawyer. She seemed to expect the two of us to trade war stories about our courtroom victories, for the entertainment of the others. I nibbled at my food and stayed where the hostess had put me, even though I'd rather be with my friends and protect Mike from Sally.

As Mr. Roberts talked on, I drank the punch, which was very tasty. Mrs. Doyle kept filling my glass.

Mr. Roberts represented landlords, I soon discovered. He made his living tossing tenants out of their apartments. "You cannot believe the way those people treat what isn't theirs," he said. "Some apartments are trashed with a vengeance. I have seen places the rats have moved out of, they are so bad." That got a laugh. "The filthy habits and destructive practices of these people—welfare recipients, for the most part—is beyond belief. They have absolutely no regard for anyone's property. Yet they are *convinced* that the government owes them a living."

The veranda in the soft evening light began to heave slowly and pleasantly, like the deck of an ocean liner, but instead of making me seasick, it gave me some kind of confidence that I don't often feel around adults. "Your welfare recipients aren't like my welfare recipients, Mr. Roberts," I said. "Why don't I send you some of mine, so you won't hate all of them?"

Mom, sitting across from me, looked startled. But Mr. Oleander smiled at me through a haze. "Ah," Mr. Roberts said as he cut through a juicy piece of meat. "Are you one of the young radical lawyers that society owes so much to these days?" His mouth smiled, but his eyes glared at me as he chewed the expensive food. "Lawyers who simply can't do enough for the downtrodden and the poor?"

"If I'm a radical, sir, don't tell Mom," I said, feeling lighthearted and glowy. "She'd send me to bed without my dinner. But the apartments I've seen are clean, even though some of my clients have halitosis that you wouldn't believe."

He wasn't having any fun. "Am I to take that as a rebuke?"

Had I made him mad at me? "Oh, no, don't do that. It's just that my welfare recipients don't all speak English, but they're very nice and I just know you'd like them."

"That isn't the point, Kate," he said. "Do they work? Do they pay their fair share of the tax burden? Or are they supported in their laziness by those of us in this room?"

"They aren't lazy, Mr. Roberts," I said. It occurred to me that he was not a nice man and I didn't like him. "Some of them can't work because they're too dumb to learn, or aren't strong enough to carry bricks and dig ditches and stuff, things like that." He didn't like me, either. "But I still think they're nice people."

Mr. Roberts quit glaring at me and looked around the circle with a knowing smile, even though no one smiled back at him. "What you don't seem to realize, my young defender of the underdog, is that those very people you wish to champion and defend are destroying our economy.

Why should the taxpayer, those of us here who actually work for a living, support those who don't?"

"Oh," I said. "My mistake, Mr. Roberts. I didn't think we were talking about the economy at all. I thought we were talking about people, you know, welfare recipients. If you want to talk about the economy you'll have to find someone else because I really don't know anything about it."

"Don't you think it's time you learned?" he snarled. "As a responsible lawyer, you should know it's the economy that drives this nation and keeps us free, something we will lose if we adopt some idiotic Robin Hood philosophy."

"Doesn't the way we pass laws have something to do with our freedom?" I asked him. "And the way our courts are run, you know, for the sake of justice? I really didn't know everything is about the economy."

Mom stood up quickly as the room continued its slow spin. "Kate, it's time for us to leave, honey," she said. "You have work to do tomorrow, remember? You and Mike?"

"Where is he?" I asked, kind of lurching to my feet. My balance wasn't great. "Nice meeting you, sir," I said, almost falling on him.

"Yes. Perhaps one day we'll meet in court."

Mom didn't exactly say goodbye to Mrs. Doyle, I noticed, and she didn't bless her with her patented smile—although everyone else got it. Even Mr. Roberts.

The two Jimmys, Linda, and Janet had left earlier with their parents. Mrs. Doyle was supposed to take Kenny, Sally, and Mike back to Denver with her, but for some reason I couldn't comprehend, Mom insisted on taking them back with us. We found them in the living room with the television set on. They weren't watching television, though. They were asleep.

They were more than that, I realized suddenly. They were drunk, and so was I. Mom managed to wake them up and get all of us in the car. Mike and Kenny sprawled all over the back seat and crashed immediately. Sally sat between Mom and me, put her head on my shoulder, and was asleep. "That woman should be executed," I heard Mom say as my eyes drooped shut.

Did she mean Mrs. Doyle? I wondered, falling asleep.

Chapter Fourteen

"WAKE UP, SLEEPYHEAD. It's after eleven." Mom's voice broke like mysterious background music into a strange dream. I was defending Law, my brother, who'd been charged with the crime of running away from home and leaving me to fend for myself, only in the dream, he looked exactly like my dad. "You and Mike are having a picnic with Miss Willow at noon, aren't you?" Mom asked.

"You're right!" I sat up so quickly that the sheet clung to me like skin. But something was wrong with me. My tongue felt thick and my head started to float. I held on to it with both hands, to keep it from drifting away. "Mom, I feel terrible about last night. You were so great about it, taking us home and tucking us in, and not blaming me for what happened. What *did* happen?"

"It was not a friendly little neighborhood gathering at

all," Mom said. "Invitations went out a month ago. We were an afterthought."

"We were?"

"Mike's dad was called out of town suddenly, and Mona needed someone to take Mike up."

I felt woozy and my mouth tasted awful, and I felt guilty without knowing what I'd done wrong, and sad, and grateful too without knowing who to thank, except my mom. The only escape for me from all these bewildering feelings was to burst into tears. "Mom, I love you so much, and I miss Zozo and Law with all my heart!"

Mom got a little weepy too. She sat on the edge of the bed and hugged me. But later, she asked me if I'd known what was in the punch Mona Doyle had given me. "Honest, no," I said. "It just tasted really good." She frowned as though she wanted to believe me but wasn't sure.

Getting Mike up in time to get to City Park by noon proved to be too much of a problem. I stuck a note on his door and went without him, wobbling at first on my bike, then feeling better. It was so beautiful out that I wished someone was with me to share it. Blue sky so absolutely clear and clean that the golden rays from the sun clung to the trees like morning dew. A few high clouds drifting around in the heavens like Casper the Friendly Ghost.

Miss Willow had spread her blanket near the lake and smiled at me when I rolled up. "Hello, dear," she said, sitting next to a picnic basket made of reeds. She looked like a sunflower in her pretty yellow dress with a blue bonnet covering her head. Was it the only dress she had? I wondered. "Where is your nice young man?"

"He couldn't make it," I said, dismounting carefully.

"You aren't catching a cold, are you? Your eyes . . ."

I couldn't tell her I had a hangover. "No, I just didn't sleep very well."

She told me she was exactly where she'd been when it happened two weeks before, and pointed to a little brown spot in the grass where the spike that tethered Herman had been planted. Mike and I had found the right general location but the wrong tree. "I wish Herman were here," she said, opening the lid to the basket. "He enjoyed picnics as much as I do. But I'd be in contempt of court or something dreadful, wouldn't I, dear?"

I nodded, and blinked. Strange things were happening in my head, as though some membrane in my brain that walled off memories had been dissolved. I could see Zozo, who grinned at me as he led me up the trail above the campground at Mesa Verde. It was steep and he couldn't carry me because the war had left him with a limp and only one arm, but he held my hand with his good one and we finally got to the top of the mesa that looked out over the Four Corners. The smells were sharp and wild, and I loved them. Piñon and cedar trees, Zozo was telling me—when all at once, two deer bolted across the trail in front of them. We'd scared them. They crashed into brush so thick we couldn't walk through it, but it swallowed them up.

I was back with Miss Willow. "I wish he was here too," I said.

She'd made sandwiches and handed me one, wrapped in waxed paper. "Peanut butter and jelly?" she asked. "It's what the young people in my day always had for lunch."

It looked gooey. The sight of it knotted my stomach into a golf ball. "No, thanks," I said. She looked wounded. "Not right now."

An old bum, tall and skinny, wandered toward us in clothes that were rags. He looked as if he hadn't washed in ages. His face was grimy, his hands and arms were dirty, and his hair was an explosion that shot out in all directions. As he stood over Miss Willow and stared at her with large, sad eyes, I hoped he wouldn't cause trouble. "Good morning, Wilma," he said. "Isn't the big dog with you today?"

Miss Willow wouldn't look at him. "Go away, Spence," she said, then tested the air with her nose. "Haven't you heard of soap and water?"

The comment didn't faze the old guy. "Who is the young lady?" he asked, pointing his head at me and sitting down on the grass at a respectful distance. "You don't have grandchildren, do you?"

"She's my lawyer. We were having a conference until you arrived."

"You don't say!" He gazed at me with interest. "Must I introduce myself, Wilma?"

Her nose was still in the air. "Miss Kate Hope, since this man won't leave, please say hello to Spencer Phipps, the valedictorian of the East High School graduating class of 1929. He was voted the Boy Most Likely to Succeed."

"Hi, Mr. Phipps," I said. He extended a grimy hand for me to shake, so we shook hands.

"Are you related to Lawrence Hope," he asked, "who has the unusual reputation of being an honest lawyer?"

"He's my grandfather." I kind of warmed up to him, even though thoughts of holding a sandwich in my right hand totally evaporated.

"You were in the newspapers recently, were you not?" he asked. "A girl prodigy who passed the bar examination at the tender age of fourteen?"

"I hated that story," I told him. "People expect me to quote Shakespeare and fill up silences with legal maxims in Latin."

"Think of your future, young woman. When you are twenty and rich and successful, you'll be ready to enter politics." His eyes drifted toward the picnic basket.

"I guess you and Miss Willow have been friends for a long time?" I asked him.

"Since childhood," he said. "We were sweethearts."

"We were not!" she exclaimed.

"Yes we were, old girl, in spite of the fact your father

never approved of me. And what is painfully obvious to me is that you have recovered from the promises and dreams that nourish the soul of those who are young and in love—even though I did not."

"You certainly fooled everyone. You were married three times!"

"Always searching for a woman with your sweet nature, but never fortunate enough to find her. You wouldn't have a spare morsel or two in that basket?"

"No!"

"Miss Willow, he can eat my sandwich," I said, patting my stomach. "I'm really a little sick today."

"Perhaps this is unkind of me to suggest, Miss Hope, but you aren't experiencing a hangover, are you?"

"Oh no, sir," I said, doing my best to keep the truth from showing on my face.

"I thought not, even though your eyes are a bit watery and your face is quite flushed. You are undoubtedly experiencing an allergic reaction of some kind. The symptoms are indistinguishable." He took the sandwich that Miss Willow held out to him. "Thank you, Wilma," he said, gazing at it with love. "Might I suggest a less formal speaking arrangement?" he added, turning to me. "You may call me Spence rather than 'sir,' and I might address you by your first name if you'll allow it." He took a huge bite.

He wasn't a bit like most old men, who expect kids to call them "sir" for no reason other than that they are old. It would be easy for me to call him by his first name. "I like the idea," I told him. "Call me Kate. Do you come here a lot?"

"Once or twice a month. I enjoy visiting with Wilma and reminiscing about the old days, even though she pretends she can't stand me."

"You were such a handsome boy," Miss Willow said to him, then turned to me. "His parents were wealthy and he had all the advantages. They sent him to Dartmouth, and he was charming and witty even before getting a degree in anthropology—which made him even wittier, although rather strange." Her head rocked with a sad memory or something. "Then he went to the war, and look at him now. A disgrace."

"My problem is not unique," Spence said. "My experiences in the war compelled me to face a most unpleasant truth. The world we live in is quite insane. Most people can blind themselves to those insanities, but many of us cannot. I drink to excess, Kate, in order to avoid the madness that surrounds me."

Was that really why he drank too much? I wondered. Grandfather had been gassed in World War I, and in World War II, Daddy had picked up the huge scar on his face and lost his arm. Both of them thought war was crazy too, but it hadn't turned them into drunken bums. "Wouldn't it be better to do something about it?" I asked.

"Would that I could," he said, peering at me with grave seriousness. "But the truth is, I would stay drunk all the time if my body would allow it. However, it compels me to surface now and again."

He was like a little boy with cuts on his knees from falling off his tricycle. Part of me wanted to dress his wounds, but another part knew he was full of germs and shouldn't be touched. "So when was the last time you were here, Spence?"

"Two or three weeks ago, which prompted my inquiry regarding Herman. I saw the noble beast that day, but not Wilma."

"Really!" I found my spiral notebook and a pen. "He's on trial for his life for attacking a baby."

"Who is on trial?" Spence asked.

"Herman. Miss Willow's dog."

The old fellow was perplexed. "They say he attacked the infant?" he asked.

"Yes," I said.

He looked saddened but not surprised. "That isn't what happened at all," he said. "Herman is a hero. I saw the whole thing."

"But he had the baby in his jaws," I said. "I've seen the tooth marks."

"Well, yes, that part is true. But don't be led astray by appearances. There will be a trial?"

"This coming Thursday," I told him. "He's been charged with being a dangerous dog, and the City wants to destroy him."

"Great Scott!" Spence declared, apparently incensed by the news. "We cannot allow that!"

"Can you be at his trial?" I asked. "You could save his life."

"Of course, dear child," he said. "When will it be held?"

"Thursday at nine, in the municipal court. Judge Steinbrunner."

His face donned the expression of a man in total command of the situation. "You may be assured of my presence. And when I tell the judge and the jury the true facts of the case, they will give the big dog a medal."

"What did you see?" I asked him. "Why did he have that baby in his jaws?"

"I cannot begin to describe to you how thrilled I was with his performance," Spence said, then turned to Miss Willow. "You wouldn't have a bit of fruit in that basket of yours, would you, old girl?"

She found an apple and gave it to him.

"Thank you," he said politely, leaning back on one hand and taking tiny, delicate bites.

"You were saying?" I asked, to get him back on the right track.

"Yes. Of course. I arrived a bit later that day than usual and saw Herman at once. The big, playful hound is impossible to miss. I did not see my dear friend Wilma, yet I was quite confident that she'd return soon—with popcorn, which she enjoys feeding to the ducks. And so I walked over to the animal, to say hello." He savored a bite of the apple and even swished it around in his mouth, like a judge in a wine-tasting contest. "The dog relishes having his stomach rubbed by someone such as myself with a knack for it . . . but all at once, he sat up and growled."

Spence sat up too, and a low, menacing rumble rolled out of his throat. "I followed the direction of his gaze," he continued, "and observed two young scamps racing along the asphalt path on those small bicycles that boys love to terrorize the citizenry with."

"The same two boys who pushed me down?" Miss Willow asked me.

Spence's eyes were alive with interest. "They pushed you down?" he demanded, as though he only wished he had been there to protect her from such an outrage. "The scoundrels! Why, my goodness, Wilma—there they are now!" He pointed a long, bony finger at two boys on Sting-Rays, chasing each other on the asphalt path around the duck pond.

Two-Fingers had said that people tend to repeat their actions from week to week, so I shouldn't have been surprised. "Miss Willow, do you recognize them?" I asked.

Spence lurched to his feet. "I shall thrash them for you, Wilma!" he shouted, running after them. *"Stop!"* he shouted again. "Stop, young scalawags!"

The boys did. They stared for a moment at the old

scarecrow stumbling toward them, then started to laugh. "It's Spencer Phipps the Third!" the short one said.

"How do, Your Majesty!" the tall, skinny one called out. They couldn't have been more than ten years old. "Where you been hidin'?"

Then they split up: one riding across the grass on Spence's left, the other on his right. "Here we come!" the short one said.

Slowly, in perfect formation, they approached the sorry old man and started circling him. As Spence lunged for one, who easily rode out of his reach, the other rode close to his backside, cuffing him. Then Spence spun around enough to make him dizzy, trying to catch the one who had just hit him. "You boys stop!" I yelled at them.

"Ya ya ya!"

I ran after the tall one, really angry at them for tormenting an old man. "Don't do that!" I almost caught the kid, but he darted to one side and then gunned it.

"She's quick, Tomato Face!" he said. "Hey! Look at the old guy!"

Spence had spun around too much. He wobbled around in a daze. Both boys charged, and Spence threw his hands in the air as though to keep them away, then stumbled back a step . . . and fell, like a long, thin board, on the grass.

"Uh-oh," the tall boy said. "Best we go." They were gone.

I ran over to Spence, who didn't move. Had he hit his head? What should I do? "Spence?" I asked, kneeling down and touching him over his heart. At least he was breathing.

"Oh dear," Miss Willow said, standing next to me. "If only Herman were here."

Why? I wondered. What could Herman do? "Miss Willow, stay with him, okay?" I said, jumping up. "I'll go get help."

But before I could leave, Spence rolled to his hands and knees, and it looked as though his body was trying to turn itself inside out. All that spinning around had made him seasick, and some of the apple he'd eaten came up. With mortification written all over his face, he lurched to his feet and ran for the street.

I followed along behind him. At the edge of the street he got down on his hands and knees and leaned over the gutter and threw up big-time. Chunks of apple were mixed with peanut butter and jelly. Very gross. The poor thing, I thought, putting my hand on his sweaty back.

"Leave me alone," he said. "I do not enjoy having you and Wilma see me in this deplorable condition." Slowly he stood up, straightened himself, and scowled at the world just as proud as a lion. Wiping his mouth off with the back of his hand, he frowned at me with that strange pride old men are afflicted with, like my grandfather, who'd rather die than let me help him. Then he saw an opening in the traffic on Seventeenth Avenue, trotted across the street, and marched off down St. Paul Street.

Miss Willow was sitting on her blanket when I got back to her, her hands in her lap. "I shall never understand him," she said.

"Uh-oh," I said, realizing that he was a witness and I'd let him get away. "Do you know where he's staying?"

"I have no idea," she said. "He sleeps on sidewalks, I think."

I ran for my bike. "Maybe I can catch him," I said. "Call me tomorrow?" I called back. "Thanks for coming!"

I rode the streets and alleys looking for him, but he was gone.

I made it to Mike's house in fifteen minutes, and found him moping in his living room with the television set on. "Come on," I said. "We've got work to do."

We rode toward the Pearsans' home in Cherry Hills, and I told him what had happened at the park. "Spence never did tell me what happened," I said, "but he told me that Herman was a hero who didn't attack the baby at all. Two-Fingers was right. Those boys must have done something, and we need to find out what it was." Ron wouldn't be there on Sunday, I went on to say in a big rush of words. Not with the whole family at home. Today we should be able to talk to Ursula without all the questions being answered by Ron, but Mike needed to hear her too, because she'd probably try to change her testimony when she took the witness stand. "I'll ask the questions, okay? When I tell her we have a man who saw the whole thing, I just know she'll tell us what really happened."

Half an hour later I rang the doorbell, keeping Mike behind me. But Ron opened the door, his big muscles stretching his T-shirt like Marlon Brando in *A Streetcar Named Desire*. "The Kate babe," he said, which kind of stunned me. Was I supposed to be thrilled at being a babe? "Just the chick I need to talk to. Hey, dude," he added when he saw Mike. "My little brother told me he flattened your nose." Ron opened the screen door and came outside.

I spoke up before Mike could answer, to avoid the trouble I saw brewing between them. "What do you want to talk to me about?" I asked.

"Ursula and I got subpoenaed. Does that mean we have to testify at that stupid trial?"

"You were subpoenaed?" I asked. "Not by my side, Ron. It means you'll be witnesses for the City."

"Witnesses?" he asked. "We sit in the witness box and answer questions from lawyers?"

"Yes. At Herman's trial."

He nodded but no longer smiled. "I want you to do me a favor at that trial, okay?" he said to me . . . and with a quick move he grabbed Mike's wrist, spun him around in a hammerlock, and started choking him! "Go easy on us, okay, Kate? I'd hate to have to break your boyfriend's arm."

"Stop that!" I shouted at him, trying to beat him with my fists. Mike tossed helplessly in his grip, gasping little breaths of pain, his eyes popping out. "We have a witness who saw the whole thing, and you're a liar!"

Ron let go of Mike, who sagged to the ground with his arm dangling like a rope. "What do you mean, you have a witness?"

"I just talked to a man who saw what really happened!" I stormed at him. "Herman was a hero! If it hadn't been for Herman . . ."—but I couldn't go on because I didn't know.

Ron knew something, though, that he wasn't telling us. He put the end of his index finger on the tip of my nose in a threatening gesture. "You want Ursula fired over this?"

I slapped his hand angrily, but it didn't even move as Mike struggled to get his feet under him. Mike was going to charge him!

"You want her sent back to Denmark because of a stupid mutt?" Ron continued.

"Mike, don't!" I said—too late. He lunged at Ron. But the musclebound football hero stepped out of Mike's way like it was something he practiced all the time, giving Mike a hard shove and a knee in his back. Mike went down again.

"Take your choice, Kate." Ron held Mike down with a foot in his back as he struggled to get up. "That dog, or your boyfriend."

He literally walked across Mike as he went inside and shut the door.

Chapter Fifteen

WHEN MIKE GOT UP and brushed himself off, he wouldn't let me see his face. I could literally hear him grinding his teeth. He yanked his bike off the Pearsans' lawn, tossed his leg over it, and took off. "Hey!" I yelled. "Wait up!"

He jammed on the brakes and I had to swerve to miss him. His chest was heaving with rage, and his face had twisted into a grimace like a crazed gargoyle's. It was as though he hated himself for getting beaten up by Ron Benson, who'd probably soon be a professional football star. What did he expect? He was only fourteen! "He assaulted you!" I told him. I wanted to call the police.

But Mike made me promise never to say anything to anyone about it, including his mom, my mom, and the Judge—and then angry tears tried to squeeze out of his eyes as he sped off in another direction. There was no way I could stay with him. "Mike! Wait!"

"Leave me alone!"

He sounded just as silly as Spence had sounded at the park. "Go kill yourself then, okay?" I yelled after him, angry because he wouldn't even talk to me about it. I wanted to tell him how great I thought he was. Instead . . .

That night I went over to Mike's house, but Mrs. Doyle said he wouldn't come out of his room. She wanted to know what had happened. "You'll have to ask Mike, Mrs. Doyle," I told her, then left quickly before she could pressure me into breaking my promise.

Monday morning when I got to the office there were clients all over the place, even standing on the porch. Grandfather was in his element, kidding with them, lofting big uglies at his spittoon without missing, and ordering Mrs. Roulette and me around like servants in his castle. I ran errands, wrote letters for him to sign, and gave legal advice to the clients who didn't really have legal problems but thought they needed a lawyer.

I called Mike, too. I felt horrible about my stupid remark, telling him to go kill himself. And there was so much I wanted to tell him about stuff. He was braver than anyone I knew, and had nothing to be ashamed of, and had stood up to Ron Benson, and . . . but he wouldn't answer. It was hard for me to concentrate on my work. I tried pushing him out of my mind, but he kept surfacing, like a toy boat in the tub that won't sink. The Alvarez trial would start the next day and the Willow case two days after that. I stayed at the office after everyone else had gone home, working on instructions until it was too dark to ride home without a light.

I wanted Mike to lead me home again on his bike, but my little plan failed. "He's in Evergreen," Mrs. Doyle said when I called again. "With his father." So I had to call good old generic Mom and ask her to come get me, which I hated. But it was better than the alternative, I concluded, which was having her kill me.

We stayed up until midnight, talking about this hypothetical boy who I couldn't identify because of a promise, and how the boy had been beaten up by the town hero. Mom knew who I meant because it was so obvious, but promised she wouldn't tell anyone, especially Mrs. Doyle, who she was having a serious problem with and never wanted to speak to again. "The male ego bruises very easily," she told me. "Just be his friend. When he's ready, he'll let you help him."

Tuesday morning dawned bright and clear. I had butterflies in my stomach, even though Grandfather would be the lawyer defending Mr. Alvarez. The Judge wore a coat with leather patches over the elbows and an old string tie, like a frontier lawyer in a fifties movie, and it was fun for me to guide the courtly old gunfighter to the courthouse. Of course, I had to carry both his briefcase and his cuspidor, neither of which went very well with the stylish new dress Mom had bought for me. "Kate darlin', I want you to see everything there is when we're in that courtroom," he said as we plodded along, "especially what's beneath the surface and can't be seen. Do you understand me?"

"How can I see what can't be seen?"

"Most of what happens when you try a case to a jury can't be seen. You learn to see by feeling it. Watch that jury and the judge, and watch the witnesses like your life depended on it. Then tell me what you think they're feeling. You won't be able to read all the faces, but some will give themselves away. Only never let them catch you at it. Some have very thin skins, like teenage boys with acne. If they think you're watching them for signs, they'll resent it."

The courtroom was filled with people who spoke in whispers. Mr. Alvarez sat in the front row, surrounded by his wife and five children, with his head down, as though he expected someone to chop it off. His tiny wife sat next to him. Her beautiful brown eyes were full of fear, which was highlighted in some way by her brilliant black hair and the baby cradled in her arms. Their two sons sat next to her, dressed in dark slacks, clean shirts, and shiny shoes, and the daughters, wearing fluffy dresses, sat next to their father. They were still as frightened rabbits.

We stopped in front of them and Grandfather put a

hand on Mr. Alvarez's shoulder. "Now don't you worry," he said in a stage whisper, loud enough for everyone in the room to hear. "The jurors in Denver are good people. You'll get a fair trial." Realizing that this was one of the unseen happenings I was supposed to see, I glanced around the room at people's expressions, trying to guess what they felt. Some watched Grandfather with little smiles on their faces while others stared at Mr. Alvarez.

I led Grandfather to the pit, which is the space between the bench and where spectators sit. It's called the pit because it's where the lawyers slug it out. We sat at our table and the prosecution sat at theirs. "Where's my spittoon?" Grandfather asked. I put it as far from the jury box as possible so he wouldn't splatter some poor innocent juror if he missed, and I dinged it with a fingernail so he'd know where it was.

I whispered to Grandfather what I'd seen so far. Most of the people in the courtroom had smiled at him and the Alvarez family when he did his little act, but not the prosecutor. Mr. Applewhite had this lofty sneer on his face, as though he had just seen a farce performed by clowns. He wore a dark suit, polished black shoes, and a handkerchief in his coat that matched his tie. A police officer in uniform sat next to him.

The door to the judge's chambers opened and a woman stuck her head out. "Mr. Hope? Mr. Applewhite? Judge Merrill would like to see you."

"What was that, Katie darlin'?" Grandfather asked in his stage-whisper voice. I told him. "Let's go, then. You'll have to lead me, blind as I am." I sort of lifted him out of his chair, as he suddenly became twice as feeble as he really was.

A big conference desk filled up most of Judge Merrill's chambers, barely leaving room for the bookcases on the walls that were loaded with musty-looking old volumes. The judge was a nice-looking man with a tanned face and black hair, about the same age as Mom, so I checked his hand for a wedding ring, saw he had one, and crossed him off my list of prospects for her. A court reporter sat next to him, hunched over a small black box on a pedestal. "The firm of Hope and Hope, I see," the judge said, standing up and shaking my hand. "Nice to meet you, Kate. I went to law school with your dad, who was a real credit to the legal profession. He'd be proud of you."

"Thank you, sir."

"Hi, Reggie," he said to Reginald Applewhite, the esteemed prosecutor, who smiled at the judge but seemed to resent the informality. "Sit down, everyone," the judge continued. We sat in the chairs in front of his desk. "This is People versus Alvarez," he said to the court reporter. The little box had keys, like a toy piano, and when anyone said anything, the reporter would tap the keys like Schroeder in a Charlie Brown special. "The defense has filed a Motion for an Indefinite Continuance, which I must say is a new one on me. Does either side have anything to say before I rule on it?"

"Yes, sir," Mr. Applewhite said. "As the Court suggests, there is no such thing as an indefinite continuance. The motion is patently frivolous and I believe Mr. Hope should be held in contempt of court for bringing it."

"Mr. Hope, I have to tell you I'm tempted," the judge said. "What did you expect to accomplish?"

"Justice, if it please the Court," Grandfather said firmly. "How in the name of justice can the prosecutor countenance what he's done in this case? I had an eyewitness— a Mexican without a work permit—who could prove my client was framed. *He*"—Grandfather pointed in Mr. Applewhite's direction—"had him deported! I asked for a continuance because someday I might get the witness into court. But I don't know when that day might be, so I filed that motion."

"Your Honor," Mr. Applewhite said, his face the color of dry ice, "I *deeply* resent that accusation and *demand* an apology! What Mr. Hope accuses me of is outrageous! His motion names one Juan Lucero as a witness who can testify that he and the defendant actually worked for Mr. Able on December twenty-third, but that Mr. Able managed— quite conveniently, I might add—to get both men drunk. The implication is that Mr. Able then framed this theft on the defendant! I can honestly represent to you that I have no idea who Mr. Lucero is or whether he's been deported or not. The name means absolutely nothing to me. I have asked Mr. Able who the man was, and Mr. Able doesn't know either. He assured me he'd never heard of the man!"

"Let me get this straight," Judge Merrill said. "The motion is to continue the case until Juan Lucero, who has been deported, comes back into the United States and can testify for the defense. The prosecution denies all knowledge of the situation. Is that right, Reggie?"

"Yes, sir. Exactly."

Grandfather frowned in thought. "You talked to Mr. Able about him?" he asked the prosecutor. "Mind telling me what Mr. Able said?"

Mr. Applewhite spoke slowly, through his teeth. "He said he had no idea who Juan Lucero was, that he'd never heard of the man."

"You don't say." Grandfather thought some more. "I'll withdraw the motion."

Something was happening that I couldn't see. I'd sweated blood over the stupid motion, and just like that, he'd pulled it off the table! "You withdraw it?" Judge Merrill asked, then shrugged his shoulders. "All right, the motion is withdrawn. Anything else, gentlemen, before we start?"

"Your Honor, my motion for contempt," Mr. Applewhite said angrily. "This has been a waste of your time, and of mine. I urge you to hold Mr. Hope in contempt of court!"

Grandfather had a funny little smile on his face as he spoke to the judge. "When this case is over, Judge Merrill, if you think I wasted the Court's valuable time, I'll just turn myself in at the jail and make it easy for you."

"Can't do better than that, Reggie," the judge said. "I'll reserve my ruling, then. Let's get this show on the road." He started to get up.

"There *is* something else we need to talk about, Judge," Grandfather said. "Photographs were taken by the police of the interior of my client's truck, but the prosecution won't give us copies. There's a clear failure to give us discovery, and the case should be dismissed."

"This is an oral motion to dismiss, Mr. Hope?"

"It is, sir."

"You're a little late with it, aren't you?"

"We just found out about it," Grandfather said.

"If it please the Court, the defense could and should have made their demand for the photos long ago," Mr. Applewhite said. "They are referred to in the police reports, which they've had for months. Yet Miss Hope waited until last week to ask about them, at which time I informed her they'd been lost. I don't have them either. The case should be tried as if they didn't exist."

"Judge, they could be exculpatory," Grandfather said. "Photos were taken. The defense has the right to see them."

"I'm certainly not inclined to dismiss the case over this," Judge Merrill said. "How badly do you need them?"

"Hard to say without seeing them." Grandfather frowned. "Why doesn't the prosecutor just continue the case long enough to find them? We won't object to a continuance."

"And the speedy-trial rule, Mr. Hope?" Mr. Applewhite asked. "Will you waive your client's right to a speedy trial?"

Judge Merrill picked up the file and looked at it. "If this case isn't tried before June twenty-sixth, it'll be in violation of the speedy-trial rule." As he spoke, I noticed a look of disdain on the judge's face that I'd have to tell Grandfather about. "Mr. Hope, that's the oldest trick in the book. Are you teaching your granddaughter all the tricks?"

"Of course," he said. "You just never know what might work."

The judge laughed. "Your motion to dismiss is denied. Let's go to work."

Everyone but the judge filed back into the courtroom and sat down. The court reporter squatted behind his machine in the middle of the room, and the clerk stationed herself at her small desk near the door to the judge's chambers. The bailiff, a small, thin black man with gray hair, stood at attention at his table near the gate that led into the pit, like a guard in his brown uniform. "All rise!" he called out.

I jumped up, but Grandfather had trouble pushing away from the table, so I bent down to help him. "I don't need your help, young lady!" he whispered loudly. "All these people will think I'm decrepit!" I heard some tittering behind me and wished a hole would open in the floor and swallow me, but no such luck.

Judge Merrill came in with his robe on, climbed the steps to the bench, and sat down. "Be seated," the bailiff said.

"Good morning, everyone," the judge said as he looked around the room. "Mr. Hope, I don't see your client. Is he here?"

"Yes, sir," Grandfather said, "over there with his wife and children. Mr. Alvarez?" he announced loudly as he struggled to his feet. "Come up here, sir."

Mr. Alvarez rose like a gladiator in a fight for his life, squeezed his wife's hand, and walked through the gate into the pit. I got up and placed a chair between Grandfather and me. "*Gracias,*" Mr. Alvarez said.

Grandfather appeared satisfied about the way all the things he couldn't see were going. Mr. Applewhite looked at the judge as if he wanted help, but all the judge did was shake his head and smile at the old man. "You may announce the case, Mr. Applewhite," he said.

The prosecutor marched to the lectern like a knight in shining armor. "This is the People of the State of Colorado versus Manuel Alvarez," he said, pointing an accusing finger at Manuel. "The People of Colorado have charged Mr. Alvarez, the defendant, with the crime of theft"—and he emphasized the words *defendant, crime,* and *theft*—"in that on December twenty-third, 1972, in the City and County of Denver, he did knowingly and unlawfully take a power drill, a power saw, and an extension cord with the combined value of fifty dollars or more but less than five hundred dollars, from Glenn Able."

Grandfather found Mr. Alvarez's hand and patted it to show his sympathy. "The defendant has pleaded not guilty," Mr. Applewhite said.

"Are both sides ready to proceed?" Judge Merrill asked.

"The People are ready," Mr. Applewhite said.

"Yes," Grandfather muttered.

Mr. Alvarez looked sick enough to throw up. It would kill him if we lost and he had to take his family back to Mexico. A horrible feeling of dread and responsibility pounded in my stomach and brain.

When Grandfather said he wanted me to feel what I couldn't see, was that what he meant?

Chapter Sixteen

THE CLERK CALLED OUT THE NAMES of six people and had them sit in the jury box, where they would be "examined" for bias and prejudice. It's called *voir dire*, which means "speak the truth" in French, and it's kind of like the first act of a play. The prosecution gets to ask questions first, then the defense, and after that each lawyer can excuse jurors who they think won't be on their side. But before the lawyers start asking questions, they usually put on a little show. It's their only chance to talk directly to the jurors, and they make the most of it.

"You may proceed," Judge Merrill said to the prosecutor.

"Thank you, Your Honor," Mr. Applewhite said. He stood behind the lectern like the master of ceremonies at the Oscar awards, introducing his witnesses to the jurors as though they were movie stars. The first nominee he presented was Glenn Able. "Will you please stand, sir?" Mr. Applewhite asked, and a man sitting in the back of the courtroom got up. "This is Mr. Glenn Able, who owns an office building in town, on South Bannock Street. He will be a principal witness for the People in this case. Do any of you know him?"

None of the jurors did. He asked them more questions about Mr. Able, trying to get them to smile, I thought—but it was hard to hear with Grandfather whispering in my ear, "What does Able look like?"

"Bald-headed," I whispered back. "Older than Mom, thick glasses on a red nose, looks like a businessman in a coat and tie."

"Do you like him? Tell me what you feel."

"He's not a nice man. He's a big act."

The next nominee the prosecutor introduced was Mrs. Able, who stood up and smiled and nodded at everyone too. Mr. Applewhite went through the same routine with her. "I don't feel anything," I whispered. "She's a big blank to me."

Mr. Applewhite presented Officer Mike Bosse next, as if the policeman was the star in a movie about a courageous cop. "He's seen it all," I whispered. "He knows what to do."

Then Mr. Applewhite made sure none of the jurors knew him, or Grandfather, or even me. After that, he questioned the jurors one at a time: first about "reasonable doubt," which could not be an imaginary or speculative doubt, but had to be a doubt based on reason; then on the "presumption of innocence," which he said was like a legal figment of the imagination; and finally on "credibility of witness." Even though he asked questions, he did it in a way that told the jurors what the answers were. "It's a performance," I whispered to Grandfather. "An old movie before talkies. Boo. Hiss." Grandfather kind of smothered a smile, and I knew we were communicating.

Then Mr. Applewhite made each member of the panel promise him that they would follow the law, and be fair and impartial to both sides of the case. When he asked that question to the last juror, Grandfather dumped a load of tobacco juice into the spittoon.

"Of course, this is not a spitting contest," Mr. Apple white said, smiling at the old man like a good sport. "If it were, the People would not have a chance. Sympathy has no place in this case either. For example, the defendant has his family here." He gestured at them. "But his wife and children are not evidence in this case. Will each of you promise me you will be guided only by the evidence, and not by feelings of sympathy you may have for the defendant?"

Starting all the way back with the first one, he made each of the jurors promise him that. Then he folded his notes and bowed to the whole panel. "Thank you," he said to his audience. "I appreciate your honesty. Pass for cause, Your Honor." He sat down.

It took me a minute to remember what "pass for cause" meant. There were two kinds of challenges: "for cause" and "peremptory." If there was a legal reason to excuse a juror, like it was against their religion to convict, then the judge would excuse the juror "for cause." By "pass for cause," Mr. Applewhite meant he wouldn't challenge any of the jurors in the box for a legal reason. We'd get to the peremptory challenges later.

"Mr. Hope, you may examine," Judge Merrill said.

When Grandfather tried to get up, his legs got stuck under the table and he struggled to get his feet under him. He felt his way to the lectern and clutched it like a bird on a telephone wire. "Kate darlin'," he asked me as he peered around the room, "am I faced in the right direction?"

The old fraud, I thought. But he was lovable about it, and the feeling I had from the jurors was that they loved him too. "Yes, sir."

He nodded. "Ladies and gentlemen," he said in a raspy old voice, "I've been trying cases in Denver since before that nice young prosecutor was born, and regret to say that most of what he told you just now was hogwash. He told you he wanted people on this jury who could be fair and impartial to both sides!" His voice had firmed up by then, and he snorted out a laugh. "Well, *he* may want jurors like that, but *I* don't. I want people who agree with *my* side of it, and I have a deep suspicion he does too, if he'd tell you the truth."

When Mr. Applewhite stood up, I made a note about his smile, which had thinned out. "Objection, Your Honor," he said.

"Mr. Hope," the judge said sternly. "Are you going to test me, or are you going to behave?"

"I certainly don't intend to test you, Judge. I'll behave."

"Proceed, then."

Grandfather leveled his sightless eyes at the jury again. "I don't see too well," he told them, "but I hear fine. What I'll do is ask each of you to talk to me for a minute or so. That'll help me to make up my mind. Let's start with you, Miss Bissle." He guessed where she might be sitting and looked off in that direction. "That all right with you, Missy?"

"'Missy'!" she exclaimed. "It's 'Ms.'" She was very definite about it.

"Mizz Bissle then," he said, aiming his face at her. "I've found out quite a bit about you already. You're a modern young woman with spirit, who won't automatically take the side of the prosecutor. You'll make up your own mind about the case. Am I right?"

She looked at me and smiled. "Yes, sir. That's right."

"Are you from Denver, Mizz Bissle?"

"No, sir, I'm from New Jersey, but I've lived here ten years."

"Do you have family here?"

"I'm married and we have two children."

He smiled like a grandfather at that. "They'll keep you young," he told her. "How old are they?"

"Five and seven."

"Well," he said. "I certainly am taken with your voice. Would you look over at Mr. Alvarez and tell me what you see?"

She did. "A man. Nice looking. His coat slightly western in style. Is that what you mean?"

"Yes," he said with approval. "Now tell me. Is he guilty or innocent?"

"I have no idea, Mr. Hope."

Grandfather frowned slightly. "That's a fair-minded answer and I compliment you for it, but it isn't quite right," he said. "You see, at this point in the trial, he's innocent," he told her. "He's *presumed* innocent, so right now, you'd have to say that the man you see sitting next to me is innocent. Does that bother you?"

"Not in the least." She stole another look at Mr. Alvarez, who had his head down, staring at his hands; then she glanced at his family. The unseen thing I saw and felt about her was good news for our side, I thought. She didn't want to find him guilty of anything.

"In fact, the law says he's presumed to be innocent, clear to the end of the trial," Grandfather told her. "You mustn't even consider if he's guilty until every bit of the evidence is in and you have gone back to the jury room and started your deliberations. Until that time, under our law, he's innocent. Will you follow the law, Mizz Bissle?" He leaned toward her in a way that told her she must speak the truth.

"Yes. I will."

"Then you can promise me, and the judge, and even Mr. Applewhite, who said he wants jurors who will follow the law, that you will cloak Mr. Alvarez with a mantle of innocence until the trial is over? That he will remain innocent, in your eyes and in your heart, until then?"

"Yes."

"I'll take a chance on you, Mizz Bissle," the old man said.

He talked the same way to everyone in the jury box, remembering all their names and instantly connecting with each one. But where the prosecutor had made it sound easy to find a person guilty beyond a reasonable doubt, Grandfather made it sound very close to impossible. And where Mr. Applewhite had glossed over the presumption of innocence, Grandfather made it sound like a high wall that was hard to climb over.

Half an hour later, we had a jury; and even though it was Grandfather who had done all the work, I was totally exhausted with the mental strain of watching all the things I couldn't see. Judge Merrill called a recess and the jurors disappeared into the jury room.

"Let's talk a minute, Reggie," Grandfather said in his still-friendly voice.

"If you wish," Mr. Applewhite said, as though to humor an old man.

"Manuel, do you mind waiting in the hall so I can talk more plainly with Mr. Applewhite here?"

"I do not mind," he said, walking toward his wife and children.

"Please ask your client to stay away from my witnesses," Mr. Applewhite said.

What did he think Mr. Alvarez would do? "Very well," Grandfather said. "Manuel, you heard and you understand?"

Manuel looked insulted but nodded his head. "*Sí.*"

"I'll go out with them, Judge," I said, "just to make sure nothing happens."

"No, stay with me, Kate. I need your eyes."

Except for the three of us, there was only one other person in the courtroom: a big man who sat in the back, behind a newspaper. He looked familiar, even though I couldn't see his face. Then he lowered it enough for me to see his eyes.

It was Ron Benson. I turned my back on him.

Grandfather worked a fresh wad of tobacco in his

mouth. "Did I ever tell you how come they allow me to take a spittoon into the courtroom?" he asked Mr. Applewhite.

"No, sir," the prosecutor said, with a pained look on his face.

"I took the City to court." He jerked his head and a stream of tobacco juice lofted out of his mouth and disappeared into the cuspidor without a trace. "When I first practiced law, in the twenties, there were ashtrays on the tables for the smokers and spittoons under them for the chewers. But that changed when the Surgeon General said smoking can kill you. And so the City passed a law banning smoking in the courtrooms, but they took away the spittoons, too!"

His beautiful old head rocked back and forth with concern over the subject, which didn't seem that important, actually. "The government bureaucrats went too far, you see, which they'll do if we aren't careful about it. Smoking can kill you, as well as the others in the room who have to breathe the air that the smokers have fouled up with their habit. But chewing isn't like that. I argued it wasn't fair to lump the two together, just because they are both tobacco." He laughed.

But the neatly dressed prosecutor didn't even crack a smile. He just sat there and stared. "I assumed you wanted to talk about the case, sir," he said, "rather than the early days."

"Just tryin' to soften you up, Reggie," Grandfather said. "Kate. How'm I doing?"

"I don't think you've overwhelmed him with your charm," I said.

"Mr. Hope, if you have an offer, please make it."

My grandfather quietly stared at nothing for a moment, then nodded with understanding, like the old professor in *The Lion, the Witch and the Wardrobe.* "My client has a good job now," he quietly told the prosecutor. "He's with a construction company and can take care of his family. If he's convicted of theft, he'll be deported and sent back to Mexico and a hard life for his wife and children. Let's plead him to drunk driving, and I'd even stipulate to some jail time. The immigration people won't deport him for a conviction like that."

"I should just dismiss the theft charge?"

"Believe me if you can, when I tell you from the bottom of my heart, he didn't do it. He did drive while he was drunk, though, and he wants to be punished for it. To set the right example for his sons."

"In other words, I should take your word for the theft?"

"Reggie, even if he did it, your evidence shows that he was angry and drunk. Jail is plenty for whatever he did. Don't have him deported."

"Thank you for your kind offer, sir," Mr. Applewhite said with sarcasm, "but Denver has too many thieves now, and far too many Mexicans. Let him go back to his own country where he belongs."

Grandfather was shocked, and let it show on his face. "That's a terribly mean-spirited attitude for a prosecutor to have, young man," he said. "You have a whole lot of growing up to do. Kate, I need to go to the bathroom."

Mr. Applewhite hurried off, looking pleased with himself, as though he'd had the last word. I led Grandfather toward the big door that opened into the hall—and there was Ron Benson, with a smile that was more of a threat, holding the door open for us. "How's your boyfriend?" he asked.

"He's okay. No thanks to you," I said.

"It could have been a lot worse, Kate. Know what I mean?"

Chapter Seventeen

AFTER THE RECESS, with the judge high on the bench like a king on his throne and the jurors nice and comfortable in their seats in the jury box, Grandfather made a motion to "sequester the witnesses." It meant that the people who would give evidence in the case had to wait in the hall until they were brought in to testify. Only a few spectators were scattered around the courtroom after that, but they included Ron Benson, the All-American thug.

"Mr. Applewhite, you may give your opening statement," Judge Merrill said.

The opening statement is supposed to be a short little speech that gives the jurors an overview of the case. The evidence will come to them in bits and pieces, like the pieces of a puzzle, and if they know what the big picture looks like, they'll understand how the bits and pieces fit together.

But most opening statements are way more than that. Grandfather told me he used to practice his "little speech" for hours, in front of a mirror. Most lawyers treat it the same as argument, using it to persuade the jury that justice is on their side, not their opponent's.

When Mr. Applewhite marched to the lectern, I knew right away he'd worked hard on his. His voice rang out in the courtroom like a soldier calling his troops to fight for the cause of freedom and decency, as he told the jury what his evidence would prove: that Manuel Alvarez was not the subdued, decent-looking family man he appeared to be in the courtroom that day, but was actually a drunken thief. Then he spun out the details that made his point.

They were devastating. How Glenn Able had given this man—a Mexican national, in this country on a work permit—a chance to make something of his life. How his kindness had been repaid with treachery and deceit. How Able had hired the defendant to be his maintenance man, but when he needed him for a repair, how he found the man in a drunken stupor and fired him on the spot. How strong words were exchanged between the defendant and Mr. Able, with the defendant vowing to get even and then angrily driving off in his pickup truck.

And how, later, a terrified Mrs. Able watched the defendant come back. From her office window, she saw the thick-shouldered, powerful, menacing man drive into the parking area with his truck, stagger into the maintenance garage, and lurch out with his arms filled with tools. How she'd locked the door to the office, frightened and afraid, then sighed with relief when he loaded the tools into his truck and drove away.

Finally, how the terrified woman had called the police, and how the police had actually found the stolen items in the defendant's truck.

Then, grim and righteous, like Robespierre sentencing the king of France to the guillotine, the prosecutor concluded, "I am confident that you will find that the People have exceeded their burden of proof in this case; and that you will do your duty, and find that the defendant, Manuel Alvarez, is guilty of theft."

Manuel had covered his eyes with his hands and lowered his head. "Please, Mr. Alvarez," I whispered to him. "You could look really guilty to the jury. Sit up straight?"

He tried, but couldn't raise his eyes.

"Mr. Hope? Your opening statement?" the judge asked.

Grandfather didn't even stand up! "I'll reserve mine until later, Judge," he said.

"Very well. Call your first witness," the judge said to Mr. Applewhite.

Officer Mike Bosse, the uniformed cop sitting next to the prosecutor, marched to the witness box like a soldier doing his duty, sat down easily like he'd been there before, and stuck his right hand in the air. "Do you solemnly swear to tell the truth, the whole truth, and nothing but the truth?" the clerk asked him.

"I do."

Bosse told the jury that on December 23, he and his partner had been sent to the Able Building to investigate a reported disturbance and a theft. They talked to Gladys Able, then drove to an address at the Santa Fe Housing project to question Manuel Alvarez. A woman who identified herself as Mrs. Alvarez opened the door, but refused to let them in the apartment. They had a description of the Alvarez truck, however, and found it in the parking lot. When they looked inside, what should they see but a power saw, a power drill, and an extension cord. These items were removed from the truck and put in their police car.

An alarm went off in my head. "Grandfather," I whispered to the old man. "The pictures they can't find? Make him admit they lost them?"

"Good for you, Kate," he whispered back.

The prosecutor pulled a box from under his table and lifted up a shiny orange circular saw for the jury to see. It had an electric motor and hand grips, with a trigger in one of the grips. He handed it to the witness. "Is this the power saw you found in the truck?"

Officer Bosse examined it carefully, then compared the serial number on the saw with a number he'd written in his notebook. "Yes, sir, I can positively identify this power saw as the one we found in Mr. Alvarez's truck." He sounded like Joe Friday on *Dragnet,* giving the facts. Mr. Applewhite put the tool on a table for exhibits so the jury would see it for the rest of the trial, and then he and Officer Bosse did the same little song-and-dance routine with the power drill and the extension cord.

"After putting these tools in your police unit, sir, what did you do?" Mr. Applewhite asked next.

Officer Bosse said they took them to the Able Building, where they met Glenn Able for the first time. He'd just returned from an errand downtown. When he saw the items found in the defendant's truck, he identified them as his.

The officers then obtained an arrest warrant and returned to Mr. Alvarez's apartment. When Mrs. Alvarez met them at the door, they explained to her they had a warrant for Mr. Alvarez's arrest. She let them in this time, and they found him asleep on the couch, reeking of alcohol. They woke him up and placed him under arrest.

"No further questions," Mr. Applewhite said.

"Cross-examine?" Judge Merrill asked my grandfather.

"Can I have a minute, Judge?" Grandfather asked him.

"Yes."

"Kate," he whispered, careful to keep his voice so low that not even Mr. Alvarez could hear him. "How does it look to the jury? What do they feel?"

I hated to, but I told him what I thought. Four of the

jurors looked satisfied and ready to convict, like they'd heard all they needed to hear, but two of them clearly felt bad about what they'd seen. The case might look hopeless to them, but they didn't want to convict Mr. Alvarez. "They want a miracle," I whispered, hoping for one myself.

The old man got up slowly, found the lectern, and peered out into the distance in the general direction of the witness on the stand. "Can you hear me all right, Officer Bosse?" he asked.

"Yes, sir, Mr. Hope. I hear you fine."

The old man nodded. "All right. Now, did Mr. Alvarez put up a struggle when you arrested him?"

"No, sir."

"He was surprised to see you, in fact, wasn't he?"

"He was pretty much under the influence, sir. Nothing surprised him much."

"My point is, he didn't know why he was being arrested. Isn't that so, Officer?"

"Well, I don't know what was in his mind."

"Now, Officer," Grandfather said like a kindly old man, "I know you are honest and have no ax to grind here, and you'll tell this jury the truth. And the truth is, my client appeared bewildered and stunned about being arrested for stealing tools. Isn't that right?"

"That's right, Judge Hope. That's how he acted."

Grandfather shrugged, but smiled. "Now, you and

your partner searched his truck without a search warrant, but you didn't need one under the circumstances of this case. Am I right?"

"Correct, sir. Exigent circumstances."

"The truck wasn't locked, was it?"

"No. We weren't forced to break in."

"And when you saw the tools, what was it you said you did next?" Grandfather asked.

"We put them in the police car."

"Very careful about picking them up, weren't you, Officer? To preserve any fingerprints that might be on them?"

Officer Bosse smiled at that. "Actually no, sir. I know that's how it's done on television, but this wasn't exactly a federal case. It was just a minor theft case, and we had all the evidence we needed."

"Oh, is that so," the old lawyer said. "So the rights of a defendant in a minor theft case aren't as important as they are in a federal case? Is that what you mean, Officer?"

"Not at all, sir," Officer Bosse said. "Fingerprints in a case like this wouldn't mean much. Of course they'd have been the defendant's because he's the one who used the tools."

"What if they'd been someone else's?" Grandfather asked. "Mr. Able, for example?"

"Objection!" Mr. Applewhite said, jumping to his feet.

"Speculation of the rankest sort. That's a matter for argument."

Grandfather smiled at the prosecutor. "Well. Certainly wouldn't want to start an argument," he said. "I'll withdraw the question." Before the prosecutor could react, he turned back to Officer Bosse. "But there is something you did first, before taking the tools out of the truck and putting them in the police car, isn't there? Something you're not telling this jury about?"

"Are you talking about the photographs?" Officer Bosse asked.

"Officer, we're in a court of law," Grandfather said. "It's the custom for the lawyers to ask the questions. Do you want me to repeat it?"

"No, sir," Officer Bosse said, then faced the jury. "My partner took some photos of the tools, you know, to show where they were in the truck."

"Well. So photographs were taken of the tools before you and your partner moved them. I'd like to see them."

The prosecutor stood up. "Your Honor, we went over this in chambers, and the defense lawyer knows perfectly well that the photographs were lost. He's merely trying to embarrass the witness. I object to this line of questioning."

"Never heard that one before," Grandfather said to the judge. "Does he mean I'm not allowed to embarrass the witness?"

A few people laughed, and even the judge smiled. "Mr. Hope, let's just move on. Ask your next question."

Grandfather rubbed his jaw and thought about things for a moment, then faced the witness. "Officer, I hope you'll believe me when I tell you that I get no pleasure at all out of embarrassing you, and I apologize to you if I've done that. But the photographs are very important to this case, wouldn't you say? Without them, how do you know where the tools were in the truck before you moved them?"

"I remember exactly where they were, sir," the officer said. "They were all wedged in behind the passenger seat, down low, so you couldn't see them."

"That's what you wanted to show with the photographs, isn't it? That the tools were out of sight, as though they'd been hidden?"

"Exactly, Judge Hope," the witness said, smiling. "Hiding them that way goes to show intent, you see. Guilt."

Grandfather did nothing when Officer Bosse gave that awful opinion! Why didn't he object? All he did was rub his chin. "Now let me see," he said. "You told this jury how you looked inside the truck and observed the tools, but the fact is, they were hidden from sight. The fact is, you couldn't see them until you opened the door and looked behind the seat on the passenger side. Isn't that true?"

He squirmed a bit. "That's what I meant by looking inside, sir."

"I see. You didn't mean to imply that you could see the tools from outside, just looking in through the window?"

"No."

"Because they were hidden to the point that you couldn't see them without opening the door and looking around. Isn't that so?"

"Yes, sir, it is."

"A man in the driver's seat wouldn't see them either. Am I right?"

Officer Bosse moved his head around as though sitting behind the wheel of a car and looking for something he couldn't find. "He might, sir, if he knew where to look."

"If he knew they were there and knew where to look, it's possible he might see them. Is that your testimony?"

"Yes, sir."

"Thank you, Officer, for your honesty," Grandfather said, searching for his chair and sitting down. "No further questions."

I made some notes about the things I couldn't see that were going on. Everyone on the jury was more interested in the case now. It wasn't what all the guys at Hill would call a slam-dunk. I had the feeling that at least we had a chance.

But that didn't last very long. The prosecution called Gladys Able to the stand as its next witness. When she came in from the hall she stared at Manuel as though she was scared to death of him, then sat in the witness box looking very brave and determined.

After the clerk gave her the oath, Mr. Applewhite asked her a string of questions to show the jury what a wonderful citizen she was, a woman who gave to charities and went to church. Then he focused her attention on December 23, 1972, just two days before Christmas, and let her tell her story.

"I was going over some accounts that morning in the office," she said. "It's on the ground floor and has a big window with a clear view of the parking area . . . The maintenance garage is right next to the office and my husband came in and asked if I'd seen Manuel . . . He was our maintenance man and had worked for us for two years . . . Yes—the man sitting between the older gentleman and the girl . . .

"I told my husband I hadn't seen Manuel, but he had to be around because his truck was there . . . Glenn looked for him, and the next thing, I heard yelling. It was loud and not nice." She sniffed and glared at Mr. Alvarez. "Some of it was in Spanish and it came from the maintenance garage and frightened me terribly."

"What happened after that?" Applewhite asked her.

"I saw Manuel stumble into his truck and just knew he'd been drinking. He drove off quite erratically but made it to the street without hitting anything . . . Glenn came into the office and was quite upset over having found Manuel drunk again, just when he needed him to fix a lamp for one of our tenants. He said he'd had it with him and fired him. A few minutes later, after composing himself, my husband drove off to the hardware store. He needed something for the lamp . . .

"Then just after one o'clock—I remember looking at my watch—Manuel came back. He drove right at the garage and I thought he would smash into the building! He jumped out of his truck, took a drink from a bottle, and went inside. I was so frightened that I locked my door— then *watched* him take things out of the garage! Tools, and an extension cord, all coiled up . . . I was terrified and did *not* try to stop him, but the moment he was gone, I called the police."

Manuel sat like a statue with his head down, staring at his hands. She made it sound so real, and I hated what was happening. She sat in the witness box with that look of determination on her face, as though nothing—not even that awful Mexican who frightened her with his anger—would keep her from telling the truth. All of the jurors seemed to believe her every word, although my two favorites looked troubled about it.

"After calling the police, can you tell us what happened next?" Mr. Applewhite asked her gently, as though he didn't want to upset her any more than he had to.

They arrived within minutes, Mrs. Able said, and she told them what she'd seen their maintenance man do. They asked for his address and a description of his truck, which she gave them. Later the officers came back with some tools and an extension cord, which they showed to her husband, who was back by then. She couldn't identify them, but he could.

Mr. Applewhite nodded at her and glanced sadly at Mr. Alvarez, like he felt sorry for him. "No further questions," he said to the judge, and sat down.

"Mr. Hope?" Judge Merrill said. "You may cross-examine."

Grandfather looked terribly frail as he struggled to get out of his chair. I felt awful—for him, for Mr. Alvarez, and for the whole Alvarez family—as I watched him feel his way up to the lectern and take it with both hands and then hold on as though he had to, to keep from falling down.

What could he do?

Chapter Eighteen

G RANDFATHER SEEMED CONFUSED, standing at the lectern, not sure of where he was. Some of the jurors looked concerned, but Mrs. Able had a comfortable smile on her face. "Have we met, Mrs. Able?" Grandfather asked her.

"No, Mr. Hope."

"Well, your voice sounds familiar, but voices are like faces and sometimes I can't tell them apart." Both Manuel and I were ready to jump up and help him if he started to fall. "Your Honor, can I talk to my associate a moment? We can do it right here if it's all right."

"Of course."

I got up quickly and put my hands on his thin old arms. "How do you feel, Grandfather?" I whispered, very low so no one could hear me.

"Never felt better," he said very softly into my ear. "I

need to know what that Able woman feels right now. Is her guard up?"

"No," I whispered as I tried not to show my surprise. "She thinks you're a pathetic old man."

He managed a feeble nod. "Go back to your chair and look like you're afraid I'll have a stroke. Go on, now." As I started to leave, he kind of lost his grip on the lectern and almost fell, but caught himself.

"Mrs. Able, you still there?" he asked in a voice so weak and old you had to lean forward to hear it.

"I haven't moved," she said.

"Did I hear you right? You said your husband fired my client that day—let's see . . . right before Christmas, wasn't it? Then Mr. Alvarez drove off and came back. Was he still drunk?"

"Yes," she said firmly. "I was afraid he'd crash that old pickup truck he drives into our building."

"But he parked it, and you watched him go in the garage or somewhere, and come out with tools in his hands?"

"Yes, sir."

"In a hurry, was he? Or did he have all day?"

"He certainly didn't act like someone who had all day."

"Well, what did he do with all those things in his hands?"

"He tossed them in his truck."

"In the back of the truck, or in the cab, or just where was it that he tossed them?" Grandfather asked.

"I'm not sure, actually," she said. "I was so frightened. The bed? I think he just tossed them in the bed."

Grandfather slumped forward with what looked like despair. "That's in the back of the truck, isn't it? Not in the cab?"

"Yes."

"I was afraid you'd say that. Didn't he take the time to hide them in the cab?"

"He did not," she said, folding her arms over her chest. "He just threw them into the bed of his pickup truck, staggered into the cab, and drove away."

The jurors looked interested again. All of them had questions on their faces, and Grandfather acted like he was very discouraged by everything she said. "Mrs. Able, you do the accounts and keep the records for the business?" he asked, as though all was lost.

"Yes, sir."

"When someone works for you and your husband, you must keep a record of it, then. Is that right?"

"Objection, Your Honor," Mr. Applewhite said. "Relevance."

"I intend to tie this up," Grandfather said.

"On that basis, I'll allow you to continue," the judge said. "You may answer the question, Mrs. Able."

"We keep careful records, Mr. Hope," she said, but it seemed to me that her antennae had poked up. "For tax purposes."

"You filed taxes for your business last year, then?"

"Yes, sir," she said. Her eyes had narrowed a little tiny bit, with suspicion.

"Your records show that you paid a man by the name of Juan Lucero for some work, don't they?"

I felt a little prickle, as if the tip of a feather was working its way up my spine. "I'm not sure," Mrs. Able said, looking troubled.

"Mrs. Able," Grandfather rasped out, dropping his act. His voice all at once got strong, like the jaws of a steel trap. "Isn't it a fact that Manuel Alvarez and Juan Lucero put tile down in a patio in your building on December twenty-third of last year?"

She frowned, as though doing her best to remember, but her breathing was jerky. "Juan may have done something for us that day, but Manuel was far too drunk to have done anything."

"You know who Juan Lucero is, I take it, don't you?"

"I . . . No. I've never met him."

"Your husband has, though, hasn't he? In fact, he hired Mr. Lucero to work for you. Correct?"

"I don't really know, sir. I'd have to look at my records."

"There is a patio in your building, and Juan Lucero laid tile in it last December, and you paid him for it. Can we go that far?"

She smiled like she wanted to be helpful but couldn't

be just then. "I can't be certain without going through my records."

The jury didn't know what was going on, but they sensed something was happening because of the way the judge and the prosecutor were glaring at her. "You knew Mr. Lucero was a Mexican without a work permit, what they call an illegal alien, didn't you?" the old man asked.

"I knew nothing of the sort!"

"It was your husband who knew that?"

"You'll have to ask him."

Grandfather nodded as though to thank her for the information. "Now, Mr. Alvarez claims you and your husband owe him some money, doesn't he?"

"Yes, he does, but I can assure you that we don't. Although perhaps that's why he stole those tools, sort of to pay himself back."

"He has sued you for over a thousand dollars, hasn't he?"

"Something outrageous," she said.

"Of course, you and your husband both know Mr. Alvarez isn't a United States citizen and that he needs a work permit to remain here. Right?"

"Yes. It was quite legal to hire him, which we did to help him."

"You also know what will happen if he's convicted of theft?"

Mr. Applewhite started to object but changed his mind. "I . . . well, not really," Mrs. Able said.

"He'd be deported," Grandfather told her. "He'd have to go back to Mexico. If that happened, there wouldn't be any way for him to collect the money he says you owe him. Didn't you and your husband know that?"

"*I* certainly didn't," she said.

"One last question, Mrs. Able. Would you mind bringing your tax records for last year to court so we can clear up just exactly when it was that Juan Lucero did that work for you?"

"Yes, I'd mind!" she said in a huff, and looked at the prosecutor for help. But the expression on his face was not friendly.

Judge Merrill glared at the clock on the wall. "It's early, but we need a recess," he said to the jury. "I'm going to excuse you now, ladies and gentlemen, but you are to return at one o'clock. You are not to talk about the case to anyone, including each other. Do any of you have any questions about what I've just said?"

The jurors shook their heads in a whole bunch of no's and got up to leave. Mrs. Able stood up too.

"Please remain seated, Mrs. Able," the judge said to her. As soon as the jurors were gone, he frowned down on her from the bench. It made her squirm. "Mrs. Able, I am ordering you to bring last year's income tax records with you this afternoon at one o'clock," he said, "as well as any other record that might indicate whether or not Juan Lucero worked for you last year."

"My goodness," she said innocently. "Whatever for?"

"Do you understand me?"

"Yes, but am I on trial here? I thought, well, it's *him*, isn't it?"

"You are excused until one o'clock," the judge said to her, and stood up. "We are in recess."

Mr. Applewhite jumped up too. He started to say something to my grandfather, then changed his mind. "We must look into this," he said to Bosse as they grabbed their briefcases and ran off.

The old judge started to wilt for real this time. Manuel saw it too and we helped him into a chair. "That was so wonderful," I said as tears came into my eyes. I hated that, because I didn't feel at all like crying.

"I caught her in a lie," he said gruffly. "Manuel, this thing could be over very soon. Can you be at my office at twelve thirty?"

"*Sí,*" he said, staring at the old man with something like wonder.

"Go eat, then."

I looked behind me to see if Ron Benson was still there. He hadn't moved, and his smirk hadn't changed either.

"Kate, I need to sit a few minutes before we go back to the office," Grandfather mumbled at me. Then, just like that, he fell asleep.

It happened so quickly that it looked like he'd died. Ron jumped up and kind of rode to my rescue. "What's wrong with him?" he asked, looming over me like The Hulk. "Should I call a doctor?"

I thought it was nice of Ron to care about the old man. "No, he's okay," I said. "Just taking a nap. Nothing to worry about."

"What just happened in your case?" Ron asked me. "Why is the judge being so hard on Mrs. Able? I don't get it."

"She's a liar," I told him. "Their whole case is a lie," I said, leaning hard on the word *lie*. "My grandfather just caught her in their big, fat lie, and the judge wants her to bring records to court, which will prove it." I watched his face for a reaction. "You don't want to underestimate my grandfather, Ron. He's very good at catching people in *lies*."

Ron smiled at me. "I can tell he likes hardball," he said. "Well, you know something? So do I. But I'm more basic about it than he is." I waited for the punchline. "He plays with words, but I tend to get physical."

"Are you threatening me again?" I asked him.

He showed me the palms of his hands and his smile got even wider. "You're way too sensitive, Kate. I just like to play hardball."

Then he walked out of the courtroom, leaving me alone with my tired, but wonderful, old grandfather.

Chapter Nineteen

When grandfather woke up, he sat very still for a moment. "Kate?" he asked, as though trying to discover where he was.

"I'm right here, Grandfather," I said. "Who did you expect?"

"Well now, young lady, at my age I never know what to expect when I wake up. Might have died and gone to heaven." He struggled out of his chair. "We'd better get back to the office. Bring my briefcase if you will, but leave the spittoon."

"Thank you, God," I said.

"I did good work today," he said as he struggled down the courthouse steps. "Trial work can fill a lawyer's soul with fine music, which you'll find out one of these days. But you have to know the tricks."

"I hate it when you tell me that the law is just a bag of

tricks! Isn't there justice? Isn't that what lawyers do? You're turning me into a real cynic, Grandfather. Stop it."

He laughed. "A little cynicism don't hurt when it comes to practicing law. But trial work isn't all tricks, Kate," he said, as his tired old legs tried to keep up with his spirits. "It takes a special kind of awareness to be a good trial lawyer, and you have it, Kate darlin'—at least, I think you do. So did your father, and so do I." Then he told me how a trial lawyer has to "get to where he feels the jury," because the jurors will watch every move he makes, even during recesses. "They want to know if they can trust him or her, if the lawyer truly believes in the case. So you must always act with total, sincere conviction in the righteousness of your cause, even when you know your client's a liar."

"In other words, a good lawyer is a hypocrite?" I asked.

"It's called effective advocacy," he said. "Mind games, your father called them. He was the best. Don't object to questions when the answers don't hurt you, for example. It helps if the other side thinks you're a dunce. Truth is, some of the mothers on the jury may even want to help you."

"Grandfather!" I said. "That's totally sexist!"

"Well, I don't care if it is."

He told me I'd have to learn how to set up a witness, like he'd done with Mrs. Able. Once she thought he was in a daze, she'd dropped her guard. Bosse was kind of a smart aleck too, and he'd enjoyed punching a hole in that big balloon of an ego the man had.

A CLOSED sign hung on the door of the office, because the lawyers were in trial, but Mrs. Roulette was there, typing letters and straightening out files. Grandfather was still hyper-full of the "good work" he'd done that day, and Mrs. Roulette had to listen to him too as he told us about the wizardry and magic that lawyers all over the nation generated on a daily basis, even though few people would ever appreciate their artistry—until she told him she'd heard it before and to leave her alone, because she had work to do. So he dragged me into his office, sat in his chair, and pulled out a plug of tobacco. I reminded him just in time that his cuspidor was still at the courthouse. "So it is," he said, putting the plug away.

"That phone should ring soon," he said, propping his feet on his desk. I hated him for doing that—if he tipped over backward and smashed into the floor, he'd shatter like a glass jar. But I couldn't stop him. "I offered to plead Manuel to drunk driving," he said. "Reggie might wish now he'd taken it. Why don't that telephone ring?"

It did, just as my stomach growled like a grizzly bear. I was starved, but watched him yank the telephone out of its cradle. "Hello! . . . Reggie? . . . You don't say! . . . Well, if you were to call the Immigration Service, I expect they'd tell you who tipped them off . . . No, Reggie, it's too late for that . . .

"You'll dismiss anyway?" He raised a fist in the air in

a victory salute. "Let's do this. I don't need to be in court when you dismiss it, and neither does my client. You go ahead and do it without us there. Then you can explain it to the jury any way you want . . . Good luck to you too, Reggie." He hung up.

"What happened?" I asked.

The old man had a great big wonderful smile that stretched from ear to ear. "The Ables got themselves a lawyer, who called Reggie and told him he don't have a case now. They won't testify. They'll take the Fifth! They'll refuse to answer any further questions on the grounds that it could incriminate them."

"What crime did the Ables commit?"

"Perjury, among others. *They* are the ones who are in trouble now, and it's serious. They lied to the police. Then they came into Judge Merrill's court and lied some more!"

"You knew it all along, didn't you?" I asked him.

"Course I did. But *knowing* it doesn't do any good if you can't prove it. The worst thing in the world for a lawyer is to know his client is innocent when he can't prove it. When all he can do is sit there and watch him get convicted anyway.

"Well, today I stopped that from happening! I made the right guesses, which you have to do when you try a case. So you see, it isn't all tricks, Kate." His face radiated with a huge grin. "A whole lot of it is pure luck!"

How wonderful, I thought. "Justice" isn't all tricks. A whole lot of it is pure luck. "What guesses?" I asked him.

"I guessed when we first got this case what the Ables were up to. They owed Manuel a thousand dollars, so they cooked up a scheme to beat him out of it. If he was deported, there wouldn't be any way for him to get paid. So they got him drunk and stuffed those tools in his truck and framed that theft charge on him. But when Juan Lucero showed up on our witness list, they knew they were in trouble. I thought it was Reggie who had Juan deported, but it was Able."

There was a knock on the door. "Señor Hope?"

"Manuel!" Grandfather called out. "Come in. Sit!"

"Judge, I'm starved," I said, thinking of the great roast beef sandwich with Swiss cheese and mustard that Mom had put in my pack.

"You go right ahead, young woman. Would you mind stopping by the courthouse and fetching my spittoon?"

I didn't want to eat alone, and hadn't seen Mike since Sunday, when he ran away from me after getting beaten up by Ron Benson. Would he have lunch with me now? The truth was, I missed him and wanted to see him, and I was fully prepared to part with half my sandwich. I called him from Mrs. Roulette's phone.

But his mom answered, and told me he and Sally Lipscombe were hanging out at Aylard's Drugstore. Knowing he was with Sally didn't exactly make me cheerful, but I wasn't going to let it ruin my lunch. I had a picnic by myself, in the park across from the courthouse, and tried to focus my mind on Herman and Miss Willow and everything that needed to be done to get that case ready for trial. I needed to find Spencer Phipps and talk to him. What had he seen? All I knew was that he thought the police reports were wrong and that Herman had been a hero. And what about Tomato Face and his buddy, who'd knocked Miss Willow down? I needed to talk to them, too. Would Willis Suggs know them?

It was hard not to think about Sally Lipscombe and all her ploys. She wanted Mike for her boyfriend, but I needed him for his skill. He was my investigator, working on a case. I finished the sandwich, then walked to the courthouse for Grandfather's cuspidor.

The CLOSED sign was still in the window, but Mr. Alvarez and Mrs. Roulette had gone. I took that smelly old spittoon into Grandfather's office where he sat behind his desk, yelling at some poor lawyer on the other end of the line. Mike and Sally were probably kissing by this time, I thought, and planning their elopement. I sat down and waited for Grandfather to hang up so I could tell him I wanted the rest of the day off.

"Are you here, Kate?" he asked as he put the phone in its cradle.

"Sort of," I told him, feeling lonely even though I was with someone.

"Tell me what you learned today."

I didn't feel much like playing that particular game, but it was better at the moment than riding home alone. "You have to be cool, I guess. Nothing really bothered you. When you stood up in front of the judge and the jury, you just seemed to know that God was in Heaven looking after you, and that Justice Will Be Done—even when it doesn't look like it will at all. How do you do that?"

"I assume the worst," he said. "Then nothing surprises me."

"You picked up on little things that I'd have glossed over. When the officer said he'd seen the tools in the truck? He made it sound like he'd just peeked in the window and seen them, but you made him admit he'd actually opened the door and looked behind the seat."

"*You* did that for me," the old man said. "You reminded me that photographs had been taken of the tools while they were still in the truck. So you pick up on little things too."

"But getting him to admit it—how did you do that?"

"I took a chance," Grandfather said. "I thought those pictures were taken for a reason, and they were. The officers took them to prove guilt, because they showed how well the tools were hidden. And you'll notice, too, that the officer didn't lie about it. He just wanted to be misunderstood."

"How did you know he wouldn't lie?"

"I didn't. But I took the chance because he's a policeman. Down deep, most of them are honest. They don't want to convict a man of something he didn't do, which is a little-known fact, especially in this day and age when everybody believes the worst about everybody else, especially the police."

Suddenly his face tightened up with pain. "Grandfather! What is it?"

"Nothin', Kate darlin'," he said a second later. "Just a wrinkle in my system, but it's gone."

I leaned back in my chair, feeling sorry for myself and wishing I could talk to him about Mike and Sally. "What's justice, Judge?" I asked him. "If it hadn't been for you and your tricks, Mr. Alvarez would have been convicted of something he didn't do, and sent back to Mexico. But he actually *was* guilty of drunk driving, and nothing will happen to him for that. Did today have anything to do with justice, or was it just a contest to see which lawyer was the best?"

He cocked his head. "Something eating you, Kate?" he asked.

"No," I lied. "Is this another trick of yours to keep from answering my question?"

"Well. I'll answer the best I can, then you go home, young lady. You need the rest of the day off before we tackle that Willow woman's case. It needs some work, I expect." He sat back in his chair. "I won't say you always get justice after a trial, but the strange fact is you usually do."

"Really?" I said. "How come it's only poor people who get ripped off, then? Not Mr. Alvarez, because he had you to fight for him. What if he'd had me?"

Was I trying to start a fight with him? If so, it didn't work. He didn't get the least bit mad at me. "It's true what you say," he said. "If you're poor in this country, you don't get justice as often as when you're rich. But the amazing thing is that you get it at all.

"Look around the world, Kate. There aren't many countries where poor people *ever* get a fair shake. But in this country, they actually do, at least now and then." Sweat popped out on his forehead, which surprised me because it wasn't that hot. "It's more than now and then, of course. Even the poor people in this country get justice more often than they don't, in spite of what you read in the newspapers."

I was ready to tell him he was full of it, when he clutched his stomach. "Uh-oh," he said, suddenly folding into himself. I jumped up and ran to his side. "Dang. Another twitch." I held him in place as he struggled to get up. "Better help me, honey."

"I'm calling a doctor!" I told him, trying to keep him from falling out of his chair.

"Don't do that," he said as he finally managed to get to his feet. "Just walk me to my hotel. I'll be all right."

And then he collapsed.

Chapter Twenty

GRANDFATHER'S EYES OPENED SLOWLY, then seemed to freeze. "Kate?" he asked, sniffing the air.

"Yes," I said. "I'm right here."

"Who's the woman with you? It ain't Mrs. Roulette."

"It's me, Dad," Mom said, patting his arm.

"Am I in a hospital?"

"Yes," she said.

"Thought so. It smells like iodine in here."

"How do you feel?" I asked from my side of the bed.

"Fine. Like I always feel after a little nap." He tried to climb out of bed, but the guardrail penned him in, so he swore at it.

"Lie down, Dad. You have to stay put. Doctor's orders."

"I'm not staying in a hospital, Annie. People die in hospitals. I don't have time for that."

"You aren't going to die," she said, brushing hair off his forehead.

He leaned back on his pillow, tired from the excitement of waking up in a strange place and complaining about it. "What happened to me?"

"You passed out yesterday," I told him, the knot in my stomach tightening.

"Yesterday! What time is it?"

"Six thirty."

"That don't tell me much. Is it morning or night?"

"It's evening," Mom said. "You were exhausted, among other things. You've been asleep for more than twenty hours."

"What!" He struggled to sit up again, but his muscles wouldn't cooperate and he settled back into his pillow. "They've loaded me up with drugs, haven't they? That's what they do in hospitals to make you sick and dependent." His eyelids drooped. "What's the prognosis?"

"You'll live," Mom said. "Some gastric problem that will keep you here a few days. They've scheduled some tests."

"Um." He relaxed . . . until his eyes popped open and he sat up. "That Willow case, Kate. When is it set for?"

"Tomorrow morning," I said, trying desperately to settle the swarm of bees in my stomach and praying there weren't any biters in the horde.

"Get my trousers." He shook the bars that kept him from falling out of bed. "Take these dang things down!"

"Judge," I said loudly. "We're partners, aren't we?"

He stopped. "Yes we are, young woman. Partners in the law."

"Then you'll have to trust me when I tell you I don't need you because the case is under control."

"Did you get a continuance?"

"No. But it's in good shape." I turned my back to Mom so she wouldn't see my quivering lips.

"*You* can't do that trial, Kate!" He was more determined than ever to get his feet on the floor. "You don't have the experience!"

That was what I'd argued to Judge Steinbrunner, but Carl Thomas said I was licensed to practice law in Colorado, so I was presumed to have the experience to try a lawsuit. He'd also said that the public interest in getting dangerous dogs out of circulation was too important to delay the case, and Judge Steinbrunner had agreed with him.

"Well, he'll get a piece of my mind, then!" Grandfather said. But moving around exhausted him, and he lay back down. "You say it's in good shape, do you?"

"Yes," I lied. The case was in horrible shape. All I knew

was that Herman was a hero—according to an old man who had seen the whole thing. But I didn't know what had happened, and that was just for starters. Picking a jury? Opening statement? Cross-examination of witnesses? I'd filled a legal pad with notes I couldn't read. And just when I needed him most, Mike had deserted me. Why was I not surprised? That's what boys are good at, I thought.

I was also thinking seriously about riding my bicycle in front of a trolley bus.

"Ask Mrs. Roulette to find *Chenoweth v. Municipal Court.* It's in the files in the basement."

"That was Daddy's case? Where he made the municipal court give jury trials to dogs?"

"How'd you know about it?"

"Judge Steinbrunner."

"Your father lost that case, but the file still might help some. I doubt that the law has changed much from then to now. There aren't that many jury trials for dogs. What's your evidence?"

"There's an eyewitness who saw what really happened that day at City Park." I didn't tell him that I didn't even know where he was.

"What will he say?"

"That Herman was a hero." I swallowed. What was the baby doing in the jaws of a hero?

But the old man wasn't listening. His head had twisted into the pillow like a puppy burrowing into his mama's stomach. Still, words dragged out of his mouth as though from a tape that was running down. "Your father didn't mean it, Kate," he said. "He couldn't help it."

I stared at him. "Didn't mean what?" I asked him. "What are you talking about?"

"Don't blame him for leaving you all alone in this world. Don't blame yourself, either."

My body was shaking all over when I felt Mom's arms around me, hugging me. "What is he talking about?" I asked her, in a voice that was barely a whisper.

An eye opened, and he looked at me as though he'd just waked up. "You've got the makin's," he said. "If the doctors haven't killed me and you have some time, come by tomorrow and we'll talk."

He was asleep.

Chapter Twenty-one

M Y BROTHER STOOD NEXT TO ME ON THE STAGE. With bright stage lights glaring in our faces, we gazed over the heads of the large audience gathered in the auditorium at Hill— when Law's cheeks started sprouting grizzled old whiskers that looked like . . . "Spencer Phipps!" The dream evaporated and I sat up in bed, wide awake.

I hadn't seen Spence since Sunday, and had no idea where the old wreck was. Had he really been an eyewitness? He was my only hope. But would he be at the trial? He'd said he'd be there, but he had not impressed me with his sense of responsibility. I had to find him!

I stared at the clock on my nightstand, the numbers glowing like red coals: 3:24 A.M. The trial would start in less than six hours! Mom had ironed a silk blouse that matched the tailored dress she'd bought me to wear, and her plan was to drive me to the office so my outfit would be clean and fresh. But I had to get there now. I stepped into my jean cutoffs, put on a sweatshirt, snuck down the stairs, and left her a note on the kitchen table:

Hi. With Herman's fate dangling in the balance I forgot all about Spencer Phipps! This will make absolutely no sense to you. Call me? Kate

I stuffed a dress and clean underwear in my panniers and wheeled my bike quietly out the back door of the garage, wondering what Mike would do if I snuck over to his house like a cat burglar and woke him up. I hadn't seen or heard from him since he rode away, his face grinding out angry tears. Did he hate me? If he knew how badly I needed him now, would he come out of his snit and help? I didn't know what to do. Would he be better at not knowing what to do than I was?

How *should* a teenage girl go about finding a drunk in the streets of Denver? If it meant searching around on Skid Row, a teenage boy would be better at it than a girl—especially a boy as big as Mike. I snuck into his backyard. His bedroom is in the back, on the first floor, and his window was open to catch the cool air, so I climbed up on my bike and scratched his screen. "Mike! Wake up!"

Nothing. The slug. A little louder this time: *"Mike!"*

I heard some movement, some grumping—and then a light went on in the house and I froze, making myself invisible. "Mike?" Mrs. Doyle asked, her shadow hovering over his bed like the Wicked Witch. I silently slipped away.

That's what happens when you try to get help from someone, I thought, realizing for the umpteenth time in my fourteen years on this planet that the only person I know I can count on is me.

It was still dark when I got to the office. Now what? I wondered, taking my panniers inside and trying to make myself think. What would Two-Fingers do? How would he go about finding Phipps?

He'd turn himself into Phipps so he could think like him. Where would an old wanderer spend his nights? Parks? Alleys? Doorways on Eighteenth Street? Flophouses? Missions? I could feel my stomach growing an ulcer. Could I look in those places without getting attacked?

A Denver Bears baseball cap hung on a hook in my office. I put it on, hoping to look like a boy with long hair, and climbed back on my bike. I rode down Broadway, past the Brown Palace and the Shirley Savoy Hotel, to Eighteenth Street, where the hobos hung out in doorways near the missions. Would he be in a flophouse? I wondered, riding by the Windsor Hotel—which was pretty up-scale for a bum, but Spencer Phipps was a pretty upscale bum. Beds were $2.50 a night, $10.00 a week.

Worth a try, I decided, putting a chain around my bike and walking into a tiny lobby where a man who hadn't shaved in a week slept with his head on a desk. I shook his shoulder. "Hi, kid," he said, trying to wake up. "Want a room?"

"No, sir." I deepened my voice, hoping it sounded like a boy, and it squeaked as though it was changing. "I'm looking for Spencer Phipps and wondered if he was staying here."

"You his grandson?"

"No, sir."

"Well, how about a drink, then?" He pulled out a flask, then stared at me strangely. "You aren't a boy. You're a girl."

"What's wrong with that?" I asked him, defensively.

"Get out of here, miss. You could be misunderstood."

I tried to hide behind the bill of my cap as I hurried out of the old hotel. There was a mission across the street with a blue neon sign in the form of a cross that said JESUS SAVES. Inside, a uniformed guard sat behind a desk. His jaw dropped when he saw me. "Miss Hope?" he asked, standing up. "Are you lookin' for me?"

I recognized him instantly, even though I'd seen him only once and he'd been totally insane that day. He'd wanted to torch the trailer house he lived in. Now, wearing a uniform and with his hair combed, he looked like a certified member of society. "Hi, Mr. Washington, am I glad to see you!"

A big smile opened up his face and he stuck out his hand, making mine disappear all the way to the elbow, which he didn't squeeze into pulp. "What are you doing down here, miss? You aren't lookin' for a place to stay, are you?"

"I'm looking for Spencer Phipps. Do you know him?"

"Old guy, never cracks a smile, talks like a professor, smells like a sewer?"

"Yes!" I said, hoping for the best.

"Saw him Tuesday but he didn't see me. Too drunk."

"I have to find him, Mr. Washington. I need him in court this morning, which gives me only five hours."

"He could be anywhere. Union Station, the railroad yard, somebody's lawn. He goes over to the lake at City Park too and sleeps under trees."

My stomach flashed red hot, then ice cold. I fought with my face to keep it from coming apart. "Thanks, Mr. Washington," I said, walking toward the door. "Maybe I'll get lucky."

"Miss Hope, sit a minute, okay?" He pulled up a chair. "You don't want to roll a drunk over to see his face. Bad idea." He lifted the coffeepot off a hotplate and poured oil into two plastic cups, and handed me one. "Four thirty in the morning is not a good time to be poking around for some down-and-outer. Let's think about it."

"But . . ."

"Let me see who's here." He opened the spiral notebook on his desk and ran his index finger down the page. It stopped. "Bearclaw. A Ute Indian who'd rather draw pictures in the sand than talk, but he and Phipps travel together." He took a sip of coffee. "A pair of squirrels, those two. Phipps brags about his family who came to Colorado in a covered wagon, but Bearclaw and his people were already here. Phipps's folks moved Bearclaw's relatives off some pretty good land, is what they've decided, but Bearclaw says he don't have any grudges over it. He'll drink with anybody." He closed the book. "If anybody knows where Phipps is, he will. How's the Judge?"

"He's at St. Luke's Hospital," I told him, which did something awful to my breathing.

"That's what I heard. I hope he gets out of there before it's too late. That's the very hospital where my wife died. They don't have a very good record, if you ask me."

Hospitals take in people who are sick and dying, so none of them do, I thought.

"This could take a while," he said as he stood up. "I'll have to sober Bearclaw up before I can talk to him, which means putting him in a shower. Why don't you get out of here now, go where I can call you? You need to get off the streets."

"I'll be at the office," I said, and gave him the telephone number. "Thank you so much, Mr. Washington."

He looked embarrassed. "Don't mention it."

There were a few more cars on the streets as I rode back, but not too many. It wasn't even five o'clock. I'd wait in the Judge's office, I decided, and spend the time getting ready for the trial.

The Judge's office had been neat and orderly when I turned on the light, which was how Mrs. Roulette always left it. But ten minutes later I'd converted it into a major disaster area, with notes, reports, questions for witnesses, scraps of paper with case citations on them, and lists of things to do scattered all over his desk, the chairs, and the floor. I'd been able to drink only half of Mr. Washington's coffee, but it must have activated my nervous system. "Time to get organized," I said to myself, putting on a fake smile and adopting a cheery attitude, just like Mom when she's frantic and out of her mind. I built piles of papers all over the place, but they didn't connect with each other. "Make files," I ordered myself, and jumped up to get file folders out of Mrs. Roulette's cabinet.

There weren't any file folders in her cabinet. Not even one. Suddenly it was after five, and the trial would start in less than four hours!

The telephone rang and I yanked it out of its cradle. Was Mrs. Roulette calling me to tell me where the file folders were? "Hello?"

"Is this my lawyer?" a voice full of uncertainty asked.

"Mr. Washington! Hi. Any luck?"

"Bearclaw wants to know what this is all about. He says Spence owes him money."

"If we can find him, maybe we can get Bearclaw paid."

"Hold on."

I heard a hand covering the telephone, but two seconds later a deep voice shattered my eardrum. "That guy Spence is bad," it said as I pulled the telephone away from my head. "He drinks from my bottle but don't pay for it. You tell him what I said."

"Mr. Bearclaw, he's an eyewitness in a case that means life and death to an old woman who needs help. Can you find him for me?"

"Spence talks crazy too. Says he's sorry his people took the land away from my people, wants to give it back. Now it's ruined with buildings and streets, he can keep it. You tell him what I said."

"The police will kill Herman if I don't find Spence," I said, more to myself than to this man who wasn't paying attention to me anyway.

"He took my coat. He's bad," he said. I started to put the phone in its cradle. "Herman?" he asked loudly. "The wolf-dog?"

"Yes!"

"I know Herman. Me and him are buddies."

"If Spence doesn't testify for him in court today, he'll be executed for something he didn't do." I waited for a reply but didn't hear anything for a moment. "Mr. Bearclaw?"

"It's me, Miss Hope," Mr. Washington said. "I'll call you later. Bearclaw just charged out of here like a cowboy after a horse thief. If anybody can find Spence for you, he can. He's gonna round up a posse."

I could feel the blood that had been squished into some little ball in my stomach gushing out, filling my veins with life and hope. What a relief! The army it would take to check all the doorways and sidewalks and parks where Spence could be sleeping it off was being formed. I could work now, knowing he'd be found by people who knew where to look for him.

The telephone rang again. "Kate?"

It was Mike! "Hi," I said. "How'd you know I was down here?"

"I don't know," he said. "Took a chance. You've got that big trial this morning. Did you try to wake me up?"

"Yes," I said, "but it didn't work. Do you still hate me?"

"I don't hate you. How's it going?"

I told him about panicking because I didn't know where Spence Phipps was, my only witness, even though I didn't know what he'd seen. Then bumping into Mr. Washington, and talking to Bearclaw, and now there was a whole posse out looking for Spence. "How are you do-ing?" I asked.

"Okay. I talked to your mom."

"You did? When?"

"Yesterday. Didn't she tell you?"

"No. What about?"

"Ron Benson, growing up, stuff like that." He cleared his throat. "Want me to do anything?"

"That's really nice of you, Mike," I said, all kind of warm and gooey inside. Maybe there were people in this world I could trust after all. "Can you talk to Willis Suggs? He might know who those kids were, on bikes, who ran over Miss Willow. One of them is called Tomato Face, and they could have seen something."

"Okay," he said. "Sally wants to help too. We'll start looking."

Sally! I almost yelled at him, and started to hang up. But I caught myself. "Mike?" I said. "Thanks for calling."

The jitters were gone. All the scattered papers and files and arguments and questions began to organize themselves in the right order. At seven fifteen, Mom called to tell me that she'd bring my new dress and freshly pressed blouse to the office at eight, and that I was to be showered so I could get all dolled up and she could take pictures of me before my first trial. "Mom!"

Mr. Washington called a little later to tell me Bearclaw and his buddies were still looking, and if they came by the office I was not to give them any money. "They'd use it to get drunk," he told me.

When Mrs. Roulette came in at a quarter to eight, I handed her a pile of stuff to type and asked her to get me some file folders while I took a shower. "Do I have time to put on the coffee?" she asked, glaring at all the papers. "You're worse than your grandfather."

Mom's eyes were wet when she took pictures of me in my new clothes. Afterward, she smiled that great smile that always brings out the best in a person, and gave me a hug. "Break a leg, honey," she said. "I'll see you tonight."

"Aren't you going to watch the trial?" I asked. I'd just kind of assumed she'd be there to pick up the pieces.

"No." She blotted up some of the wetness around her eyes with a tissue. "I'll be at the hospital with your grandfather. Mrs. Roulette will keep us posted."

"Oh." I was disappointed, which surprised me, but relieved, too.

Mr. Washington called again at eight fifteen, sounding worried as he told me not to worry. But at a quarter to nine there was still no word from him, and I had to be in court at nine. I called him to get the latest.

He said Bearclaw and his posse had given up. They didn't handle failure well, he added, and most of them, including Bearclaw, were drunk.

That was the beginning of a very long day.

Chapter Twenty-two

My HIGH HEELS CLICKED WITH OPTIMISM and my smile was in place as I left the office for the courthouse, but it was an act. I seriously considered walking down the middle of the street. Maybe a car would hit me—softly, nothing permanent, but a broken leg would be nice.

I felt like a convict walking the last mile. So much had gone wrong with my case. The day before, I'd met with Judge Steinbrunner and Mr. Thomas to plead for a continuance. But not only did the judge refuse to give me one, he ordered Herman to stay out of the courtroom during the trial. I'd wanted the big dog there so he could gaze at the jury with his soulful brown eyes and wag his tail at them from time to time. But Mr. Thomas convinced Judge Steinbrunner that Herman might bite someone and sue the City. Miss Willow was ordered to take the dog to a storage room in the basement of the courthouse during the trial, where there would be a cage for him and someone from Animal Control to watch him.

At five minutes before nine, I found the room in the basement and looked in. "Hi," I said to a woman in a dog-catcher's uniform who sat next to a cage in a corner of the room, reading the paper. "I'm Kate Hope, the lawyer for Herman and Miss Willow?"

"Hi, honey," she said. "Where's your client?"

Neither Herman nor Miss Willow was there! Miss Willow had never been late for anything in her life. Her genes wouldn't allow it. "Not a problem, I'm sure," I said, lightly trying to shrug off another disaster while my imagination pictured the worst possible scenario to explain their absence. She'd run away with her dog, knowing it was hopeless with me instead of the Judge as her lawyer. Now both of them were fugitives from justice. "Miss Willow must not have been able to find a place to park or something," I said, "but they'll be here in a minute or two." I blessed her with Mom's smile. "Thanks. I'd better get upstairs."

The courtroom was jammed! Every seat was taken, the aisles were filled with bodies, and people leaned against every available inch of wall space, forming a big ring around the room. But it was not the average cross-section of humanity summoned for jury duty. Most of them were kids my age and older. It looked as though the entire eighth-grade class at Hill was there, as well as the East High School football team, the cheerleaders, and half the student body. "The Great Mouthpiece!" someone yelled out at me as one of the football players drew his fingers across his throat with something like malicious joy in his eyes.

Mom's smile struggled, but I managed to keep it in place as I hurried through the gate into the pit, my briefcase in my hand. "Judge would like to see you in chambers, Miss Hope," the bailiff said.

I made my way through the door behind the bench for judges and lawyers and was greeted by Judge Steinbrunner as I entered his chambers. He sat behind his large conference desk. Carl Thomas nodded at me from one of the chairs like an executioner who loved what he did for a living. "You look very nice, young woman, as I expect lady lawyers to look in my courtroom," he said. "Sit down. How's your grandfather?"

"I wish he was here!"

"But he's all right?"

"As far as I know, sir. My mom is with him, so I don't think he has a choice."

"You be sure and give him my best. Do you have a set of instructions for me?"

"Yes, sir," I said, pulling them out of my briefcase and sliding one set to the judge and another set to Mr. Thomas, who pushed a huge pile of instructions toward me. "Why all the young people, Kate?" the judge asked. "I've never seen it so crowded. Civics classes bring in perhaps twenty children at a time, but there are fifty, seventy, who knows how many students out there, and it's summer vacation! You aren't planning on a demonstration or some kind of foolishness, are you?"

"Oh no, sir! I didn't invite them. In fact, I wish they'd go away."

His thin eyes adopted sort of a wait-and-see attitude. "Well, it's a public trial and they have the right. Anything else we need to talk about before we start?"

"I have a tiny problem, Your Honor," I said, squirming. "My client hasn't arrived yet, which worries me because she's always on time."

Thomas glared at me. "The dog?" he asked. "Where is he?"

"He's with Miss Willow, and I'm sure they'll be here, but . . ."

"Judge, I was afraid of this," Mr. Thomas said, aiming an I-told-you-so expression at the judge. "That dog should not have been allowed to go back into the community— although I certainly don't blame you for allowing it," he added hastily. He faced me. "Kate, how are you going to feel when you read the paper and find out he's bitten another baby?"

"I don't think that will happen," I said. "Carl."

Not a huge victory in the infinite scheme of things, but if he was going to call me Kate, I was going to call him Carl whether he liked it or not. I could tell from his expression that he did not.

"Your Honor, I'm asking you for a warrant for the arrest of Miss Willow and her dog."

The judge looked worried as one hand nervously stroked his chin. "Let's not rush into this just yet," he said. "Do you have any idea where she'd go with her dog?" he asked me. "Relatives? Friends?"

"She lives alone, sir, and her only friend in the world is Herman. I really don't understand this, but I know she'll be here. It's just that sometimes she puts things off to the last minute, and she's scared to death. But I talked to her last night and she promised me she'd be here." Then another emotion chose that moment to thrust its way to the foreground: total defeat. My smile caved in on itself, and a tiny whimper pushed out of my mouth. My eyes betrayed me too, filling with humiliating tears.

Neither of the men knew what to do and I didn't either, but I yanked out a hankie and blew my nose, wiped away the unwelcome moisture, and smiled with all my teeth. "Hay fever."

"My daughter's out there in that crowd of kids," Mr. Thomas said, to my surprise. "She wants to meet you during a recess. That be all right?"

"Of course," I managed.

"Just so we're straight, Kate," he went on, "I don't want *you* to go to jail. Just that sweet little old lady who hired you."

That was really so nice of him, I thought, smiling at him and laughing along with the judge at Mr. Thomas's sudden flash of humor . . . when we heard the barking of a dog! "Well now," Steinbrunner said. "Unless my ears are going the way of my eyesight, we may not have a problem after all. That could be your client I hear, barking! Why don't you go take a peek, young woman?"

For an instant Mr. Thomas looked relieved too, until his expression changed into suspicion. "This isn't a trick, is it?" he asked, pushing away from the table. "I'll go with you."

We looked into the courtroom and there was Miss Willow, sitting in one of the chairs along the rail in front of the audience with Herman at her feet. A man I'd never seen before sat next to her, rubbing Herman's ears. He was as thin as a scarecrow and had tiny blood-soaked pieces of Kleenex stuck to his face like pimples and wore an old-fashioned suit that looked like it had been made out of gunnysacks. Ankles as white as a movie star's teeth hung out below the suit, as though the trousers had been made for a shorter scarecrow. The man saw me and waved. "Good morning, counselor," he said.

Spencer Phipps, without that scraggly beard of his!

The blobs on his face must have been where he'd nicked himself shaving.

Thomas was not amused, to put it mildly. "Your grandfather's idea?" he asked me. "This is a clear violation of the judge's order, and . . ."

He stopped when a hush settled over the courtroom. Herman's back had stiffened, his yellow eyes had narrowed into thin slits, and a menacing growl rumbled in his throat. I couldn't figure it out . . . until I saw what he was growling at. Ron Benson! I'd seen him earlier, standing in the back with an army of his jockstrap buddies, and now I watched helplessly as he strutted to the seats behind the front rail where Ursula Jespersen sat.

Spence grabbed the leash out of Miss Willow's hand and held it in both of his, as Herman seemed to put up his dukes, ready for a fight with Ron Benson. Suddenly Mr. Thomas pushed in front of me. "Get that vicious dog out of here!" he demanded loudly, as everyone in the audience near Herman—except for Ron—shrank back. "Quick!" Thomas hollered. "Before he goes berserk!"

I did my best to come to the rescue. "Spence, there's a storage room in the basement," I said. "Can you get him there?"

"I can indeed." Spence pulled Herman into the aisle past Ron, and everything was going okay—Herman's tail was even wagging a bit—until Officer Milliken, the dogcatcher intent on executing Herman, burst into the courtroom.

"Out of my way!" he shouted, charging down the aisle like a hero. "I'll take that, sir!" He yanked the leash out of Spence's hand and started dragging the poor animal, choking him, as people jerked their hands and arms up to protect themselves from attack.

Miss Willow had her fist in her mouth. "My poor dog!" she cried. "What will they do to him?"

"Fear not, Wilma," Spence said grandly, trying his best to keep up. "Officer, unhand that dog!"

"Out of my way, old man, before you get hurt!" Milliken shouted as they disappeared into the hall.

"Don't worry, Miss Willow," I told her. "Spence is right there. Herman will be fine, if we can keep him away from certain people."

But my client had not made the right impression at all. He'd acted like a dog with a wild streak in his nature: one that could suddenly go berserk.

He'd acted like a dangerous dog.

We'd picked the jury, and after a short recess, we sat in the courtroom like fish in a fishbowl, watched by a hundred eyes. Carl Thomas and Officer Milliken sat next to the jury box at the plaintiff's table with relaxed and confident expressions, but Miss Willow huddled next to me at the defense table like a little girl trying to hide. Only there was nowhere to hide. The spectator area was filled with kids waiting for the curtain to go up, and the six jurors who had been picked earlier that morning were staring at us from another angle.

During the recess I'd had a chance to talk to my star witness for five minutes, which helped a little, but wasn't anywhere near enough time because he couldn't stick to the point. But I thought I'd gotten the gist of what he'd seen, and it gave me hope. At least we had a fighting chance. Yet I had horrible misgivings about the jury we'd picked. During *voir dire*, I didn't bring up anything that would help my side of the case, as Grandfather would have done. All I'd been able to do was smile and agree with them when they told me they'd be fair and impartial; but now they were seated in the box and ready to sit in judgment. How could a sixty-year-old grandfather with three daughters and seven grandkids, and five middle-aged mothers with children, be fair and impartial to a dog charged with biting a baby?

"You may give your opening statement, Mr. Thomas," the judge said.

"Thank you, Your Honor." He positioned a notepad on the lectern and faced the jury, obviously at ease as he looked into their faces. "Members of the jury," he said, and then, turning toward me with a big smile, "and Miss Hope."

I have a better, richer, cuter, and more devastating

smile than he does by far. My teeth are whiter, too, so I smiled back.

Thomas quickly went on with his statement, deflecting the attention of the jurors back to him. When he told them what an opening statement was, he trotted out the same old analogy lawyers always use, but made it sound like something he'd just thought of. "Trials are like jigsaw puzzles, and the evidence often comes in bits and pieces. But if you see the big picture first, then you know how they fit into the puzzle. And so, before the evidence is taken, both sides have the opportunity to tell you what they believe the evidence will show. Because the burden of proof is on the City, I go first, but please pay close attention to Miss Hope when she gives you her version of the evidence."

How nice of him, I thought, as my stomach wrapped around my spine. I was certain my vocal cords would snap and my brain would take a holiday and I would drool. You had to admire how smoothly he played the part of a nice lawyer who would never in the world take advantage of his inexperienced opponent who was a mere fourteen-year-old girl.

"The City's evidence will be testimony from these witnesses," he said, gesturing toward the six handsome and well-dressed people who sat in the front row of the spectator area, directly behind me. They looked judgmental and righteous, like Puritans during the Salem witch trials. "But before I introduce them to you, let me tell you a little about this case. You will meet a dog named Herman, and will be called upon to decide whether or not the animal is a 'dangerous dog.'"

I hated knowing what he was doing during his opening statement and not being able to keep him from doing it. In one sentence, he'd transformed Herman from a dog with a name to an animal. "Of course, a dog can be loyal to its owner and still be a danger to others," he said, "which is what the evidence in this case will show. There is no doubt in my mind that the animal is loyal to its owner, that nice-looking woman sitting with Miss Hope. In spite of that, you will learn he's extremely dangerous."

There was something I should do, but my mind had frozen as I tried to thaw it out, then realized he was arguing! Would Grandfather let him argue during the opening statement, when you are only supposed to tell the jury what the evidence is? I started to object, but instead of standing like you're supposed to in court, I put up my hand like a kid in school. The judge frowned at me with annoyance, and Mr. Thomas didn't even slow down. Then it was too late to object, because he'd moved on to something else. "Now let me introduce the witnesses for the City. Mr. and Mrs. Pearsan, will you stand, please?"

A man and wife with television-perfect faces like Ozzie and Harriet stood up and smiled at the jury. They were dressed in simple but expensive clothes and holding hands. "The Pearsans are the mother and father of the four-month-old baby girl who was attacked by the dog." Mr. Thomas spoke matter-of-factly, like a butler announcing that dinner was served, but the jurors were shocked. "Little Monica can't be here with us today," he continued, as though she couldn't attend because of the horrible injuries she was healing from, "but you will meet her even so. The proud parents will show you photos of their child."

They sat down as Mr. Thomas introduced the next person in the row. "This is Miss Ursula Jespersen," he said as she stood up. "Ursula is a live-in nanny from Denmark who is employed by this hard-working couple," and she smiled and blushed nicely like a princess in a fairy tale who smiles and blushes on cue. "She will tell you, among other things, of her feelings when she saw little Monica in the jaws of the animal."

When Ursula heard Mr. Thomas say that to the jury, it was obvious that she knew exactly how she had felt . . . and an electric jolt touched off another shock, this one in my stomach. The big thing I knew I'd forgotten about flashed in my mind. The witnesses for Mr. Thomas were hearing his opening statement! No lawyer wants the witnesses for the other side to hear what that lawyer says he intends to prove, because then they'll know exactly what to say and how to act. "Your Honor?" I said, jumping up. "I make a motion to exclude all witnesses from the courtroom!"

"You do *what?*" he demanded. "Approach the bench."

My legs, strong enough to push me up the steep climb of Lookout Mountain on a bicycle, trembled like stilts in a windstorm as we huddled around the court reporter, our voices down so the jury wouldn't hear us. "Miss Hope," Steinbrunner whispered at me through his teeth, "I will grant your motion *after* Mr. Thomas's opening statement, but not *during* it. If you didn't want them here *during* his opening statement, you should have made your motion *before he started.*"

Mr. Thomas, in a big display of courtesy, let me go first, and I stumbled back to my chair with the wind completely out of my sails. I tried not to look at Ron Benson's happy smile or the satisfied smirks on the faces of the kids in the spectator area—when I saw Mike in the middle of them, staring at the floor. He sat next to Sally Lipscombe, who was trying to hold his hand.

As Mr. Thomas got behind the lectern, where he stood like the president addressing Congress, Miss Willow clutched my arm, her blue hands cold with fear. "They won't take Herman away from me, will they?" her tiny voice pleaded.

"We don't know yet," I whispered.

But I knew. Mom's smile, so full of optimism and faith in the power of right to overcome wrong, deserted me. Justice was a joke in the real world of the legal system, I thought. It was nothing but tricks and tactics the lawyers used to keep the jury from finding out the truth. The truth about Herman had nothing to do with this case. All that mattered was which side had the slickest lawyer.

Kate, that don't sound like you at all! a voice called out from somewhere I couldn't see. *I thought you was a lawyer! Don't blame the system. Use it!*

Grandfather? Had they let him out of the hospital? I twisted my head around, looking for the speaker, but all I saw was Mike, smiling at me with his thumbs up.

Had Mike tried to give me a stiff-upper-lip lecture from where he sat? Not like him at all. And I was certain the voice belonged to the Judge, my law partner. "Grampa?" I asked, forgetting where I was. "Where are you?"

Judge Steinbrunner stared at me. "Did you say something, Miss Hope?" he asked.

Mom's smile was back on my face. "I guess I did, sir, to myself."

"Well now. I won't try to keep you from talking to yourself, but I will ask you to keep your voice down."

Ursula wasn't the only one who could blush prettily, I discovered as laughter washed over me like surf. The judge let it roil and swirl around the room for ten seconds, then whacked his gavel on the marble plate. It sounded like a pistol shot and was followed with total silence. "Listen to me, all you young people," he said. "This is a court of law.

You have the right to be here, but only if you conduct yourselves properly. I will not tolerate any foolishness. Do you understand me?"

They did. Mr. Thomas continued with his introductions. "Mr. Benson, would you stand up, please?" As Ron stood up, his flashing blue eyes touched mine with pity, then shined on the jury. He was all blond wavy hair piled on top of a Greek god's body, with muscles bulging beneath a suit. "Mr. Benson may be known to some of you," Mr. Thomas said, like he was the best friend the jurors ever had, "because of his high school athletic career and his prowess in football at Penn State." Why not throw in the fact that the mayor wanted to change the name of Leetsdale Drive to Ron Benson Boulevard? "Today, however, you will meet him as a friend of Ursula Jespersen. Mr. Benson also witnessed the attack."

After Ron sat down, Mr. Thomas put a large chart on an easel, angling it so the jury could see what was on it. A map of the sidewalks, streets, benches, trees, and shrubs along a piece of the shoreline at City Park Lake hung in front of them as big as a blackboard. Using a pointer, he described what Miss Jespersen and Mr. Benson would tell them, starting with wheeling little Monica around the lake and showing exactly where they'd stopped to rest.

My pulse banged around inside of me like a jackhammer as Mr. Thomas told the jury what Ursula and Ron had seen. How a large dog charged out of nowhere and attacked the sleeping infant in the buggy. How the animal had run off with the baby in his jaws. The jurors were paralyzed with horror by his description, but the story had a happy ending. Thank God for the presence of a gifted athlete, Mr. Thomas said, telling them that if Ron Benson hadn't been there to stop the carnage, no one knows how the frightening scenario might have ended.

The cop who had been called to the scene of the crime stood up next, looking sharp in his uniform, and grim. Then the doctor who examined little Monica was introduced to the jury. "At the conclusion of our evidence, I feel certain you will arrive at the only responsible verdict there is in this case," Mr. Thomas sadly proclaimed, like a preacher at a funeral. "The animal, the dog named Herman, is a dangerous dog." He sat down.

Judge Steinbrunner peered down his nose at me as I did my best to look confident in spite of the odds. "You can talk to someone other than yourself now, Miss Hope," he said. "It's time for your opening statement."

Chapter Twenty-three

I JUST KNEW SOMETHING AWFUL would happen when I tried to give my opening statement, and it did. I couldn't stand up! I was frozen in an invisible block of ice! *Stuck, are you,* Grandfather's voice said, followed by his low chuckle. *Happens to the best of 'em. It still happens to me. Get up now, Pumpkin. Dazzle them with your teeth.*

It had been years since anyone had called me Pumpkin, and it activated some reflexes I didn't know I had. I jumped to my feet, feeling warm and gooey inside. My dad had called me that, telling everyone within earshot that it was his favorite name for his favorite daughter. I glowed with pride, until my brother pointed out to me that I was Zozo's *only* daughter.

The damage had already been done, though, because I continued to glow with pride. "Your Honor, can the witnesses be excluded now?" I asked, Mom's smile beaming at the judge with memories the judge didn't know anything about.

Judge Steinbrunner peered at the six people in the row behind me who Thomas had introduced to the jury. "Miss Hope has made a motion to exclude witnesses," he said to them. "Officer David Milliken and Miss Willow can stay, but anyone else who expects to testify in this case must leave the courtroom." They shrugged like good sports and got up. "Please wait in the hall until you're called," the judge told them, "and don't discuss the case among yourselves."

Lawyers are supposed to stay behind the lectern when they give their opening statement, but when I stood behind it, the only part of me the jury could see was my smiling face. "I'm a little short for this," I said to the judge, patting it. "Can I . . ."

"You may."

Good start, I thought as the jurors watched me with expressions that said "Isn't she cute?" For the moment, at least, they were on my side. "Thank you, Your Honor," I said to him, then threw all my charm at Mr. Thomas. "And thank you too, Mr. Thomas, for asking the jury to listen to me carefully, because the defense evidence tells a very different story from the one you've told." They weren't exactly on the edge of their chairs, but they were listening, as I called myself Pumpkin to bring on the glow.

"You see, we have an eyewitness who saw this whole scary incident, and he'll tell you what *really* happened. It's very, very different from what Mr. Thomas would have you believe."

Mr. Thomas stood up. "Your Honor," he said, "I had hoped this kind of thing would not happen. But I feel, sir, that I must interrupt."

The judge stared at me with that awful expression he'd used on me before, as though I'd committed a crime. "Ladies and gentlemen," he said, smiling with patience at the jurors, "something unexpected has occurred and I anticipate the need for a short argument. The bailiff will escort you to the jury room. These things happen in the course of a trial, and you should not concern yourselves over them or consider them in your deliberations."

It was apparent to the whole world that I'd done something terrible again, but what? The bailiff led the jurors into the jury room and I wished the kids would leave too, but they didn't budge. They were glued to their chairs, waiting gleefully for the ax to fall—except Mike, whose face was a deep, violent red.

"Miss Hope," Steinbrunner said when the jurors were gone, "the Court file doesn't show that your side had any witnesses, except perhaps your client, Miss Willow. Is she your eyewitness?"

"No," I said, as my back stiffened on its own. Mom's genes wouldn't let me back down. "She wasn't with

Herman, sir, when this happened. She was being taken care of by a couple of paramedics."

"Miss Hope, when you have witnesses, you must let the other side know who they are. Didn't you get a witness list from Mr. Thomas?"

A witness list! "Yes, sir."

"Well, why didn't you give him yours?" he asked, doing his best to control himself, but close to losing it. "He doesn't like surprises, and neither do I. That's trial by ambush and has no place in a court of law."

I had no explanation, other than that Grandfather had collapsed and all the clients had been dumped in my lap and a thousand things were on my mind and it was only the second trial I'd put together in my life. Should I make an excuse, like there was a power failure and Mrs. Roulette's electric typewriters shorted and I thought she'd done it but hadn't? *Don't make it worse than it is,* Grampa said. "I have no excuse, sir. I just forgot."

"Well. At least you're honest about it," he said, frowning. "You leave me in a very difficult position. Who is this witness?"

"His name is Spencer Phipps, sir, and he—"

"Spencer Phipps?" the judge asked as he and Mr. Thomas exchanged glances of recognition. "Is he out?" Out of *what,* I wondered, looking over at Miss Willow who had almost slid out of sight under the table. But enough of her remained visible to show an expression on her face like a squished lemon. "I'll do this in the interests of justice, young lady," the judge said. "You may call your witness in spite of the rule, but the trial will have to be delayed to give the city attorney time to prepare for him. I hope you have learned your lesson here and that it won't happen again."

"Thank you, Your Honor. It won't."

"Mr. Thomas, how much time will you need?" the judge asked him.

He and Officer Milliken smiled at each other, which wasn't a good sign at all. "I can prepare for him during a recess, Judge," he said. "No need to delay the trial. Mr. Phipps is well known in the city attorney's office."

The judge nodded. "Bailiff, go get the jury."

As we waited, I asked Miss Willow what the deal was. "Spence acts crazy sometimes," she whispered.

"How crazy?"

"He gets committed to the state mental hospital."

My star witness, whose version of what happened was the one the jury had to believe if Herman was to have any chance at all, was looney tunes!

As the jurors filed back into the box, I considered my options. Was suicide an alternative? No, I thought, trying to cheer myself up. Mom would kill me. "You may continue, Miss Hope," the judge said.

When I told the jury who my star witness was, two of them were surprised, but all of them listened patiently to every word. I outlined what I thought Spence would say, claiming that Herman was a hero who saved the infant, in spite of the way it might have looked—but it sounded like the figment of an imagination that needed fertilizer, even to me. None of the jurors would look at me after that.

The judge declared a recess for lunch.

Every kid I'd ever known in my life was in the courtroom, but I was invisible to them as they erupted with chatter once the judge and the jury were out of sight. They were laughing about the cranky old judge, the slick city attorney . . . and Kate, the Great Mouthpiece, whose head would soon be handed to the jury on a silver platter. Out of the corner of my eye I saw Mike disappear with Sally. He could at least have waved at me, I thought.

I took Miss Willow to the storage room in the basement, where she could eat with Herman and Spence. She'd packed food for them and offered me a sandwich too, but my stomach wouldn't allow me so much as a bite. I should have tried to get more information out of Spence, but I couldn't face him just then, and hurried to the office instead, smiling with confidence at everyone along the way, knowing I'd soon be able to lock myself in Grandfather's room and scream.

Someone was following me. I felt eyes on the back of my head, so I stopped in my tracks and turned around, ready to confront whoever the offender was. A creep? I wondered, as two huge eyes focused on me through what could have been identical magnifying glasses on each side of his nose. "Hi," he said. "Aren't you Kate Hope, the lawyer?"

He wore a short-sleeved Hawaiian shirt with a row of pens in the left pocket, and he had a spiral notebook in his right hand. "Yes."

"I'm Max Briar, *Rocky Mountain News.* How's it going?"

"Busy," I said, hoping he could take a hint.

"You're involved in that trial that's packing them in, aren't you?" he asked, opening his notebook and pulling out a pen. "The one all the kids are watching?"

"Yes."

"What kind of case is it?"

"It's a jury trial for a dog."

"No kidding!" He looked interested, which I didn't need because any publicity it generated would not enhance my self-esteem. "Who's the judge?"

"Steinbrunner."

"He's tough. Do you like practicing law?"

"Some days are better than others," I said. "You'll have to excuse me, Mr. Briar, but I'm in kind of a hurry."

"Don't worry about it. Say hello to your mom."

There were two telephone messages I had to return at the office before I could close the door and be alone and cry. "Hi, Mom," I said, my jaw quivering. She was at her office instead of the hospital. "How's Grampa?"

"I just left him. Sleeping soundly, but I've been instructed to stay near a phone. Otherwise I'd be down there, cheering you on. How are you doing?"

"Great," I lied. "We've given opening statements and the evidence goes in next. I still have my head on my shoulders." I wanted to tell her about Grandfather's voice, but couldn't.

"You'll do just fine." She went on to tell me I was to consider myself hugged and that she knew I must be exhausted. I was also to eat the roast beef sandwich she'd left with Mrs. Roulette and be home in time for dinner.

"Anything else?" I asked.

"Yes, honey. Break a leg."

The other one was to Mike, who was waiting by a phone booth on Colfax and had to talk. He picked up the phone before it finished its first ring. "Kate?"

I hate it when I get emotional, but knowing he hadn't deserted me after all to run off with Sally and get married put me on the edge of tears. "Hi. What's up?" I asked in as professional a voice as I could manage.

"We found them."

"We?"

"Sally and me."

"Found who?"

"The kids who knocked Miss Willow down. I told Willis Suggs one of them was called Tomato Face, and he knew right away who they were. Do you know what else they did?"

"Gave the baby carriage a shove?"

"Right! How did you know?"

"It's what Spencer Phipps told me. Mike, this is so great," I said, coming back to life. "They can back up his story. Except . . ."

"Except what?" Mike asked. "We'll get them to the courthouse and you can put them on the witness stand and the jury will know that crazy old Spence isn't a total nut case."

More surprise witnesses? "Steinbrunner will explode into shrapnel, Mike, you heard him. He'll unglue me if I do that."

"So?" he asked, like it wouldn't bother him in the slightest for the judge to unglue me. "Nobody's gonna believe that old man, Kate. Now they will. Besides, I thought defense lawyers tried anything."

He was right on both counts. Grandfather wouldn't hesitate a second. He'd jump into the lake of the law with both feet, just to see how high the water splashed. He'd fight back with "the interests of justice," and "the search for the truth," and ask the judge how the new witnesses could have been included on a witness list when he didn't know until they'd been found what their names were. "Ooooh," I said, letting my voice shake, mocking my own terror, "this will be so bad. I need their names, telephone numbers, and addresses."

"All I have are names so far," he said. "Bean Pole and Tomato Face."

"Those are their names?"

"That's all I've got."

"It will have to do, then. Can you get them to the courthouse this afternoon? So Mr. Thomas can interview them if he wants?"

"You got it," he promised, as I choked on tears because of what I was feeling that I couldn't say. "Anything else?"

"I . . ." There was so much stuff in my head that wanted to gush out, in waves of gratitude.

"See you in court!" Mike called out, hanging up as though to save me from embarrassment.

Mrs. Roulette typed the witness list without saying a word to me about it, which was nice of her. I felt encouraged enough even to try some of the sandwich, but it didn't do well in my stomach, so I wrapped it back up for Herman. I tried to gather my thoughts in the quiet of Grandfather's room, then took a deep breath, put the witness list and sandwich in my briefcase, and walked back to the courthouse, where I would slay the dragons of injustice that slithered around. But first I stopped in the basement to give Herman the snack and make sure Spence was still on the scene.

The dog filled up the cage he was cooped up in, his jaw flat on the floor, as his tail thumped with happiness at the sight of the roast beef, which he ate in one gulp. Spence and Miss Willow were with him, sitting next to each other and holding hands, which I thought was really sweet. "Well!" Spence said, full of heartiness and cheer like an actor playing the part of a senator meeting a voter. "Our lawyer, Wilma. Did you have a decent lunch, Kate?"

"Yes, thank you," I said, sitting down. "I am so glad you made it, Spence, and I like your suit," I lied, ignoring the way it fit and the blood-soaked bits of paper on his cheeks. "How did you sleep last night?" I asked, fishing for answers to questions that popped into my mind, like where he'd spent the night and how Bearclaw's posse had missed him.

"Wonderfully well," he informed me. "I slept with Herman in Wilma's backyard. She knew nothing about it, of course. Had she known that a man spent the night on the premises, she'd have been scandalized."

"Spence!" she cooed as she tucked her hand comfortably in his.

"Yet she was extraordinarily hospitable to me this morning, and even allowed me the use of her shower."

"The bathroom is a mess."

The last place the posse would have looked would be Miss Willow's backyard. "Why did you spend the night with Herman instead of, you know, with your buddies?" I asked.

"Because I'm incurably irresponsible," he explained. "Had I remained with my companions, I would have missed the trial. And so, in order to ensure my attendance, I retired earlier than usual to a location of little or no temptation." He smiled that sad smile of his that had its own stamp and strange appeal. "To make a promise to a human and break it is forgivable. Humans don't deserve any better. But to let a dog down is absolutely unpardonable. I would never have forgiven myself had I let Herman down."

It was ten minutes before one and I had to face the judge with the witness list, so I told Miss Willow to be sure and be on time and then went upstairs, hoping to find the judge in a good mood.

Ron Benson was sitting on a bench in the hall as I walked by. "Hi, counselor," he said. "Nice try."

"What are you talking about?"

"You'll find out."

The judge hadn't come back from lunch, so I left the witness list with his clerk who shuddered when she saw it and said, "I don't know about this, Kate, are you sure?"

I shrugged at her, smiled, and nodded.

"Go, girl," she said.

Back in the courtroom, Miss Willow waited like a little mouse, and Mr. Thomas and Officer Milliken nodded at me from their places. I gave Mr. Thomas a copy of the witness list and watched his eyes roll out of sight. "I don't believe this," he said.

Kids were filling up the courtroom again, and the reporter from the *Rocky Mountain News* was in the front row winking at me. "Pull out all the stops, okay?" he said.

"Why?"

"This could make the front page."

Chapter Twenty-four

"WILL THE LAWYERS APPROACH the bench?" the judge asked, not even looking at me. But he stared at my witness list as if it was the dead body of his favorite pet. We moved forward. Mr. Thomas wouldn't look at me either. Here it comes, I thought, hoping Grandfather's voice would help me again.

"Miss Hope," the judge whispered so the jurors wouldn't hear, "your witness list should have been filed three days before trial. It's too late now. If there's good cause for an exception, you need to state what it is in a proper motion."

Ask for an oral one, Grandfather's voice said. "Sir, can I make an oral motion, then?" I asked. "In the interests of justice?"

The rays from Judge Steinbrunner's eyes were hot enough to light a fire. "At the first recess I'll hear you, young woman. Not now. We are going to finish this case this afternoon."

At least he's taking me seriously, I thought as I walked back to my chair. He isn't sending me to my room like a naughty little girl. "Mr. Thomas," the judge said, "you may call your first witness."

The bailiff brought Mrs. Pearsan in from the hall, her casual summer suit perfect for Denver, with turquoise earrings framing her face. She sat in the witness box like an Indian princess, raised her right hand, and swore to tell the truth. I smiled at her to see if she'd smile at me, and she did, showing me and the jury an open and friendly attitude, with nothing to hide. It matched her appearance. I liked her, and so did the jurors, who listened with approval when she told them where she lived and worked, what her husband's name was, and that their little baby's name was Monica.

But when Mr. Thomas showed her pictures of the little girl, she smiled at each snapshot, then dabbed at tears I didn't see in her eyes. "Poor baby," she said, which sounded like a line she'd memorized. "Her legs are still bruised." The pictures were passed to the jury.

When I got up to cross-examine her, the butterflies in my stomach reminded me I'd never done this before. I slipped around the lectern so she could see all of me, rather than just my face. "She's so cute," I said. "It must have been very scary for you."

"Much more than scary," she told me—and the jury. "I almost fainted. I will never forget how shocked and distraught I was when I first heard about it."

I empathized with her totally. "Was it Miss Jespersen who told you?"

"Actually, I heard it from my husband first. But Ursula and I talked too, as you can imagine."

"You're lucky to have Miss Jespersen," I said. "She's an au pair, isn't she? From Denmark?"

"Yes."

I asked her what an au pair was, hoping there were some poor people on the jury who would hate her for having so much money that she could bring a babysitter all the way from Europe—which was mean of me, but Grampa seemed to be watching, and nodded his old head with satisfaction. After that, cross-examining her was easy, like chatting it up with a friend of my mom's. I asked her where the baby had been taken for treatment, and was told the emergency room at Denver General Hospital. Baby Monica's pediatrician dropped everything, she said, and rushed out to the hospital to examine her. After treating her, he released the tiny baby to Mom and Dad. "How is Monica now?" I asked, and was told she was fine, except for a tiny bruise still on her leg. "She's back to laughing and giggling and playing with toys in her crib," Mrs. Pearsan said, glowing with love for her baby.

I was proud of myself when she stepped down from the box, because at least the jury knew Herman hadn't chewed Monica into bits. But my confidence evaporated when Carl Thomas brought Mr. Pearsan to the stand. Mr. Pearsan told the jury he'd been devastated by the call, which came from the emergency room at the hospital, and he added that his wife became hysterical. He described in detail how everyone at the hospital, even Ron Benson, had cried. Although he didn't say it, the message written on his face was easy to read: That dog needs to be killed.

That man won't help you, Grampa's voice said as I stood up, ready to take him on. *He wants to hurt you. Leave him alone.* "No questions, Judge," I said. "Thank you, Mr. Pearsan," I added.

Even that was too much. "Don't thank me, young woman," he snarled. "Don't even talk to me. I don't know how you can look at yourself in the mirror."

As I tried to recover my poise, Ursula Jespersen walked down the aisle and mounted the stand. At least she was a nice distraction for the man on the jury, looking sexy in a miniskirt and a revealing blouse. All the guys in the audience sat up straight too, and so did the judge.

Mr. Thomas guided her through her testimony. In a soft voice with a delicate Danish accent, she told the jury how she and her boyfriend, Ron, had taken the baby to the park in the Pearsans' car, with Monica in a portable baby carriage instead of a stroller because she was so tiny she couldn't sit up yet. They wheeled her to a grassy spot near the lake, then sat down next to her and watched the ducks. Mr. Thomas had Ursula get out of the witness box and go to the chart, so she could point out exactly where things happened. Then she returned, and he asked her to tell the jury what happened next.

Her soft voice became even softer. It was Sunday and quite lovely, she said, with happy people everywhere . . . but suddenly her manner changed. "Such a large dog! From nowhere he came, huge, like a wolf!" Her eyes glazed over then, and her face turned white as she seemed to see him again. "He smash into Monica's carriage and I scream when it crashes to the ground. My baby tumbles out! And Ron jumps to his feet. The animal take Monica in his jaws and run away with her!" She covered her face with her hands to blot out the nightmare vision.

But Mr. Thomas wouldn't let her forget. He made her tell all of it: how Ron grabbed the chain around the dog's neck, forcing him to drop Monica—but then the animal turned on Ron! Ron courageously fought the dog, whipping him with the chain and beating the beast into submission, while "I rush to protect my poor baby who cry with such fear in her voice, such terror, so afraid of the dog. I feel so bad for my poor baby."

Had Spence made his story up? He'd told me that no

one was sitting near the baby carriage when he arrived on the scene. That Ron and Ursula busted through a hedge or something, after the commotion started. Yet Ursula sounded so honest and convincing. The pain she'd suffered seemed very real in her mind. "Would you recognize the animal if you saw him again?" Mr. Thomas asked.

Her eyes flashed angrily. "Yesss! I see him this morning."

"That may be," Mr. Thomas said, "but he must be identified for the record." He turned to the officer sitting next to him, who looked glamorous at that moment, like a Canadian Mountie in a blue uniform instead of a red one. "Officer Milliken, bring in the animal, please."

I'd seen the way Milliken had dragged Herman away that morning, trying to make him look like the Hound of the Baskervilles, and knew he'd do it again just to make him look fierce. "Your Honor, Miss Willow can get him," I said, jumping up.

Mr. Thomas smiled at me as though I was too young to understand all the ramifications. "I think we'd all feel safer, Miss Hope, if Officer Milliken got him. Just in case."

"In case what?" I demanded. "Herman won't hurt anyone."

"You lawyers stop," the judge snapped. "Approach the bench."

I was sick of Mr. Thomas and his grandstanding about

Herman the wild beast, and decided to grandstand right back. I even held my own with the judge, who ruled in my favor. Miss Willow could get the dog, he said, once some "protections" were in place; and a few minutes later, she and Herman came through the doors into the courtroom. I almost died when I saw him. He looked wild and vicious, with the hair along his back standing up like wire and his teeth hanging out.

But as soon as he saw all the kids in the courtroom, his ears lay down, a big doggie smile rearranged his face, his tail wagged back and forth, and he barked with friendliness. What had set him off, I realized, was seeing Ron Benson, whom Herman had passed in the hall before entering the courtroom. Two sheriff's deputies stood behind Miss Willow with pistols in holsters on their hips. They were the "protections" the judge had ordered, and one of them said, "Easy does it," his hand on the pistol grip, obviously ready to yank it out and start shooting.

When Herman saw me, he dragged Miss Willow over, put his front paws on my shoulders, and licked my face, almost tipping me over in my chair. Officer Milliken charged over as though I was in terrible danger, grabbing the chain out of Miss Willow's hand. "Officer, let go!" I told him, taking the leash. "Herman likes to lick my face. I think it's the salt."

Some of the kids laughed, but Mr. Thomas was clearly nervous and so were most of the jurors—except two of them who might pet him, I thought, if I could manage to get him close to them. "For the sake of all of us, let's do this quickly," Mr. Thomas said, maintaining his distance from Herman and leaving no doubt in anyone's mind that he thought Herman was vicious. "Miss Jespersen, have you seen this animal before?"

Herman seemed to understand that the witness was the center of attention, and he pulled on the leash, his tail wagging, as though he wanted to go to her and say hello. "I have seen thees animal," Ursula said, shrinking back in her chair as though terrified of the beast. "He take my baby away from me in his jaws!"

"For the record, the Court notes that the dog named Herman, belonging to Miss Wilma Willow, has been identified by the witness," Steinbrunner said.

"Good. We're done with the creature," Mr. Thomas said. "Get him out of here, please, before—"

"Your Honor?" I asked, interrupting Mr. Thomas before he had a chance to spit out all his dire predictions. "There is lots of room under our table. If the jury has to decide whether Herman is a dangerous dog, wouldn't it be better to leave him where they can see him? He's on a leash, the protections Mr. Thomas has insisted on are in place, and he could stay where he is at Miss Willow's feet."

Two more jurors were interested in him. One woman even leaned over the rail to see him better, which perked Herman up. He crawled under the table and tried to reach her, with his tail wagging and his nose working and a friendly expression on his face. "Be careful!" Mr. Thomas warned. "Keep the animal away from the jury!"

Herman stopped, like a well-trained dog obeying an order, and looked at Mr. Thomas with a question on his face as I pulled him toward me and gently rubbed him around his ears the way Mike did, knowing he liked it. "I can't allow him to stay," Judge Steinbrunner said. "Have your client take him away."

That's the way to mix it up, young lady, Grampa's voice said. It startled me, but I liked it because he wasn't usually very generous with his compliments. "Of course, Your Honor," I said, handing the leash to Miss Willow. "Take this vicious monster back to his cage, please," I said, "before he licks someone to death."

"Enough, young woman," the judge said when a few people laughed.

Herman eagerly led Miss Willow out the door as Mr. Thomas looked at me with a tighter smile than I'd seen before. "Your witness, Miss Hope," he said. "You may cross-examine."

"Thank you, Mr. Thomas," I said, and adopted a lawyer-like expression, deciding to get tough. "Miss Jespersen, you didn't see Herman smash into the baby carriage at all, did you?"

What are you doing? Grampa's voice thundered at me.

Giving her another chance to beat you up? Think *like a lawyer, Kate. Don't worry about* looking *like one.*

Ursula did just what he said she'd do. She leaned forward angrily. "Thees dog that day was not so very nice and so friendly as with you, Miss Hope," she said. "He knock down the carriage and my baby fall out, and he pick up my baby in his jaws!"

"How do you know that?" I asked, trying to regain my footing. "You didn't see a thing because you and Ron Benson were behind a lilac hedge. Isn't that the truth?"

For God's sake, Kate, the voice said. *What kind of answer do you expect from a dumb question like that?*

"We were not behind a lilac hedge!" she gasped, as though insulted beyond her endurance level. "What do you suggest?"

My brain had hemorrhaged. I tried to stop the bleeding with a tourniquet. "Wasn't there a lilac hedge near you?" I asked.

"I do not know how far away. I hardly see this hedge."

"But it's there on the chart, isn't it?" I asked.

"There are many bushes on the chart. Ron and I watch the ducks."

I couldn't think of anything else to ask her and started to sit down. *Don't leave it there!* Grandfather stormed. *Ask her something that can help your case! Did she see the boys on the bikes, for example . . . but lead up to it so she'll agree with you.*

Hammering people on the head works on Perry Mason, *but it's bad cross-examination.*

I smiled, but she didn't buy it. At all. "Miss Jespersen, where did you and Mr. Benson park your car?" I asked, sliding behind the lectern where I could hide from her and the jury.

"There is a parking lot near the big yellow building."

"The streets in the park were blocked off, weren't they?"

"Yes."

"So you weren't parked near where you were sitting?"

"That is true."

"And there were lots of people walking on the streets, and kids on bicycles?" I asked.

"Yes."

"There were even some kids on Sting-Rays, weren't there?"

"I do not know this word."

"A Sting-Ray is a kind of bike, with little wheels and a seat like a banana, and wide handlebars," I told her. "Do you remember kids on bikes like that?"

She shrugged. "Not really."

"Kids on Sting-Rays ride them on the grass and the walkways as well as on the streets. Didn't you see some of them?"

"Perhaps."

Ideas started forming in my brain again. "You testified

earlier about the fight between Mr. Benson and Herman, do you remember?"

"Yes."

"And how Mr. Benson had to beat the dog into submission?"

"Yes."

"The dog just got what he deserved, don't you think?"

"I certainly do."

"Because after the fight his coat was bloody, and even one eye had been battered and bloodied and was swollen shut. Isn't that right?"

She shrugged. "That animal was not a pretty sight."

Now you're being a lawyer, Kate. Good questions!

It was so nice of Grandfather to cheer me on, but I knew I had to be careful. "You've seen Herman in the courtroom today, and how friendly and nice he's been?"

Her arms crossed. "Not always," she said. "Not this morning, before the trial begins. He growl with fierceness."

"That was when you were sitting with Ron Benson, wasn't it?" I asked.

"Your Honor," Mr. Thomas said, "objection. Facts not in evidence. Relevance."

"But Your Honor," I said quickly, before the judge could rule, "I think it's very relevant. Whenever Herman smells Ron Benson, who beat him bloody with a chain, he gets hostile. Other than that, he's just a sweet and gentle dog. Isn't that relevant?"

"Enough of that, Miss Hope!" the judge stormed at me. "Save those comments for argument. Objection is sustained. Now move on!"

"Thank you, Your Honor," I said quickly, smiling at him. *Bully for you!* Grampa said, and it felt like a hug. *You got the makin's!* "Just so I'm real clear about your testimony," I said, "you are very sure that you and Mr. Benson were not behind that lilac hedge"—I walked over to the chart and pointed to the one that I hoped Spence would say they were behind—"at any time that day?"

"Absolutely not!"

"Did anyone see this happen other than you and Mr. Benson?"

"Many others."

"Do you remember seeing an old man in dirty clothes?"

Her nose wrinkled prettily, which was the way she did everything—prettily. "Yesss. He smell badly. He need to wash himself."

I could go on, Grandfather said, *but* you'd *better stop. Good work!*

"Thank you, Miss Jespersen," I said, sitting down.

"Call your next witness, Mr. Thomas," Judge Steinbrunner said.

"Yes, sir. I'll call Ron Benson to the stand."

Chapter Twenty-five

HAVING FIVE MOTHERS ON THE JURY might not be so awful, I thought when Ron Benson took the stand. I tried to see him the way they would, rather than through the eyes of the one man on the jury, or the kids in the courtroom who thought he was so great because he could play a stupid game like football. What was the big deal about that, other than fame and glory and large bucks from the National Football League when he finished college? Mr. Thomas treated him like a god too, as did the judge, proving that men are way too impressed with sports. But the mothers, even though they were interested in him, weren't ready to get down on their knees in worship.

With Mr. Thomas asking the questions, Ron repeated the horrible story that Ursula Jespersen had already told, except that he was oh-so-modest about the brave way he'd stood up to the beast. When he moved over to the chart to show exactly where he and Ursula were sitting when the dog attacked, Mr. Thomas took him through his testimony all over again.

Ron moved like a panther when he walked back to his seat in the witness box. "No further questions," Mr. Thomas said. "You may examine."

It wasn't as hard as I'd thought it would be to smile at Ron. "We've met, haven't we, Mr. Benson?" I asked from behind the lectern.

"Yeah, you could say that," he said. "When you and your boyfriend came by to talk to Ursula."

"That was a week ago Tuesday, wasn't it, Mr. Benson? When we met the first time?"

"Yes," he said, his hands balled into angry fists. Did he want to smack me?

I realized he didn't scare me at all. "It was around one in the afternoon at the Pearsan residence, right? You wore short pants and no shirt?"

He blushed suddenly. The muscles in his jaw got huge and started thumping. "Yeah."

"Your Honor, I object to this line of questioning," Mr. Thomas said, standing. "It's not relevant to the issues here."

"I agree," the judge said. "Let's move on, Miss Hope."

"Thank you, sir," I said, as though the judge and I were together on the objection. But one of the mothers on the jury had an eyebrow up, and I wondered if I could make Ron lose his cool. He was on the edge now. Could I give the jury a taste of the real Ron Benson, a musclebound bully and a liar, willing to sacrifice the life of a dog to save himself and his girlfriend from embarrassment?

I tried a patient-mother voice, as though he was a child who needed a good mom to help him understand things. I'd used it on my older brother when I was only six, and it could drive him up a tree. "Do you remember that day at City Park . . . well, for the record, it was Sunday, May twenty-seventh, 1973, about three weeks ago. Try to remember that day, okay?" I asked.

"Duh," he said, with annoyance. "Sure I remember it."

"Good for you," I said, as though encouraging him. "There were other people at the park that day, weren't there?"

I loved watching the muscles in his jaw send angry vibrations through the courtroom. There were lots of other people, he said. After the incident with the dog, a crowd. Did he remember an old man in dirty clothes who might even have had an odor about him? "Oh yes," Ron said, then described the man as "a mess. Tall, thin, hair every which way, and the rottenest beard I ever saw."

You might be a lawyer yet, Grandfather's gruff voice said. *Keep working on his attitude. Good job using the City's witnesses to prove up your case. Now that jury knows Spence was there.*

In my best "If you don't understand, just ask me" voice, I asked Ron if he'd seen the dog today that had done this awful thing. "Yes," he said, ready to explode, and leveling a stare at me that no doubt would have terrified a lineman on the opposing football team.

"You and Herman aren't really buddies, are you, Mr. Benson?"

"You mean, do I like that dog?" he demanded, snarling at me. "Would I want that animal in my house? Around my children if I had any?"

I started to object. *Don't*, Grampa's voice said. *He's close to helping you.* "Actually, I meant that every time he's seen you this morning, he's acted aggressively. You understand what I mean by 'aggressively,' don't you?"

"Yes, I know what you mean!" Ron said, his neck all swollen and red . . . and then he seemed to catch himself. "But it isn't me that sets him off, Kate. Excuse me. Miss Hope." He threw me a beautiful smirk. "He's just plain vicious and dangerous. Mean enough to attack a little *baby*."

"Really," I said. "You mean he acts that way around everyone?"

"That's exactly what I mean. Didn't you see how he was with the animal-control officer?"

"You're talking about the man who dragged him down the aisle earlier today, before the trial started?" I asked.

"Could have. I don't know."

"You don't know? You whipped him with it, didn't you?"

"Your words, Kate," he said. "I protected myself from him. When he dropped Monica, he went for my throat."

"How awful," I said. "That must have terrified you, to have a vicious, snarling animal charge you and go for your throat. Were you terrified?"

He leaned back in his chair and smiled, as though nothing really bothered him very much. "Not really."

"Then why did you whip him with the chain and spike hard enough to cut him and make him bleed?"

"That's a lie. I didn't hurt him. I just protected myself."

"Oh," I said. "Miss Jespersen testified a few minutes ago that you beat the dog into submission. Did she lie to the jury when she told them that?"

"She never said that," he snapped at me. "You're making that up."

"I'm not making it up, Mr. Benson," I told him. "She even testified that Herman's coat was bloody afterward, and that one of his eyes was swollen shut. Would you like to have the record of her testimony read to you?"

He cleared his throat and looked at Mr. Thomas, who was busy writing on a legal pad. "I told you I was protecting myself," Ron said. "What would you have done, Little Miss Angel-face? Petted him? Given him a dog bone?"

"He wanted to get that animal out of here before he bit somebody," Ron declared.

"A dog like that would never wag his tail at anyone who got near him, would he?" Ron frowned at me but didn't answer, so I went on. "Or lick somebody in the face, or allow someone to rub his stomach?"

Some of the jurors smiled. "I'd be real surprised," Ron said.

"Is it possible that there's just some bad chemistry between you and Herman that makes him aggressive?"

"Do I have to answer a stupid question like that?" he asked, glaring at the judge.

"You do, Mr. Benson," the judge said.

"No." Ron folded his arms in front of him and stared pointedly at the clock. "How much longer will this go on?"

Don't object, Grampa's voice said. *He's showing himself well.*

I smiled at him, letting the moment take its own sweet time. "Mr. Benson, in the park that day when you saw him, he was dragging a chain behind him, wasn't he? One of those thin chains that people use as a dog leash?"

"Yes," he said, like a grizzly bear in a cage who wants out so he can get at the squirrel on the other side of the bars who is teasing him.

"The chain had a spike on the end, didn't it?" I asked. "The kind of spike that gets hammered into the ground to tether a dog?"

It was fun, dancing around the big bozo. He would flatten me on a football field, but I could dance circles around him in court. *Nothing like it, is there?* Grandfather's voice said. *But be careful. It can change in an instant.* "Did Herman reach your throat, Mr. Benson?"

"No."

"Or your hands, or your arms or legs?"

"No."

"So there were no dog bites or scratches on you at all, isn't that right?"

"He tried, but he never got me."

"What about your clothes?" I asked. "Did he get a fang into a sleeve or a pant leg?"

"He did not."

"In fact, all Herman managed to do was get himself beaten bloody by you?"

He stared at me without saying anything. I could have asked the judge to order him to answer the question, but the stare was so venomous and awful that I wanted to give the jury plenty of time to see it.

"It must have felt wonderful to give Herman exactly what he deserved, and to punish him so thoroughly. Am I right, Mr. Benson?"

"Objection, Judge," Mr. Thomas said, as though he was bored. "Relevance. Argumentative."

"Sustained. Miss Hope, this has gone on long enough. Move on, young lady."

"Thank you, sir. Can I ask a couple of questions from the chart?"

"You may."

I got next to it and picked up the pointer, like a teacher in school. "This is an accurate map of where the action was that day, isn't it, Mr. Benson?"

"It's okay."

"Just okay? Is there something you'd like to add to it, or take off?"

"No."

"For example, it shows the shoreline of that little lake, and lots of little meadows and shrubs"—I pointed to things as I talked about them—"and that asphalt path that kind of wanders around and gets real close to the lake." I stuck the tip of the pointer where the map showed that. "That's the way it was that day, isn't it?"

"I already said it was."

You are so angry at me, I thought happily. "Mr. Benson, I have a witness who saw you and Miss Jespersen over here," I said, touching a place on the other side of a lilac hedge. It was exactly where Ursula had been absolutely certain she and Ron had not been. "Is that where you and Miss Jespersen watched the ducks?"

"Objection," Thomas said. "Assumes a fact not in evidence."

"Sustained."

Keep trying. "You and Miss Jespersen were over here before this happened, weren't you, Mr. Benson?" I asked, pointing to the same place.

"No."

"Did you hear Miss Jespersen's testimony?" I asked, as though I'd caught him in a lie.

"No," he said, glaring at me with suspicion.

"Didn't you spread your blanket over here when you first got there?"

"We might have. I'm not sure."

"You were on the other side of the lilac hedge just some of the time you were in the park that day. Is that fair to say?"

"What of it? That isn't where we were when the dog showed up."

"You weren't there very long, I guess. Is that what you mean?"

"We weren't there more than two minutes. So what?"

So one of you is lying, I thought, hoping the jury saw it too. "Thank you, Mr. Benson," I said, and sat down and waited to hear what the voice in my brain had to say about my performance. It had a little smile inside, and some gruff grandfatherly pride. *You've got the instincts,* it said.

But the glow didn't last. "Ladies and gentlemen," the judge said, "we'll have a short recess now." He frowned in my direction, and I kind of ducked. "Bailiff, you can escort the jury to the jury room, and I'll ask the lawyers to meet me in my chambers."

Here it comes, I thought. My motion for additional witnesses. Before following Mr. Thomas through the door that led to the judge's office, I looked for Mike and my two witnesses. I saw Sally get up with Kenny Benson and scoot toward the hall, but there was no sign of Mike. And what was Sally doing with Kenny? I wondered. Hadn't she been with Mike?

"Hey, Kate," someone said, turning me around. Willis Suggs! "Uncle Two-Fingers asked me to say hello."

"Willis, hi! Thanks for helping. Did you bring Bean Pole and Tomato Face?"

"No," he said, looking down. "They changed their mind."

"What do you mean? What happened? Where's Mike?"

"Pickin' hisself off the ground, the last I saw. Sorry, Kate. Nothin' I could do, only watch."

"Watch what?"

"Two big dudes, buddies of Ron Benson, messed it all up. They gave Bean Pole and Tomato Face T-shirts, then took them someplace, you know, like for ice cream."

"What happened to Mike?"

"He tried to stop them," Willis said. "Big mistake."

"You mean he let them take my witnesses?"

"He couldn't stop them, Kate. They didn't hurt him bad, but they hurt him."

My motion for additional witnesses was denied, naturally. I spluttered around helplessly in Judge Steinbrunner's chambers, but I had no proof of anything, and no witnesses, either. It was almost a relief to crawl back to the pit and sit next to Miss Willow, where I could smile with confidence even though my case teetered on the brink of disaster. "Call your next witness," the judge said to Mr. Thomas, and Dr. Donald Webb trotted to the stand, as fit and trim as a marathon runner.

He had four color photographs of Monica and at least they weren't gruesome, which was a relief. There was some bruising on her legs and two little red dots on her right thigh, and the doctor used them to describe the trauma to the baby, which included an assault on her feelings. "She howled long and loudly," Dr. Webb said, "I should say expressing outrage, indignity, and pain."

How did he know what the little baby was expressing? She might have been hungry. But I didn't object, because what would have been the point? I wanted him to like me, in case he could help me with my case.

As a medical doctor, he could give expert opinions, to help the jury interpret the facts. Mr. Thomas asked him if he had an opinion as to what had caused the bruising on Monica's legs and the red dots on her skin.

"In my opinion," he said, "she'd been picked up in the jaws of a large animal, such as a dog."

I floundered around on cross-examination. But it wasn't on purpose like Grandfather had done. I wasn't trying to trick the witness into thinking I was dumb. My brain had stopped working. I'd switched it to ON at four that morning, and it needed a rest. It sorted through what it knew about asking questions of expert witnesses, and came up empty. I asked what the two red dots were, which was stupid: "Tooth marks." The jury didn't need another reminder that the baby had been in Herman's jaws.

Then I thought of a way to soften the blow—one that might even please Grandfather. The doctor had treated several dog-bite cases, he said when I asked him about it. He agreed with me that this was not a severe case. The skin had not been torn, and no surgery was required, or stitching of wounds. In fact, the baby's skin had barely been punctured. After cleaning her wound and bandaging it, he'd released her to her parents. There hadn't been any need for her to spend the night in the hospital.

But it got embarrassing when I tried to get him to give *me* an expert opinion, one that would help my side of the case. Mr. Thomas kept objecting to the questions I asked, and the judge always ruled with him.

I thought Grampa would come to my rescue, but it was as though he'd gone away, just as my dad had done to me when I was six. Couldn't the old man hang around long enough to help me frame a hypothetical question?

That's what I needed, I realized as my mind dredged up some law on the subject. A hypothetical question that assumed a lot of stuff! I'd never asked one before, but I'd read about them. "Doctor, when you look at the bruises and tooth marks on Monica's thigh, and where they are, and the way there aren't any other tooth marks on her, or anything to show that Herman tried to chew on her or anything like that, isn't it true that the little injuries you found on her are just as consistent with Herman picking Monica up to keep her from rolling into the lake, and then bringing her *to* Miss Jespersen, as they are with Herman snatching Monica off the ground and running *away* with her to eat her up?"

Thunderbolts were tossed at me by Mr. Thomas, who could hardly wait to object, and Judge Steinbrunner, who was even quicker to sustain the objection. But I weathered the storm with a smile and had the feeling that some of the women on the jury were proud of me for standing there without even a raincoat for protection.

But where was Grandfather? I wanted him back inside my head, where *he* could be proud of me. Had he deserted me too? I wondered angrily.

If that was the way he wanted it, fine.

Officer Smith, who arrived on the scene right after it happened, was the City's last witness. I tried to focus on what he was saying, but I couldn't get past the badge on his chest and knew it would be impossible for me to get tough with a cop. Mr. Thomas took him through the preliminaries, then asked him what he'd learned in the course of his investigation. "A German shepherd police dog, unattended, had gone berserk," he said. "The animal knocked a baby carriage down, then grabbed the infant who'd been inside—picked her up in his jaws—and tried to run off with her. But a man who didn't want to be identified at the time—he's okay with it now—stopped it from happening."

"Have you subsequently learned the identity of the man who stopped it from happening?"

"Yes, sir," Officer Smith said. "Ron Benson." He nodded with pride, cheering for a hometown boy. "Running back for Penn State, an All-American."

From the way he testified, it sounded as though he'd seen it happen, but he hadn't even been there! I should have objected! It was Grandfather's fault that I hadn't caught it, but it was too late now. I stood up to cross-examine him and tried to make the best of it, knowing I'd been deserted again. "Officer," I said, "when you testified just now, I had the feeling you were there and saw it happen. But you didn't see it happen, did you?"

"No, Miss Hope, I investigated it. Talked to people, found out about it, you know."

"Then when you said a dog had gone berserk, that's just what people told you. You didn't see it happen and can't say, of your own knowledge, that the dog actually went berserk, can you?"

He laughed, kind of at me, just a kid. "The people I talked to were pretty convincing, Miss Hope. But you're right. I didn't see it, and can't say, of my own knowledge, what happened."

"Thank you, Officer. The people you talked to were Ron Benson and Ursula Jespersen, and that's about it, isn't it?"

"A couple of others, but I didn't get their names."

"Was one of them an old man, not very well dressed, with a beard?"

He smiled. "That'd be Spencer Phipps."

"Mr. Phipps didn't describe the incident like that, did he?"

"I can't honestly say," Smith said. "Spence was babbling his usual nonsense. I didn't pay much attention."

"So you decided not to ask him what he'd seen?"

"He may have seen something, Miss Hope; you can't really tell with old Spence." He smiled at me and the jury. "Mr. Phipps is known to the Denver Police Department as 'certifiable.' Do you want me to explain?"

"Not really," I said as the gray matter inside my skull went to sleep again, protecting itself from reality. I sat down, and Mr. Thomas rested his case.

"The City has rested," the judge announced. "It is now

the defense's turn to put on evidence. Are you ready to proceed, Miss Hope?"

"Of course, Your Honor," I said, shining a confident smile in his direction that was pure lie. What was the use? I looked around for Grampa in my mind but saw my dad instead, driving away from me, with Law, into a snowstorm.

"Justice" was a cruel joke, like everything else in life. I had two witnesses to prove my side of the case, my poor, tired brain pointed out to me. The first was Wilma Willow, who owned the dog that was on trial for his life and would say anything to save him, and the second was a certified nut.

Chapter Twenty-six

"YOU MAY CALL YOUR FIRST WITNESS, Miss Hope."

"Thank you, Your Honor," I said, standing next to the lectern and facing my client. She sat at the defense table, looking wilted and very alone. I couldn't look at her. Instead, I waved a welcoming arm in her direction in a theatrical gesture I'd practiced in front of a mirror the day before, when I'd believed in justice. "I'll call Miss Wilma Willow."

"Yes, dear?" her tiny voice quavered back, filled with anxiety.

"Come testify, Miss Willow," I said, with all the encouragement I could muster on short notice. "Please?"

"Oh dear."

At first the jurors sympathized with her shyness, but later they squirmed in their seats with embarrassment. She babbled on forever about how brave and loyal and protective her Herman was, who could not possibly have done anything so awful as bite a baby. When I finally got her to focus on what had happened, she told of tethering Herman to a chain leash and going to the concession stand to buy popcorn for the ducks and being *almost* there when two boys on bicycles knocked her down! And a man made her lie in one position until an emergency ambulance arrived with two nice young people who made sure nothing was broken, but it must have taken at least half an hour before she could get back to her picnic blanket . . . and Herman was gone! And when she saw him later at the animal shelter, he was a bloody mess and they wouldn't let her take him home or even pet him and . . .

"Objection, Judge," Thomas said. "The issue is whether or not the animal is a dangerous dog. What happened at the animal shelter isn't relevant."

"Sustained."

"Thank you, Your Honor," I said, still smiling. But my smile was a mask. "No further questions."

"Cross-examine, Mr. Thomas?" the judge asked.

"No questions, if it please the Court."

"Call your next witness, Miss Hope."

It was after four o'clock when Spencer Phipps walked to the witness box, looking like a puppet made out of sticks. His trousers were too short and his pitifully skinny legs hung beneath the ragged cuffs like toothpicks made out of marble. But his head was high and I tried to suck up some of his courage—or foolhardiness. He looked proud and regal, like the king of Narnia checking out the far reaches of his kingdom, and he nodded royally to the jury, the judge, and all the kids in the courtroom, as though they were his subjects.

"Mr. Phipps, will you spell your name, please, for the court reporter?" I asked, knowing that disaster loomed hugely, over him, and Herman, and Miss Willow.

"Glad to, young woman," he said grandly, then pronouncing the letters of his name carefully and investing each one with importance. It was obvious that Miss Willow had fallen head over heels in love with him, now that he'd showered, shaved, and donned a clean suit—in spite of the fact that no one else could see him as a knight in shining armor. In fact, people were laughing at him. The judge had covered his mouth to smother his laughs, as had two of the jurors, and snorts of malicious joy drifted in from the peanut gallery. All that anyone else could see was a sad old fool.

He often went to the park on Sundays, he said, to visit with his dear friend Wilma Willow. When he arrived that day he found Herman tethered on the grass at his usual place of residence when on a Sunday picnic, within a stone's throw of the lake. But, alas, no Wilma. And so Spence sat himself down on the grass next to the dog and waited, when two boys on small bicycles appeared.

They were riding on the paved pathway near the edge of the lake and all at once, one boy gave the other boy a mighty shove!

Spence mimicked the action, letting his hands fly out in front of him, then described the desperation of the boy who had been shoved: how desperately he fought to keep from falling down. "A baby carriage was there," he said, "and the youngster reached out with one hand and grabbed it!" Spence gripped the rail of the witness box with all his strength to demonstrate the situation. "And as soon as the lad regained his balance, he sent it sailing!" and he threw the offending hand away in a dramatic display of scorn and contempt.

His voice ricocheted around the room like that of a Shakespearean actor delivering a soliloquy. "Herman, brave and splendid hound, saw the baby carriage careen for the lake!" Spence thundered in full, rich tones. "At that moment, his true nature came to the fore! He was simply magnificent! The noble animal flew into action, yanking the tether out of the ground with the ease of a grown man snapping a thread!"

The jurors smiled at him and nodded, the way mothers encourage two-year-olds to keep them talking. Spence thought it meant they were hanging on his every word, and believing in the scene he drew for them to see with all their hearts. But it didn't mean that at all. With grand, flourishing movements of arms and hands, he described the further heroics of the dog, who flew through the air toward the baby carriage as it careened recklessly and directly toward the water! A bare moment before it splashed into the water, Herman knocked it over, and a tiny infant popped out and began rolling down the grass and into the pond! Just in time, the magnificent animal prevented that from happening, by tenderly picking the squalling baby up in his mouth.

A young couple, who Spence assumed were the parents, emerged from behind a lilac hedge. They were somewhat disheveled, he recalled. The woman rushed hysterically to the child and picked her up, frightening her terribly. The man, a muscular fellow who apparently was threatened by what he imagined, grabbed the leash and viciously beat Herman with the chain. "Poor Herman," Spence said, lifting his arms and shielding himself from unseen blows. "He covered himself and tried to dodge and run away, but he simply could not defend himself from this powerful man, who yanked the chain with great force, choking Herman, as he continued slashing and whipping the dog with the chain.

"I tried to inform the young couple of what had actually transpired, but they would not listen." He shrugged his shoulders. "A crowd quickly gathered, of course, and instantly, it seemed, everyone leapt to quite the wrong conclusion."

"Then what did you do, Mr. Phipps?"

"I was gravely disheartened, Miss Hope. All minds had closed to the truth. There was nothing I could do for Herman. And so I departed."

"Thank you, Mr. Phipps," I said. "No further questions."

I might as well have thrown the lovable old bum to the wolves. When Mr. Thomas took him on cross-examination, he dismantled his ego one piece at a time. He had documents in his hands proving that Spence had been in the state mental hospital in Pueblo, but he didn't need them, as Spence cheerfully admitted he'd been hospitalized many times. Following his experiences in World War II, he explained, he'd developed an addiction to alcohol, and at precisely the same time, the State began to persecute him.

Mr. Thomas asked him if he'd once seen a herd of flying horses stampede through the skies above Denver. Quite true, Spence readily agreed. Hadn't he also been forced to flee when several buildings chased after him? That happened as well, Spence stated with the same degree of certainty, adding that he doubted that others believed him, apart from those who'd had similar experiences.

Mr. Thomas then told Spence he'd noticed that he and Miss Willow had been holding hands earlier in the day, and asked him if she was special to him. Indeed she was, Spence said, and Mr. Thomas asked for details. Spence may have thought he was Romeo in *Romeo and Juliet*. He gazed at his old sweetheart with fondness and told the world of his love for her—how he'd been smitten by her charms in high school, forty years before, and had worshiped her from afar ever since.

"Do you love her enough to lie for her, sir?" Mr. Thomas asked.

"Of course," Spence said. "It would be a lie for me to tell you otherwise. But there is no need to tell lies concerning this matter." He smiled at Miss Willow.

Only to find that she could no longer look at him. An expression of shock, as though he'd suddenly fallen off a cliff, registered on his face as rows of people in the gallery hid behind their hands and tried not to laugh. Most of the jurors had to stare at the floor, and it was awful for me to watch the old man drop out of his dreamworld, into a nightmare of humiliation. "Wilma?" he begged with his voice. "Miss Hope? You believe me, don't you?"

It was after five when Spence was excused from the stand. He ran down the aisle without even seeing Miss Willow, shaking and looking like what he was: an old bum who needed a drink. Miss Willow watched him go with tears in her eyes and as the doors closed behind him, I wondered if I would ever see him again.

Judge Steinbrunner wanted to finish the case that night, as all that was left was final argument and jury deliberations. But the mothers on the jury had to get home to fix dinner for their husbands and children, so the judge continued the case until nine the next morning. Miss Willow started to stand, but the judge made a gesture with his hand that told her she should stay in her chair. "The parties will stay for a few minutes," he said. "There is a matter we need to discuss out of the presence of the jury."

What else could go wrong? I wondered as the jurors and many of the spectators left the courtroom. "Miss Hope," the judge said, "we need to decide where Herman will spend the night."

"We do?" I asked. "I thought that had been decided, sir. He stays with Miss Willow until the case is over."

"The situation has changed, unfortunately. I cannot ignore the testimony that's been presented today. Of course, it's still up to the jury to make a final determination, but the evidence I've heard to this point is enough to convince me that the animal may very well have a vicious streak in him that could erupt at any time. He could even turn on Miss Willow. Therefore—"

"But Your Honor," I blurted, "the evidence shows that the only person Herman even touched was little Monica, and that was to keep her from rolling into the lake and drowning!"

The roof didn't fall on my head, and lightning didn't strike me dead for interrupting a judge in the middle of a sentence. In fact, the expression on his face showed kindness and concern—even though it was way too firm. "That is certainly one way to view the evidence," he said, "but I can't take that chance. It is therefore my order that Herman be remanded to the custody of Officer Milliken, to be transported by him to the Denver Animal Shelter until further order of this Court." He whacked the marble plate on the bench with his gavel before I could say anything more, and he quickly stood up. "Court is adjourned."

I tried to move, but the muscle had drained out of my legs and they wouldn't respond to the demands of my brain. "What did he mean, 'remanded to the custody of Officer Milliken,' dear?" Miss Willow asked me.

"He means Herman will spend the night at the animal shelter," I said. "But they'll let you go say good night to him. Won't you, Officer?"

Officer Milliken had been listening to us talk, and shrugged. "Sure, as long as she doesn't get too close. You heard the judge."

Mr. Thomas, Officer Milliken, and Miss Willow weren't having problems with *their* legs. They were able to walk out of the courtroom without help, but I couldn't. I nodded my goodbyes to them, but couldn't stand up, feeling numb all over. Then I heard sounds behind me and turned to see what it was.

Kenny Benson was staggering around like a drunken puppet with Sally and some other kids for an audience. "I have a vision," he said. "A heroic dolphin will descend from heaven above. See you him, my children?" he asked, weaving around and throwing a heavenly gaze at the ceiling with his hands outstretched. "Hark ye! Off in the distance I observe Kate Hope, fair attorney. Madame!" he called out to me, almost falling but grabbing the rail to keep his balance. "Will you join me in a toast to Herman, noble and gallant beast?" He raised his free hand invitingly, shaped like a goblet ready to clink against mine.

At least his jeering comments brought some energy back to my legs. I stood up and packed my briefcase, ignoring him.

"Tomorrow then, O Great Mouthpiece, defender of the innocent!" he called out, leading his band of merry men into the hall.

The reporter from the *Rocky Mountain News* watched the whole charade from his front-row seat. "How do you feel, Kate?" he asked me. "What are your chances?"

Mom's smile came to the rescue. "Don't count Herman out yet, Mr. Briar," I said. "You cover sports, too, don't you?" I asked with cheerful breeziness.

"Yeah."

"You know, like they say in baseball, it ain't over till it's over."

But it was over. Herman would die. "Why, Daddy?" I asked, as though he could give me an answer.

I forced myself outside with a manufactured spring in my step, and walked for the office.

Chapter Twenty-seven

I F I GIVE UP NOW, I thought, walking toward the office where I would grab a cushion to crush in my arms and cry on, then Mom and I can go see *Mary Poppins* tonight. I'll be able to sleep until eight in the morning, and I'll let Mom drive me to the courthouse where I can model that black party dress I got for Christmas. Mr. Briar will take my picture for the *Rocky Mountain News,* and I'll smile all the way through final argument, then hold Miss Willow's hand tenderly when the jury comes back with its death sentence.

Kate, that ain't like you a bit.

I stopped. "Grandfather?"

Just who did you expect it to be?

"Where did you go? I thought you'd—"

Deserted you, same as your father? Well, I haven't and neither did he. Don't you remember what I said?

"You've said a lot of stuff!" I cried. A woman who had passed me on the sidewalk slowed down and looked back at me. I turned away in embarrassment. You can't expect me to remember *everything*, I said in my head.

I told you he didn't mean it because he couldn't help it. Isn't that what I told you?

What a wretched place for this to be happening! I started to cry, big-time, as I remembered the rest of what Grampa had said: Let him into your heart. Trust him to be there for you, and he will.

"Are you all right, honey?" the woman who'd been watching me said.

"I could use a hug," I told her.

Feel better? Grandfather asked, a few minutes later.

Much better, I said in my head, walking on toward the office. The woman had been so nice. She hadn't done anything except give me what I needed just then, which was a hug.

Then watch where you're going! the old man said.

An ant materialized on the sidewalk. I almost stepped on him, but he swerved out of the way in time to escape being mashed. Fascinated by his quick reaction, I watched him scuttle to safety. How had the ant saved himself from disaster?

Think on it, Kate.

Why do that? I wondered, but kind of teased myself with the feeling that the ant, somehow, had handed me an argument that would give me a fighting chance. The ant had acted out of instinct. Somehow he'd felt my foot dropping on him and had known just what to do. Hadn't Herman, in saving the baby, done the same thing? If I told the jury the story of how that ant had escaped my foot, could I convince them that what Herman had done was not the act of an animal gone berserk, but a natural instinctive response that was part of him?

"Be an ant," I mouthed silently, as though standing in front of the jury and pleading for Herman's life. "That tiny insect I almost snuffed out of existence must have felt some force coming down that would mash him, but his instinct for self-preservation kicked in and he managed to get out of the way. Just as Herman's instinct kicked in when he saw the baby carriage, headed for the lake. Put yourself there, ladies and gentlemen," I continued mumbling, staring at the sidewalk to make sure I didn't step on any ants. "Go over to where Herman is tethered, and see what he sees. Be him."

If they thought *Spence* was crazy, wait until I asked them to be a dog! But my mouth and brain were too engaged to quit.

"Would you just suddenly have this urgent, terrible desire for raw meat or something?" I heard myself ask them.

"An irresistible drive that grabbed you by the throat and sent you flying after that carriage, knocking it over so you could get at a sleeping infant hidden under the covers?" I shook my head. "It makes no sense at all for you to take a baby in your jaws. You need a powerful and compelling reason to do something as drastic as that. Dogs are driven by instinct. They are driven by the forces buried in their soul that were planted in them millions of years ago." Wow. Out of me? "We *know* what drove Herman to fly into action because Spencer Phipps watched it happen and *told* us."

The corner of Thirteenth and Bannock, and the office of Hope and Hope, was only two doors away, and I realized how tired I was after a long day in court. I realized too that an argument pitting the word of a certified crazy against the word of a lovely au pair and a football hero had no chance. The wind went out of my sails, leaving me stranded in the middle of the ocean. If I was on that jury and had to choose between the testimony of the City's witnesses and Spencer Phipps, it wouldn't take me long to make up my mind. I needed more than words to save Herman's life. I had to *show* them . . .

Put yourself there! See what the dog saw! Can I do that? I asked as an idea exploded in my head like a stroke, forcing me to stop in my tracks, paralyzed. *Now you're being a lawyer!* Grandfather's voice rang in my head. *That's what you do!* Show *them!*

Something happened to me then that I can't explain because my ego had nothing to do with it. "I love you so much!" I blurted out, as some poor man, walking in the other direction, wondered what in the world was going on.

"Were you talking to me, miss?"

"Oh no, sir," I managed, as emotions I couldn't control just then made a mess out of my face. "It's so wonderful, because I *can* put them there!" I ran for the office and smashed through the door without even thinking that if Mrs. Roulette had been standing on the other side, I'd have flattened her.

The office was closed and no clients were anywhere to be seen, but Mrs. Roulette was at her desk, thank goodness, far enough away to avoid injury. When she saw tears gushing out of my eyes and heard funny little sounds coming out of my mouth, of joy and love and at-least-I-have-a-fighting chance, which I tried to control but couldn't, she hurried over to me and wrapped me up in her arms. "It's all right, dear," she said. "It's all right. You'll feel awful, but you'll get over it. Your grandfather will be so proud of you, honey. You did your best."

A real, live shoulder warmed with the blood that flowed through veins felt a whole lot better than a cushion as a source of comfort. I let her pet me, soaking up the strength in that old and wonderful heart, then told her what was going on in mine. "I'm not done yet," I said as my face at last took charge of itself and quit blubbering. "I can still win!"

"Yes, dear," she said, letting go and handing me a Kleenex. "Of course you can. You have a visitor, did I tell you?"

"No. Mom?"

"Go see. He's in your grandfather's office."

A "he"? I blotted the guck off my face and went in. "Mike!" He'd been slouched in a chair in front of the Judge's desk, but when he looked at me I could tell he'd been crying too. "You okay?" I asked, staring at a Band-Aid on his lip and some bruising and swelling under his right eye. "What happened to you?"

"Nothing."

"You big jerk," I said, afraid to give him a hug even though I wanted to. "Willis told me how you almost brought in Bean Pole and Tomato Face. What happened?"

"Sally told Kenny about our witnesses," he said, snuffling and wiping off his nose with the back of his hand, which is a guy thing that's very annoying. "So two buddies of Ron's showed up, and I couldn't . . ." I didn't tell him how disgusting it was. "How's it going with you?" he asked, his eyes searching me out with sympathy. "I saw what happened to Spence."

"Actually, I'm starved," I told him, kicking off my shoes. "Got any money?"

"Aren't you going home? I thought I'd ride with you and—"

"There's this great idea that started with an ant on the sidewalk, but I can't handle it on an empty stomach, and I'll need help. Can you afford a large pizza, Pizza Palace on Colfax? I'll pay you back."

"Yeah." He got up, kind of grinning but with that typical bewildered expression on his face as though he wasn't quite sure what to do next.

"Well, move out then," I told him, and like a good soldier he was gone.

I hopped across the hall to my room, changed into jeans and a clean T-shirt I like. It's from NASA, and on the back it's got my favorite picture of the Earth, blue and beautiful, as seen from the moon, and the writing on the front says *Anything is possible.* I slipped into a pair of Mom's old saddle shoes and trotted into the reception room, where Mrs. Roulette was dabbing on lipstick and getting ready to leave. "Your young man said he'd be back with some food. Shouldn't you go home, dear? I know your mother wants to see you."

I shook my head. "We could be here all night."

"I don't think so," she said, glaring at me.

"Mrs. Roulette, you don't understand," I said. "I really have a chance to pull a rabbit out of the hat and win tomorrow. But I need help to put it together, and Mike is perfect because he does what I tell him, and I can count on him." It felt wonderful for me to admit that to myself.

"You're sure you know what you're doing, young woman?"

"I'm positive. Can you come in early tomorrow morning and type a motion for me? It'll be short, I promise, but I'll need it before I go to court."

She shrugged as she picked up her purse. "Would your grandfather approve of what you're doing?"

"Absolutely no question about it," I told her, and almost added that he already had, but it would have sounded too weird. "He'd say, '*That's* what you should do!' or something."

Her bony old hand reached out for me and touched my face. "I have a feeling about you, young lady, that is . . . quite wonderful," she said, peering at me through her bifocals. "Be sure and lock up when you leave," she added, turning for the door. "And call your mother."

Chapter Twenty-eight

"Honey?"

I recognized the voice as Mom's, then turned my back to her and hugged the pillow.

"It's after eight, Kate. Aren't you supposed to be in court at nine?"

"*Mom!* Why didn't you wake me up?"

I bounded out of bed, but my eyes were sewn shut and it took a second to find my robe that I couldn't get into because it was backward. "I *did* wake you up," Mom snapped at me, as though I'd accused her of murder. "Come downstairs now and eat. You haven't been eating."

"I have to get dressed."

"*Now.* There's time because I'm taking you and we need to talk."

I didn't have time for a lesson in life, but I did need a

ride, so I compromised my principles and tried to bargain with her. "Can't I even brush my teeth?"

"Yes."

Downstairs, she had the ironing board out and was pressing the pale green button-down miniskirt she thought looked so cute on me that I couldn't stand. "Are you borrowing my clothes now?" I asked her. "I don't think you can wear that."

"It's for you. It's the only dress you have that's clean."

"My Christmas dress?"

"All wrong. It's dark, too long, and too dressy for what you need today. I talked to Mrs. Roulette last night, and she told me you really think you have a chance. But not in something designed for parties and subdued lighting. This is daytime, and you want to look cheerful and optimistic. Trust me."

So she didn't like my Christmas dress. I decided not to argue.

"Sit down and eat," she commanded, pointing at the kitchen table with its cereal, milk in a pitcher, orange juice, and a toasted bagel. "There's an article in the *News* this morning about you that doesn't paint a very pretty picture about your case, but I want you to know something." When she snuffled, I realized she was worried about me, and it really surprised me. "If you lose, if your scheme or whatever it is doesn't work, it won't be the end of the world. Okay?"

"It will be for Herman," I said, pouring milk on the bran flakes but feeling safer with her on my side.

"Is there anything you want to tell me about your relationship with Mike? I mean . . . well, you know what I mean." Mothers are so suspicious. I waited for the rest of it. "Gladys called me last night at ten o'clock, looking for him. I called the office and no one was there. You told me that's where you'd be, and you weren't. Neither was he. Where were you?"

"Having sex in the law library, but don't worry, I've been reading *Ms.* and know how to protect myself from babies." I glanced at the clock on the wall. "It's eight thirty!" I said, jumping up.

"Your dress is ready," she said, through the slit under her nose where her mouth used to be. "We'll talk in the car."

But the drive to the office wasn't much fun for me because my stomach tipped upside down, almost ruining the dress Mom had gotten ready for me. She must have seen it coming and pulled over in time for me to empty my breakfast into the gutter. "Oh, honey, you've inherited my nervous stomach," she said, with her hand on my back. "Take these," and she handed me Tums for my stomach and mints to sweeten my breath. "Do I take you to the courthouse or the office?"

"Office," I said miserably, hiccupping but getting the meds down. "I need to pick up some things."

"Shall I wait for you?"

"No thanks, Mom. I need to walk."

"Promise me something?" she asked as I opened the door. "When the jury comes back with its verdict, you'll call me?"

I nodded at her and we traded smiles. "Thanks for breakfast," I said. "I love you."

"Break a leg."

The usual assortment of wonderful old leftovers and discards waited patiently in the lobby to see a lawyer. But they seemed to know I was in a trial, and they smiled at me. Mrs. Roulette was at her desk, helping a young girl with a baby in her arms fill out a form. "Is Mike here?" I asked her, searching the counter for my motion.

"No, but he was when I arrived this morning." She stared at me suspiciously. "He looked like he'd been up all night."

"I hope not," I said. "Where is he now?"

"Home, I think. He wanted me to give you a message." She found a note on her desk and read it aloud. "'Everything is ready, but it took forever to get the truck running. It needed a fuel pump.' What is going on?"

"I'll explain later." My stomach took another major twist. Thank you God, I thought, for making sure there's nothing left to throw up. A thousand things could go wrong, and if just one of them did—curtains for Herman. I found the motion with two copies the sweet old woman with gnarled fingers that looked like twigs had typed for me, then searched everywhere for my briefcase . . . "It's in your grandfather's office," she said. I found it on his desk and stuffed the motion and copies inside, then blew Mrs. Roulette a kiss as I rushed for the door. "Wish me luck!"

"You look very nice, even though that dress is awfully short. Did you see the story in the paper?"

"No, but Mom told me it was awful."

"Your grandfather called about it. I told him you were up to something, and he said, 'You tell her I'm not worried one bit!' "

It was two minutes after nine when I walked into the courtroom with my stomach under control and Mom's smile on my face—and it was like walking into a freezer. Judge Steinbrunner glowered at me from the bench through an absolute and total stillness, even though every seat was taken and kids were lined up against the walls. The only sound came from my heels that missed a beat, then marched down the aisle. Mr. Thomas and Officer Milliken watched from their places in the pit with snide little smiles on their faces, Max Briar sat in the front row with his head down, scribbling in the open notepad on his leg, and Miss Willow shivered in a huddle at the defense table, cold and frightened and alone, like a bag lady in March.

Even the court reporter and jurors were in place. My confidence level was not high, but I aimed my smile at the judge anyway, with no effect. "You are late, Miss Hope," he said. "Do you have an excuse?"

"No, sir," I said. "I just overslept."

"Overslept?" He leaned over the bench to get a better look at me. "Miss Hope, you do *not* keep a jury or this Court waiting so you can *sleep!*" My hands sweated like sponges as my heart, at two hundred beats a minute, fired blood through my veins like water jets. "Approach the bench," he ordered ominously.

I set my briefcase down, let my hand drag across Miss Willow's back, and realized Spence was nowhere to be seen. Neither was Mike. I walked up to the bench with Mr. Thomas and the court reporter. "Miss Hope, what are you doing in my courtroom wearing a miniskirt?" the judge whispered angrily.

"What?" Mom's smile can usually handle surprises, but not this one. It vanished as I checked the hemline, less than two inches above my knees. Not extreme at all. What was his problem?

"In my court, lady attorneys are required to wear dresses that are modest and not revealing."

"But . . ." I was going to tell him that my mother had picked it out, but how would that help? "Would you like me to go home and change, sir?" I asked, fighting to keep my real feelings of anger and humiliation from showing.

"No. But an apology would be nice."

"I can't do that," I said without thinking, meeting his stare with one of my own. But I pulled my eyes away rather than get into a contest with him, which he'd have lost.

"Your Honor," Mr. Thomas whispered, "I noticed that two of the jurors are in miniskirts. I don't like it any more than you do, sir, but . . ."

"We will talk about this later, young lady," the judge's whisper-covered-with-ice informed me. "Let's get started."

Mr. Thomas and I returned to our places. I hated having been made conscious of my knees hanging out, as though that were a crime. But I refused to hide them as I sat down and managed a smile at Miss Willow, who gave me a quick and timid one in return.

"Ladies and gentlemen, this trial has been more of a trial, perhaps, than any of us expected," the judge said, "but we're finally approaching a conclusion. The evidence is now before you, and it's time for—" I stood up—"final argument." He frowned at his hands but wouldn't look at me. "What is it, Miss Hope?"

"Your Honor, the defense has more evidence to put on."

"It's too *late* for that!" he exploded. "I will *not* allow you to put on another surprise witness! This is the third time you've made that request and the Court has been extremely lenient with you, but now we will have final argument! Are you ready to proceed?"

"It isn't another witness, Judge," I said, in a very reasonable voice that was loud enough to let him know I would not back down. "Furthermore, I would remind the Court that the defense has not rested."

"*What?*" But then he thought about it, and looked at the court reporter. "Very well. Miss. Hope. You may proceed."

"I have a motion, sir. May I tender it to the Court?"

"A *motion*," he said, as fire shot out of his nose. "Give it to me, please. It would have helped, you know, if you'd gotten here early enough this morning to go over this with me and the city attorney."

"I know, sir, and I'm very sorry, and apologize to you both." I dug the motion out of my briefcase and handed him the original and gave a copy to Mr. Thomas. I could smile at them with ease now. Anyone as sensitive as they were about a girl in a miniskirt would never fill my heart with terror again.

"Miss Hope," the judge said in a voice weary with exasperation, "this needs to be signed."

"Uh-oh," I said, trying to make light of it. "Not a good start for me, is it, sir?" I asked, taking the motion to the table to sign it. My pen didn't work. "Judge, can I borrow your pen?"

He laughed! "You may," he said as he handed me his pen. "Please do me a favor, Miss Hope. Don't break it?"

"No, sir."

Way to handle the old fuddy-duddy, Grandfather's voice said.

"What is it you're asking for?" the judge asked as I handed him the motion and his pen.

"A demonstration, sir. Demonstrative evidence?"

"Really," he said, reading aloud with interest that wasn't an act. "You want to stage a demonstration for the jury, using the dog. You say you can re-create the conditions that, according to your evidence, the dog was faced with. You want the jury to watch the dog's reaction. And we don't have to go to City Park Lake, you say, because you can stage your demonstration across the street, on the Civic Center lawn." He nodded at me with something like respect. "How long will it take you to get ready?"

"If my assistant is here . . . ," I said, looking into the mass of humanity for Mike—and spotting my mother! She was way in the back of the courtroom and tried to duck her head out of the way, then realized she'd been caught, and blessed me with her smile. "Hi, Mom," I mouthed. Having her there with me in the courtroom that morning felt like being wrapped up in a warm blanket on a cold night.

But where was Mike?

He'd been hiding too, sort of, behind two tall boys who were standing along the wall near the door. He blushed, raised his hand, and stepped away from them into the aisle. I waved at him with a huge sense of relief because he wasn't still crashed in his bed at home. "Judge, the person with his hand in the air," I said, "is Mike Doyle, my assistant. He can answer your question better than I can, sir."

"Young man," the judge called out. "How long will it take?"

Mike didn't do as I expected and collapse, but came through with a guess as good as any. "An hour?"

"What's your position, Mr. Thomas? Do you need time to look up the cases she's cited?"

"I'm familiar with the law, Judge," he said, standing, "but how do we know this isn't something they've rehearsed?"

"How could we?" I asked. "Herman was in dog jail last night and he's still there."

Mr. Thomas ignored me, but that didn't matter. I knew I'd made my point. "Your Honor," he said, "the evidence the defense has put before this jury to justify this motion is the testimony of a man who is mentally unstable. It isn't credible evidence, sir. It should be ignored. This so-called demonstration won't prove anything. Instead of wasting half the morning, we'll waste all of it. How much time should this Court give to this case?"

"Well now. It's true Mr. Phipps has a history of seeing things that aren't there, but it's nevertheless possible he saw what he claimed. I certainly can't rule, as a matter of law, that his evidence should be excluded. It may not be the best evidence in the world, but my ruling is that it's enough to support Miss Hope's motion."

Mr. Thomas shrugged. "Very well then, Judge," he said, smiling at me a bit like Dracula before the kiss of death. "We shall see what we shall see."

Chapter Twenty-nine

MOM BLEW ME A KISS AND DISAPPEARED, but I knew she'd be back to watch the show. With Mike in charge of the Alvarez family and help from three sheriff's deputies and two animal-control officers, the demonstration was ready to go at a few minutes after ten. It was an absolutely gorgeous day. The temperature was in the seventies, a cool breeze carried the scents of blooming flowers, and a few white puffy clouds floated in a sky that was so blue it throbbed.

The Civic Center, where the action would take place, was a large, open park across the street from the courthouse. Its big lawns with gardens and trees stretched east to west from Broadway to Bannock, and south to north from Fourteenth to Colfax. An amphitheater at the south end of the big park was connected to a sizable fountain at the north end by a sidewalk as wide as a road.

A path at right angles to the sidewalk started near a larger-than-life bronze statue of an Indian on horseback. The path went fifty yards to the east, then arced slowly back to the sidewalk sixty yards north of the statue, kind of marking off a large piece of lawn. That was where the demonstration would take place. Yellow caution tape had been strung all the way around it.

The judge, the jury, and Mr. Thomas sat in folding chairs on the path along the north boundary of the enclosure, under some trees to shade them from the sun. Kids and spectators gathered to the east of the enclosure, where there was a low stone wall, waist high. A lot of them sat on the wall to have a great view of the action. I waited with Mike, Miss Willow, Officer Milliken, two sheriff's deputies, and Herman on the path at the south boundary near the statue. Herman was cooped up in a cage so small he couldn't stretch all the way out.

The piece of lawn needed for the demonstration waited like an empty stage. With a pulse rate in the low two hundreds, I walked onto the stage and faced the judge and the jury, who were more than thirty yards away. It was as though the curtain had been raised, dropping stillness— except for the sounds of traffic in the distance. "Shall I start, sir?" I shouted at the judge.

"The sooner the better, Miss Hope."

"Can you hear me, ladies and gentlemen?" I asked the jurors in the same loud voice that proved my existence.

"Yes," a few of them chorused.

"Judge Steinbrunner has allowed me to put on a demonstration," I explained as Mike, right on cue, spread a blanket at the center of the stage and put a picnic basket on a corner of the blanket. "You'll have to use your imaginations, though. We're really at City Park, and it's Sunday, May twenty-seventh, but the year is the same. We're still in 1973. Okay?"

They nodded their willingness to use their imaginations.

"Miss Willow?" I said, gesturing to her as Mike led her over to Herman's cage. Officer Milliken opened it while the sheriff's deputies watched, holding pistols in their hand. Mike handed a chain leash to Miss Willow, who clipped it on Herman. The dog looked around with his senses on high alert, then cautiously crept out of the cage and placed himself between the men with drawn guns and Miss Willow.

She looked sweet in her yellow dress. Herman saw the blanket on the grass with the picnic basket and pulled her toward it with his tail wagging. "As you may have guessed, Miss Willow has brought her dog Herman to the park for a picnic. Tether him, please, Miss Willow?"

She tried pushing a metal spike, six inches long that was hooked to the end of the chain leash, into the ground. But it wouldn't go in. With Herman stretched out on the blanket, she stepped on the spike with her foot, and this time it grudgingly slid into the lawn. "We haven't re-created all the conditions as they existed that day," I said as she sat on the blanket and tucked her skirt under her legs. "For example, there isn't any lake nearby." Herman sidled over to her and she rubbed his ears, as his tail thumped on the ground. "But the basket has fruit inside, and a sandwich, and . . ."

Herman pulled away from Miss Willow and started growling! His ears flattened, and he sat up like a loaded spring aimed like the needle of a compass at someone perched on the stone fence. Ron Benson! In a Penn State T-shirt, he looked ready to leap at Herman and attack. He grinned at me, then glared and kind of growled at Herman. They locked up in a staring contest, but the difference was, Herman bared his teeth.

There was nothing I could do about Ron without stray-ing from the script that the judge had approved, and stray-ing from the script was not an option. "It's a different baby, too," I said to the jury, pointing at Manuel Alvarez. He stood next to a baby carriage on the sidewalk with a baby in his arms. "This is Mr. Manuel Alvarez, who donated a baby for the demonstration."

People laughed, as I had expected. "The distance be-tween Herman and the baby carriage is forty yards, the same as the distance between Herman and the carriage little Monica was in." How could I get Herman to look at the baby? "Miss Willow, can you make Herman watch what Mr. Alvarez is doing?"

She had to grip the dog's face in her hands and turn him around, forcing him to take his eyes away from Ron Benson, but she managed as Mr. Alvarez lifted his baby high enough for everyone to see. Herman let off a little bark and wagged his tail. "Put her in the carriage, please," I said as the dog squirmed, trying to check his back, while Miss Willow used all her strength to make him watch. Mr. Alvarez gently placed the tiny girl in the carriage. "Good, Miss Willow," I said, and she let go of his face. The big dog snapped back into his staring duel with Ron Benson, with nothing moving other than the fur on his back that ruffled like a wheat field in the wind.

"Now we wait for a minute," I said, "while Mr. Alvarez takes his baby out of the carriage and gives him to his mother. My assistant's idea," I continued, "who didn't think we should use a real baby." I encouraged the ripple of laughter with a smile. "Later, Mr. Alvarez will put a Raggedy Ann doll in the carriage. With five children, he has dolls to spare."

The jurors seemed to be enjoying themselves, making it easy to fill up enough time for Mr. Alvarez to do what he had to do. "The idea is to let Herman think there's a real baby in the carriage," I said as Mr. Alvarez found his wife and handed her the infant, then climbed into his battered pickup truck. It had been parked on the sidewalk behind the statue. "Will the deputies take their places?" I asked, as one walked over to a spot near the jury, and the other patrolled the path on the east. "These men are armed. If something goes wrong with Herman, they'll protect us from him."

Then Pablo Alvarez, Manuel's oldest son, lifted a Sting-Ray minibike out of the bed of the truck, aimed it at the baby carriage, and sat on it. All I could do was hope that Herman was not so locked up by the sneering face of Ron Benson that he couldn't see Pablo. As Mr. Alvarez started the truck, sweat popped off my forehead. "When I give the signal," I told the jurors, "Mr. Alvarez will drive on the sidewalk going north. At the same time, his son on the minibike will ride as fast as he can toward the carriage. He will push it into the sidewalk, directly in the path of the truck. From Herman's point of view, it should look very bad for the baby in the carriage. It should look as bad to him as it did a month ago, when—according to our evidence—the carriage with Monica Pearsan was rolling into City Park Lake."

My knees hanging beneath my miniskirt trembled so horribly that I pressed them together, hoping no one had noticed. "There won't be any reruns like they have on TV when the umpire makes a questionable call. The whole point is to see if Herman will try to save the baby." I raised my hand at the same time my heart stopped, then dropped my hand. "Go!"

Pablo started riding toward the baby carriage on his Sting-Ray, picking up speed. Herman didn't want to, but he pulled his eyes off Ron Benson and watched. His ears lifted when the truck started creeping forward. Then Pablo found the carriage with one hand and shoved it into the sidewalk, right into the path of the truck.

Mr. Alvarez gunned the truck so that it bore down on the baby carriage like a freight train . . . and Herman took off! The tether that Miss Willow had struggled to punch into the lawn was yanked out as Herman raced across the lawn and smashed into the baby carriage, knocking it out of the way before the truck could hit it. Mr. Alvarez slammed on the brakes and swerved, barely missing the big dog.

It worked! Mike ran for Herman to make sure he hadn't been hit, and the dog climbed all over him, licking his face . . . and I heard cheering! The jury, the judge, and all the kids and people were cheering!

Grampa's old face grinned at me from a place inside my head. *Now!* his voice said. *Do it now!*

"If it please the Court!" I screamed with all my breath to make myself heard above the din. "I rest my case!"

Chapter Thirty

CITY PARK WAS CROWDED with people when Mike and I found Miss Willow at her picnic spot, wearing her yellow dress and sitting on a blanket with Herman stretched out on the grass. He barked when he saw us, bounding out as far as the chain would allow, his tail whipping back and forth so hard it wagged his whole body. When the hellos were over we sat on the blanket with Herman tending Mike's black eye like a nurse, examining it then probing it with his tongue.

"Thank you for your help, dear," Miss Willow said to Mike. "Kate told me she couldn't possibly have put on that demonstration without you."

"She did?" Mike asked. "She didn't say anything to me."

"I bought you a pizza, didn't I?" I told him. "I was

hoping you might share some of it with me but you didn't, which was no surprise." He grinned at me. He actually has a very nice grin. "I also let you carry my briefcase."

"Big deal."

"Will you children have an apple?" Miss Willow asked, poking around in her picnic basket and pulling out two of them. "I brought extra food in case . . . well." She blushed. "One never knows who might come by unexpectedly."

I shook my head at the apple, but Mike took one that didn't have a chance. It was gone within seconds.

"That was an awfully nice article about you in the paper, wasn't it?" Miss Willow said to me. "Did you like it?"

"I . . . well . . . I didn't really read it," I said.

"Oh-h-h!" Mike said. "You framed it! It's hanging on your wall!"

"Your grandfather must be awfully proud of you."

"I guess," I said, "but he doesn't say much." Actually, he'd said a lot, but I wanted to be modest.

"Well. You tell him for me that you were worth every penny of the twenty dollars he charged me, and that if I ever have another legal problem, I'll just bring it right to you."

Was twenty dollars *all* Grandfather charged for all that work, sweat, and tears? "I'll tell him, Miss Willow, and thank you for your confidence in me, but the truth is, Herman's the real hero." The big dog had been listening and barked, letting us know he was in on the conversation.

A heavy man wearing Levi's and cowboy boots, with long black hair and skin the color of stained wood, walked toward us carrying a neatly folded stack of clothes. "Herman," he said in a deep voice that resonated like a bugle as he bent down so Herman could smell his hand. "The wolf-dog."

I recognized his voice from our telephone conversation at five in the morning. "You're Bearclaw, aren't you?" I asked him. "Spence's friend?"

"I am Bearclaw," he said. "I know Spence, but not his friend. He drinks too much." He put the clothes down on the blanket. "He said these belong to you," he said to Miss Willow.

"Why yes, they do. That was an old suit of my father's, and it's been cleaned and pressed. How nice of him! But . . . why did he send you?" she asked, suddenly anxious. "Is he hurt, or in the hospital? Couldn't he come himself?"

Bearclaw shook his head slowly. "'Tell her I'm too busy,' he said."

The words weren't at all what I would expect from Spence and I felt terrible, watching Miss Willow crumple under their coldness. "Did he tell you to say that, Mr. Bearclaw?" Mike asked. "I mean, he didn't get a job and go to work or anything, did he?"

Bearclaw frowned at Mike. "Who are you?"

"He's my investigator," I said, realizing that Mike was

getting better at his job. "It's perfectly okay for you to talk to him."

"That's right, what you say," Bearclaw said to Mike. "Spence don't want important people to see him now. Important people who will laugh at him behind their faces."

"What does he mean by that?" I asked. "Who's so important to him?"

"You. A young girl, but a big lawyer. Her." He pointed at Miss Willow. "Important people laugh at crazy drunks."

Miss Willow couldn't keep her hands still. "Oh dear," she said as they held each other for comfort.

"Is Spence with you now, Mr. Bearclaw?" Mike asked.

"He don't want me to say."

"You don't have to say anything," Mike told him. "Just point."

He pointed at the lilac hedge near the edge of the lake. Mike had figured that out? "I'll go get him," I said, standing and starting to run over there.

"No!" Bearclaw said, stopping me. "He would run away."

I sat down. "*You* get him then, Mr. Bearclaw," I said. "Tell him Miss Willow would love to see him so she can thank him personally for his help."

Bearclaw shrugged, then ambled off for the hedge.

"Dear, you shouldn't have done that," Miss Willow

said as her hands fluttered to her hair, "but I'm awfully glad you did. Will he come over?" She opened the lid of her basket and closed it. "I just know he won't."

I got up. "It was very nice seeing you again, Miss Willow, and Herman too, but Mike and I have to go. He's working on another case for me. Let's go, Mike."

"I am?"

How can anyone be so smart and so incredibly dumb at the same time? "Come on," I said, walking off in a hurry in the hope that it might make him walk in a hurry too. "We're leaving."

"Goodbye, children!" Miss Willow called out.

Mike caught up to me. "What case?" he asked.

I grabbed his hand and dragged him along so he'd keep up. "I just want to make it easy for that old man to come over and sit with her and I just hope he isn't as thick-headed as you are."

Six or seven people wandered across the grass in front of us, blocking our view of Miss Willow and hers of us. "Over there," I said, ducking behind them and running over to a hawthorn bush where we could hide and spy. "Take a nap if you want," I told him. "I want to see if Spence shows up and whether she'll let him kiss her without taking a shower."

"I'll go get some popcorn. Want some?"

"You're such a romantic. Sure."

I lay on my stomach on the grass with my chin on my

fists and watched with droopy eyes because I hadn't caught up on my sleep . . . when my eyes closed all the way. I was no longer watching Miss Willow at City Park; I was at the office, watching Grampa teeter in a chair with his feet on his desk. He glared at me in my miniskirt. "Kate darlin', you'd better change into something a wee bit more appropriate before the dinner. You know how the judge is."

"I can't do that," I said angrily. "Two of the jurors are in miniskirts and they'll be there too."

"But they aren't getting the Outstanding Trial Lawyer of the Year Award."

"This is my lucky outfit and I'm going to wear it always, this year and into the next century, no matter how long it takes."

"You don't need to wait that long, you know," the old man said. "He's there for you now."

"What are you talking about?" I asked him, trembling. "Who is there for me now? I don't believe you."

"Zozo will introduce you. He's the master of ceremonies."

"But he's dead!" I started to cry. "He ran off and died!"

Grampa sat up to see me better, and watched through eyes that worked. "I'm proud of you, young woman," he said, but he looked angry. What had I done wrong? "You've forgiven him."

The scene morphed into the kitchen. Mom's arms

wrapped me in a warm blanket, and she smiled her beautiful smile at me. "They're back."

The door from the garage opened, and Law and my dad came in. "Hi, Pumpkin," Zozo said to me. "How's my favorite daughter?"

I felt so wonderfully safe, with her hugging me and Daddy in my heart, and then someone grabbed my shoulder and shook it. "Kate? Want some popcorn?"

"Mike!" I woke up and tried to get my bearings with my nose in the grass. "You're back," I said. "What took you so long?"

He had that lopsided grin on his face, where most of his mouth was under his black eye. "Look," he said.

I raised my head high enough to see Miss Willow and Spence in the distance, sitting on the blanket with their shoulders touching, holding hands. Herman was stretched out on the grass, looking comfortably bored but still included in the family circle.

"Ready, Grampa?" I asked the old man, gripping his elbow.

We were leaving his room at the hotel, and Mom was waiting in the car. "Let go of my arm!" he demanded. "I ain't a cripple. And don't call me that. We're partners."

"Can't I call you Grampa when you come to dinner?" I asked. "I want you to be my grandfather on Sundays. Not my partner."

"So that's what you want, is it?" He put his hand on my shoulder when we started down the steps. "I'll allow it. I expect you're pretty full of yourself after your big win." He even leaned on me for support. "But don't get *too* puffed up, young woman. The truth is, you didn't win at all."

"I didn't?" I asked, surprised. "Mr. Thomas thought so. So did the judge."

"Well, they're wrong, which perhaps you'll learn with experience, though I doubt it." We stopped so he could get his breath. "When I beat the socks off that stallion from the DA's office, I didn't win either. The system won." We started moving again. "No one believes in the system now, with all the people who want to get rid of it or trade it in for something else. But there ain't no better system in the world than what we have right here in this country. Do you see that, Kate?"

I didn't want to get in a big argument, but the way it seemed to me, "justice" was a crapshoot.

"You don't see it, do you?" he asked, sadly. "Well, it's clear to me and maybe one day it will be to you, too. The firm of Hope and Hope had two trials last week, and both times, justice got done. I don't know why, but it *happens* that way. Not all the time, but more often than it don't."

I wanted to believe him. Daddy had. "Maybe all I need is more experience," I said.

When we got to the street, it was three o'clock, and hot. Mom had all the windows open in the car because

Grampa wouldn't use an air conditioner. I helped him into the front seat. "How are you, Annie?" he asked when he was comfortable.

Mom's eyes were wet, but that was all right because Grampa couldn't see that she'd been weepy. She'd gotten emotional because he was on his feet and walking. "I'm fine, Dad. You're looking well."

"At my age, it don't matter how I look, but I feel good."

I jumped in back, and Mom pulled away from the curb. "Have you read the stories about Kate?" she asked him.

Even from the back seat I could see his smile. "She'll need some new hats, I expect. Tell me, young lady. Does your head fit in the car, or do you have to hang it out the window, where there's enough room for it?"

"It's right here," I said, grabbing it with both hands. "But you're the one who should have the big head, Grampa. It was you who really tried the case."

"*I* tried it! How could that be? I was in the hospital!"

"That may be," I said, "but you were in my head too. The whole time, giving me advice." That wasn't all he'd given me, but I didn't go into the rest.

He turned around and tried to find me, looking strange. "That's a peculiar thing for you to say," he said. "I had the dangdest dreams Thursday and Friday.

"I'd a sworn I was there, too."

Author's Note

THIS BOOK ASKS THE READER to believe that, in 1973, fourteen-year-old Kate Hope practiced law in Colorado. Would that have been possible? Or does that stretch credulity to the breaking point?

The author of this book is a lawyer as well as a writer, and so of course he has an opinion on the subject. But first, let him find his lawyer's hat: a dress fedora, with a feather in the brim . . .

There. He put it on, and adjusted it so it sits at a suitable angle over his right eye, out of which he is squinting.

In his opinion, though there'd have been hurdles to clear, it would have been possible for a fourteen-year-old girl to practice law in Colorado in 1973. He briefed the question, and what follows is his memorandum on the law.

Points and Authorities

Colorado was a United States territory before it became a state. It was organized as a territory on February 28, 1861, and was admitted into the Union as a state on August 1, 1876.

Even as a territory it had laws, courts, lawyers, and politicians. Those laws were updated annually by a legislative assembly, and were first published in 1868. That one-volume work was—and still is—called the *Revised Statutes of Colorado, 1867.*

Chapter VII of that work is on "Attorneys at Law." Though it has more than twenty sections, the first three are the only ones that matter as far as this opinion is concerned, because they regulated the "rules of admission to the bar." In other words, they spelled out the conditions that had to be met by those in the territory who wanted to be lawyers.

The first section provided generally that anyone who wanted to practice law in Colorado had to get a license from the Supreme Court. The second and third sections were on what applicants had to show the Supreme Court before it would give them the license. Applicants had to show, first, that they were "of good moral character"; second, that they'd been "engaged in the study of law for two successive years"; and third, that they had passed an examination on the law, given to them under the direction of the Supreme Court.

That's all it took to be a lawyer in those good old days when Colorado was still a territory. Age was not a factor then. Many individuals who practiced law in those days had not reached the age of "majority," usually defined as twenty-one years. It isn't likely that there was anyone as young as Kate Hope, but there could have been.

When Colorado became a state in 1876, the chapter on "Attorneys at Law" was adopted in its entirety by the First Session of the General Assembly. The language is the same, word for word, as it was in the *Revised Statutes of Colorado, 1867,* except that wherever the word "territory" appeared, it was replaced by "state."

The constitution of the state of Colorado was also adopted in 1876. It included a "Schedule" that provided, in part, the following:

> *That no inconvenience may arise by reason of the change in the form of government, it is hereby ordained and declared: . . . That all laws in force at the adoption of this constitution shall, so far as not inconsistent therewith, remain of the same force as if this constitution had not been adopted, until they expire by their own limitation or are altered or repealed by the general assembly . . .*

That brings us to the main point. Because the territorial laws regulating the rules of admission to the bar had not been repealed, then even if other laws were passed on the subject, the territorial laws would still be in effect. In other words, there would have been another way to get a license to practice law.

It would have required some serious lawyering skills to persuade the Supreme Court of Colorado, in 1973, that the original laws had not been repealed by later enactments of laws on the same subject. But in the opinion of the author, Judge Hope had those skills. The old lawyer would have argued that the original laws had never been *specifically* repealed; therefore, they were still on the books. He'd also have argued that the old laws were in substantial agreement with the new ones anyway. Both provide that only persons of good moral character who have studied law for a defined period of time can take the bar examination, and both require that, before getting the license, the person must pass the examination.

Getting a license to practice law would not have been the end of Kate's problem. There would still have been hurdles she'd need to clear before she could actually represent a client. She'd have to disclose her age, and the client would have to sign a waiver. Judges would also need to be satisfied that there had been full disclosure of her age, and that the client was represented by the lawyer of his or her choice.

You may wonder why those legal maneuvers weren't included in the book. Here's the reason. When the author took off his lawyer's hat and put on his comfortable Colorado Rockies baseball cap, his writer's hat, he knew that if those boring details were included, they'd become so tedious that many readers would go to sleep. He didn't want that, so he used a device writers are allowed to use when they tell stories: poetic license. In other words, he ignored those boring details because they would have slowed down the story.

It may not be as accurate that way. But it reads better.

Acknowledgments

This book was a long time in the making. Without the help and encouragement of a whole host of angels, it would have wandered around forever in "book hell," that awful pit in a corner of the underworld where unpublished manuscripts are consigned.

At Houghton Mifflin, my thanks go to Amy Flynn and Kate O'Sullivan, for keeping the project alive. And I am in awe of Erica Zappy, my talented editor, for her in-depth critique. Thanks also to Katya Rice, a copyeditor who is without peer.

Prototypes, character wrinkles, and legal twists were provided by a lot of lawyers: my older brother, Richard, younger brother, "Chuck," my sister's husband, Dick Schmidt, and my father and grandfather.

For insights as to how a judge might treat a fourteen-year-old lawyer in court, thanks go to Judge John D. McMullen of the Denver District Court.

Herrick Roth, a legendary educator in Denver, introduced me to some of the teachers who taught at Hill Junior High School in 1973: Dave and Meredith Jones, Mary Ann Ross, and Ruth Huebner. Thanks to them all for their time as well as critiques. Other sources regarding the period and the place were Patrick Thornham, Jeffrey Downing, and Betsy McIlhenney.

Many readers were equally generous with their time and helped with their honest critiques: The Wild Ones, a writer's group I belong to composed mainly of talented and outrageous women (and you know who you are), Linda and Larry Drake, Katherine Pearson, and Nancy Hawkins.

I'd like also to acknowledge two old and dear friends: William B. R. Reiss, my first agent, then with the Paul Reynolds Agency, and Jane Chelius, then the senior editor at Pocket Books and now a literary agent. Without their guidance and help, I'd never have been a writer.